An ArtScroll Novel®

THE EXILES OF

by Henye Meyer

Published by

Mesorah Publications, ltd

CROCODILE ISLAND

FIRST EDITION
First Impression ... June 1984
Second Impression ... December 1991
Third Impression ... February 2003

Published and Distributed by
MESORAH PUBLICATIONS, LTD.
4401 Second Avenue / Brooklyn, N.Y 11232

Distributed in Europe by
LEHMANNS
Unit E, Viking Industrial Park
Rolling Mill Road NE32 3DP
Jarow, Tyne & Wear,
England

Distributed in Australia and New Zealand by
GOLDS WORLD OF JUDAICA
3-13 William Street
Balaclava, Melbourne 3183
Victoria Australia

Distributed in Israel by
SIFRIATI / A. GITLER BOOKS
6 Hayarkon Street
Bnei Brak 51127

Distributed in South Africa by
KOLLEL BOOKSHOP
Shop 8A Norwood Hypermarket
Norwood 2196, Johannesburg, South Africa

ISBN:
0-89906-779-4 (hard cover)
0-89906-780-8 (paperback)
Typography by CompuScribe at ArtScroll Studios, Ltd.
Printed in the United States of America by Moriah Offset
Bound by Sefercraft, Quality Bookbinders, Ltd., Brooklyn N.Y. 11232

AUTHOR'S ACKNOWLEDGMENT

Besides the patient, understanding ArtScroll Staff, a remarkable number of people helped me write this book — friends, neighbors, and acquaintances who provided everything from moral support to indispensable items of information. I want to thank in particular Rabbi Hersh Goldwurm, who shared his knowledge and his library with me; my unwitting strategist Mrs. Debbie Maimon, who showed me the kind of book I ought to be writing; and my tactician Mrs. Chana Sokol, whose constructive criticism taught me how to do it. Most of all, however, I want to assure my family that I still know they're there and I do appreciate them: my husband, who was mechazek me; and my children, whose forebearance is, I hope, rewarded.

H.M.

To the reader:

This historical novel is based on a sidelight in the commentary of *Abarbanel* to Exodus 7:26. The great commentator was the finance minister of Ferdinand and Isabella, the Spanish monarchs who instituted the Inquisition and finally expelled the Jews of Spain in 1492. Don Yitzchak Abarbanel was so valuable to the royal court that he was exempted from the decree, but when his intercessions on behalf of his fellow Jews failed, he led them into exile.

Abarbanel writes of an island in the Atlantic known as Crocodile Island and says:

The king of Portugal forced many children of the Spanish exiles to adopt his faith. He sent them to [Crocodile Island] fourteen years ago; all of them children without any blemish, boys and girls, more than two thousand souls. They have already multiplied there, and most of the island is inhabited by them. The island is not far from the equator.

CHAPTER ONE

I WISH WE COULD WALK a little faster," Luis Navarro said with uncharacteristic peevishness. The late-July sun beat down on his shoulders.

"What for? There's nowhere to go."

Luis glanced at the slight boy beside him who had spoken. He was right, as he was so often. Ahead, the road was thronged with people trudging into the dusty distance; behind, a stream of refugees choked the road from Spain. He thought of the swaying, creaking carts piled high with a pathetic jumble of possessions. How does one choose a single cartload to salvage out of a lifetime's accumulation? he wondered.

As if to mock their misery, a musician was playing a merry dancing-tune somewhere in the crowd. And it was the Nine Days too, Luis thought resentfully; even he had learned that much.

"Saadya, we're supposed to be mourning the Beith Hamikdash. Can't your father stop the music?"

The slight boy looked gravely at Luis. "My father told him to play to keep people's spirits up."

"It isn't working very well."

"What do you expect?" asked Saadya. "The king's only allowing us eight months in Portugal. By Spring of 1493 we'll have to be on the move again."

Luis twitched his sleeve. "Saadya, why did you all decide to leave Spain, to give in like this? Plenty of people converted, or became Marranos, and kept all they owned and stayed in their homes. My own grandparents converted fifty years ago when the mob was after them. They practiced some Judaismo secretly, but they kept the family wealth! You should have seen what we had

— chandeliers, carpets, tapestries, fine horses, coffers of jewelry — "

"And what happened to your parents, Luis?" Saadya's father broke in gently. "There was no mob after them, was there? They could have taken some of their wealth and gone to Italy or Holland but they were so attached to their luxuries that they couldn't bring themselves to escape to a place where they could be Jews openly. What happened to you? They were afraid to teach you so you grew up knowing hardly anything about your own Judaismo. And in the end the Inquisition caught your parents anyway."

"My parents died because they were Jews," Luis protested.

"Yes, they did," agreed the rav, "but everyone on this road feels that it's more honorable, more worthwhile, for a soldier to die fighting in battle defending his cause than to be shot deserting. We haven't given in. This is how we fight our battle: by throwing away everything that doesn't matter in order to hold fast to the one thing that does — our Judaismo. No matter what happens to us," he added. "Do you understand that?"

Luis gazed at Saadya's father in silence. He could understand. But he didn't like thinking of his parents as deserters. Perhaps it was better not to remember them at all.

But he could not forget. As the long walk continued into Portugal, from Beja to Evora, from Evora to Lisboa, through waving wheatfields and barren hot charneca, through lush coastal farmlands to Lisboa's twisting alleys; and as the weeks went by from summer heat to winter's wet winds, he remembered that last afternoon in his parents' house because his dreams at night would not let him forget:

☙ ☙ ☙

"Por favor, Rosalia," Luis wheedled, his knee on the rough wooden bench that stood on the stone-flagged kitchen floor. He leaned across the table towards the cook. With a practiced motion she sprinkled the coarse salt over a chicken she was making kosher, and she did not look up. "Rosalia, if I tell you how kind you are, will you give me a piece of cake?"

Throwing a furtive glance over her shoulder as she slid the

chicken into a cupboard out of sight, Rosalia looked sternly at Luis. "Eleven is too old to be still twisting people around your finger like that."

Luis laughed. "You will give it to me! Oh, Rosalia, you're wonderful, you're — "

"Get on with you!" Cutting a slab of the cake, she put it in his hand. "Now get back to that Latin or Greek or whatever it is before your parents catch you!"

"Latin. It's boring me silly. Gracias, dear Rosalia — "

"Rosalia!" The fat little cook from next door burst into the kitchen. "Quick, Rosalia!" Seizing the woman by the hand, she pulled her to the door. She caught sight of Luis. "You, too!" She snatched at his hand. "Run!"

They dashed with her to the villa next to the Navarros'. "The Inquisition!" The small woman pointed a trembling finger at the men-at-arms running around the building to guard the back exit they had just left.

"The chicken!" Rosalia flung a hand out helplessly. "I left the salted chicken — it's all the proof they need that we're still Jews!"

The other cook clutched at her. "You have to leave this house! Everybody knows Marranos have Marrano servants. If they catch you here they'll suspect us!"

Luis was shaking all over as though he had had a fever and was trembling now with chills. The Inquisition has come, he told himself. They're taking Mama and Papa away. I'll never see them again. But none of it seemed real except that he was frightened and shivering.

"Rosalia," he said suddenly, "where are you going to take me?"

"You'll have to go alone," she said hurriedly as the little cook pushed them out a side door, "we can't be seen together — go to Barcelona — Granada — Ecija — "

"Don't leave me, Rosalia!" He clung to her apron but she tugged it out of his fingers.

"I'm going to Lisboa, I can't take you, child — here, let me dirty your doublet for you, it's too fine, people will notice you — oh, child, you still have the cake in your hand!" She burst into tears and disappeared into an alley.

Luis ran after her. "Rosalia, come back! Rosalia! Rosalia!"

❧ ❧ ❧

Someone was shaking him and calling his name softly. He opened his eyes to rain-drenched cobbles and sodden straw. Drawing a deep, shuddering breath, he ordered his heart to stop pounding. It had happened nearly two years ago. There was nothing to fear, now. He was in Lisboa. The Inquisition could not reach him here.

"The same nightmare again?" came a sympathetic whisper.

"Yes. Sorry."

"Not your fault. The wind's driving the rain into your corner. Squeeze in with me. We're in the lee of the building; you can dry off."

"It's all right, Saadya; I can never go back to sleep after that dream, anyhow," Luis whispered back. "I'll go find a dry doorway."

"Wait for me; I'll come with you."

Not far away there was a sheltered place; they huddled against each other, their arms around their knees. In the darkness Saadya said, "You told me the nightmare, once; but you never said what came afterwards. Where did you go? If you don't mind talking about it, that is."

"After Rosalia left? Oh, I lived rough in the streets. I got the hang of it pretty fast after I found a bunch of street urchins who took me on. They sold my fancy clothes and gave me this outfit; made a good profit out of me, I shouldn't wonder. I didn't care; I figured the Inquisition would never expect to find me dressed like a beggar."

"So how did you come to Lisboa?"

Luis grinned. "Followed my food supply, that's all. Truly. See, all I knew about being Jewish was that we had different holidays and ate kosher food. So I scavenged in the Juderia for what I ate. Suddenly all the Jews were leaving, so I did, too. There was nothing to keep me in Sevilla any more. I kept wanting to leave every time I saw the processions." His tone was no longer light. "My parents died like that, condemned heretics wearing yellow San Benitos." There was an unhappy silence.

"Luis?" Saadya's voice was hesitant. "What do they look like? San Benitos, I mean?"

"Like a huge yellow talith katan, down to your knees. Without the tzitzith. That's why your father had such hard work getting me to wear a talith katan. It had a different meaning for me."

He fell silent, remembering the grandees in black robes, banners waving; priests and cardinals, their embroidered robes magnificent in the sun; black-cloaked Dominican friars chanting solemnly as they herded their victims along the street to the Quemadero, the place of burnings. The condemned all looked alike — all in tall caps, all carrying long green candles, all in shapeless San Benitos, yellow for confessed heretics: they tortured you, so of course you confessed, but they burned you anyway, only they gave you a yellow San Benito instead of a black one to die in. You had to be very strong or very crazy to win a black San Benito.

"Luis?" Saadya's voice was gently questioning.

"Yes — never mind; I shouldn't think about those things. So I left Sevilla and just went along with the crowds, begging food from them. I got stuck at the border — didn't have the eight cruzados to get across, of course — until your father let me hang on underneath your wagon and smuggled me into Portugal. I'm just glad I found your family."

"Because Abba's a rav?"

"Yes, and because you were willing to teach me Judaismo. Everyone else seemed to know what they were making sacrifices for. I didn't."

"Mm." After a pause Saadya asked, "Did you ever find Rosalia?"

"No." Luis sighed. "I think I asked at every house in Lisboa, even ones that weren't Jewish. Maybe she changed her mind and didn't come here after all, I don't know." He gave Saadya a little shove. "Go back to sleep. You've had your bedtime story."

"Come on, I'm only a year younger than you," Saadya protested.

"Sure, I know. But you're still part of a family, you've got parents who worry about you. Thanks for the company."

He sensed, rather than saw, Saadya leave the dark doorway for the shadowed street. A few minutes later a gust of wind sent the rain pattering against the stone at Luis's feet. He hoped Saadya had made it back to his family in time to stay dry. He was the youngest Toledano child and they all fussed over him. Family. It seemed centuries since he had had a family, or maybe it had been someone else entirely. Leaning against the stone wall beside him, he listened to the rain and the December wind around the corners of the crooked streets, and tried not to remember being a child in Sevilla.

❈   ❈   ❈

A hundred years before, when the Castilians had sacked Lisboa, the Judiaria had already been the best part of the city. In the intervening century the Jewish quarter, nestled midway up Alfama's hillside, had grown still more gracious and elegant, each house finer within than the last, each with a charming view of Lisboa's harbor from the screened balconies. Flights of steps led from one narrow, paved street to another in such a bewildering maze that newcomers could be lost between the Rua da Judiaria and the Rua Nova a stone's throw away.

For the immigrants who swarmed into the quarter that summer of 1492, however, the quaint streets and delightful alleys became their homes because there was nowhere else; and the fine paved surface made hard beds.

In a gray March predawn, Reina d'Ortas woke to see her brother already up, standing on the wet cobblestones. "Yosef!" she whispered, her eyes wide with fear. "What's wrong?"

"Nothing," he whispered back. "I want to go down to the harbor to see if a ship needs unloading. If I'm really early I might get work, and even finish in time for another job later on."

Carefully, so as not to rouse her mother, Reina crept away from the thin layer of straw that they slept on. In the alley they were sheltered from the worst of the winds, but storm clouds scudded across the sky and it had been raining off and on for days. Reina washed quickly and caught at Yosef's sleeve.

"You're going down to the harbor? In this?"

"There might be a ship," insisted Yosef.

"They say it's been blowing at sea for nearly a week. There won't be any ships; they'll all be in harbor already." She understood his desperate search for work; they lived so close to the border between hunger and starvation. But there was no sense in wasting effort.

"I have to go, just in case. What if there is one?" He held out his hand. "Come with me."

With a quick embarrassed shake of her head Reina looked at the ground and confessed, "I'm afraid."

"You're always afraid, afraid of everything," her brother accused. "Why don't you grow up? Come down with me. It's perfectly safe; nobody will be about."

She could see from his face how silly he thought her. He was right; she *was* afraid of everything. She hated the way Yosef looked at her at times like this; it made her want to writhe. Yosef was brave; Mama was quite unexpectedly brave; but she herself had never risen to the challenge of their new life, never found the courage within her that Mama assured her must be there. "All right," she said at last.

Together they walked down the narrow streets cramped between buildings, their shoulders hunched against the wind and the rain. Down a flight of steps into the Rua da Judiaria, and they could see the harbor clearly, their view widening as they came out at the foot of the hill. Seagulls encrusted the roofs of every quayside building as thickly as barnacles on a ship's bottom, and in the sheltered places near shore little islands of clustered gulls rode uneasily on the restless water.

"Look at all the gulls sheltering here," Reina exclaimed. "It must be terrible at sea. How could a ship —" she stopped.

For there was a ship, just dropping anchor near the wooden quay. Once a graceful, sleek caravel, she was storm-battered now, sails ripped, rigging hanging uselessly, yards splintered. As she swung in the wind they could see *"Niña"* painted on her transom, half-obliterated with encrusted salt. They saw a boat lowered and a man climb down into it, his white hair blowing in his face. His crew rowed toward the steps that led down to the water near the blue-roofed housing of the harbor crane.

As the boat tied up, Yosef went forward to meet the captain. The man came up the steps briskly enough, but he looked tired out.

"Need a hand with unloading, Senhor?" The wind whipped the words out of Yosef's mouth so that for a moment he was not sure the captain had heard.

"I'm not unloading here." The white-haired man tried to push past Yosef.

"Take you to a ship's chandler, Senhor?" Yosef persisted.

"I know the way better than you do, boy," snapped the man. He strode off confidently, clearly familiar with the port of Lisboa.

Yosef watched him go. "*Gam zu l'tova*," he said quietly.

Although Yosef's face showed nothing, Reina felt his humiliation as keenly as he did himself. It was so hard for him to bring himself to beg for work that being refused so brusquely was like a slap. She felt herself blushing.

There was no reason to remain on the quay. There would not be another unlikely ship defying the storm. Slowly they climbed back up the hill into the Judiaria, through the passages between blank whitewashed house-walls.

People were beginning to stir. Out of doorways and alleys men stepped into the street, slightly grumpy and only half-awake, on their way to the synagoga.

Yosef touched Reina's arm. "Go back to Mama. Tell her I've gone to meldar. I'll see you tonight." And he was gone, a small, neat figure in rusty black velvet, lost almost at once in the throng.

Reina glanced down at her worn gown of silken baldaquin, too shabby to sell. They were all shabby, now, she and Mama and Yosef. But it bothered Yosef most.

Being poor gnawed at Yosef's self-respect like a rat at a rope. When Reina laughed at Yosef brushing his once-fine velvets as fastidiously as a gentleman, he said savagely, "Being poor is having to look ugly and ridiculous. Every speck on my suit is a step closer to being poor, to looking like Luis."

She knew the boy he meant, the stocky one who slept in the next alley. She thought he looked pleasant, with his friendly face and quick, wide grin, his sunburnt cheeks and shaggy brown hair. But his clothes *were* poor, a hodgepodge of castoffs:

threadbare hose, peasant's trousers too frayed to tie over the knees any more, an oversize doublet he would take years to grow into, badly mended and with no belt but a bit of cord.

Reina sighed. It mattered so much to Yosef to remain the rich man's son, the boy who carried himself like a young grandee, erect and self-possessed. He was striking anyway, with his black hair and pale aristocrat's skin, his high proud nose and clear, direct eyes. One hardly noticed how grim his mouth was.

She thought she could remember him before he had been like that, when he had been an ordinary, teasing older brother. But that had been when Papa was still alive. She remembered Papa clearly: handsome, dignified, sitting proudly on the best horseflesh money could buy. She had admired Papa, but she had been a little afraid of him, too, the stern disciplined man who would not tolerate disorganization. Even Mama, she thought, had been a little afraid of him.

After Papa died Yosef tried to fill his place. Overnight he seemed to grow up into a copy of Papa, dignified and disciplined as Papa had been. He tried very hard to keep the business going, too; she remembered the time she had peeped into the accounts and found them kept as punctiliously as Papa had, in a hand that was so similar she could hardly tell the two apart. She found herself standing in awe of him, and after a while she did not think of him as her older brother any more but as a sort of distant relation she respected but did not know very well.

But he was, after all, only a boy; and when people heard that the Jews had to flee Spain, creditors sprang up like weeds to take advantage of the child trying to manage the man's tasks. The perfectly kept accounts never seemed to help; the courts always decided against them; and Papa's flourishing business lay in ruins long before the final date arrived. In the end there was nothing left for Yosef to do but say, as Papa had always done, "Gam zu l'tova."

Gam zu l'tova. So often they had heard Papa say that phrase: when a business deal fell through, when something was lost or broken, whenever things didn't go the way they would have liked. Always it was "gam zu l'tova." Even when Papa knew he was dying he looked at her and Yosef and said fiercely, "*Gam zu l'tova.*"

Now they were so poor that she and Mama had to scrub other people's floors to live, so poor that they possessed nothing but their pride. Yet Yosef kept his back straight and his head high and said "*Gam zu l'tova*" as if it cost him no effort. Once, when she had asked him about it, he had said, "You can have no money and still keep your pride; it is when having no money makes you humble that you become poor." Never, she thought, never would Yosef be poor.

She did not mock his courtier's airs any more; only she felt a little sorry for him for his fierce pride, so like Papa's, because it made his life so much more difficult. For herself, she cared not at all about being proud or humble; it was not her self-respect that made her hate being poor but having to go hungry too often and having to live in an alley, like a stray cat.

Mama was awake. In Spain she had been little and plump and helpless, hardly able to cope with the house. Reina and Yosef had grown up feeling protective about her. But she was not plump and helpless anymore; she was tiny and tough and determined and she worked harder than any servant they had ever had. To Reina's eyes Mama did not seem to notice that they were poor, or remember that they had once been well-to-do. Reina did not understand how a person could shut off part of her mind like that.

Looking up at the stormy sky, Mama said, "I hope it's not like this at the end of the month."

"Why then, especially?" Reina asked, puzzled.

"Because we'll be traveling again, Reina. This is the last of the eight months we're allowed to stay in Portugal. Whether or not the king keeps his promise to give us ships, we'll have to leave Portugal somehow."

"Already?" Reina faltered. "I hadn't realized it was so soon."

So soon. Scarcely two weeks later they stood among thousands of others on the wooden quay that stretched along the harborside. King João really had sent ships; they lay in the harbor now, tying up a few at a time and letting people swarm aboard until each captain called a halt; then casting off and making room for more. In the bright April sunshine Reina could not help but feel hopeful.

Thousands of homeless Jews from all over Portugal are here, Reina thought, and Mama and Yosef and I; and together we'll all build new lives where the king's ships take us. Mama and I won't have to scrub floors and Yosef will find work and we'll live in a house again. She gazed happily at Mama. But her mother's face was grave.

"Mama, why aren't you happy? We're finally leaving Lisboa!"

"Think, Reina!" her mother said sharply. "What community can cope with these thousands of paupers? It will be worse than it was here. Here, we slaved for a few coppers; there, we'll be begging. Here, we were hungry; there we may starve."

Reina's mouth opened in silent horror. Not better. Worse. Not better. She felt tears coming into her eyes and her lip trembling. Yosef gave her a quick shake.

"Don't you dare cry! Be brave for once," he snapped.

"But Mama, we have no choice; we have to leave Portugal. What can we do?"

"We say 'gam zu l'tova', as Papa would have. Whatever happens is right and good, whether or not we can see it. You must have that bitachon, Reina, you — "

"There aren't enough ships," Yosef said suddenly. "The last lot are moving away but there aren't any more."

"What!" Reina craned her neck to see, but she was as tiny as her mother and too many people were in the way.

There was a sharp scream. From behind them a young woman thrust her way through the crowd, clutching two small children so tightly against her that they had started to cry. Soldiers pushed their way after the woman but they had not caught her by the time she reached the edge of the quay. With hardly a moment's hesitation she leapt into the water, the children still in her arms. The crying of the children stopped almost at once.

Stunned by the suddenness of the incident, Reina did not at first understand what she had seen. Only gradually did she realize that the woman had been escaping from some unknown threat. She twisted around to where the woman had come from — and screamed.

She was looking directly into the face of a monk.

Jerking away, she tried to run but the crowd pressed in too tightly to let her through. She clung to her mother and turned toward Yosef but Yosef was gone. Out of the corner of her eye she saw the monk reach out slowly — slowly. His hand seemed to inch across the distance deliberately, relentlessly until the dry fingers touched her arm and curved around it little by little, tighter and tighter. He pulled at her but her arms were around Mama and she would not let go. She felt Mama's arms laced firmly around her. She buried her head against Mama's shoulder.

There was a sharp, vicious wrench. Mama was not there any more. Twisting and writhing in the monk's grasp, Reina saw her mother struggling against a soldier double her size. The soldier shoved her roughly. Reina saw her stumble and fall, saw her head strike the cobbles of the fine paved street, saw her roll over slightly and lie still. Someone bent down and examined her. Someone else rolled the body aside with an indifferent foot.

"Mama! I have to go to Mama!" Reina dragged against the monk's hands. He would not release her. With a swift motion she bent and bit him. For an instant his grip relaxed. She broke free and dashed frantically toward where her mother lay.

But before she reached her, Reina felt herself captured again in a hold that was no longer firm but brutal. The dry fingers bit into her arms and the monk's breathing was heavy and angry in her ear. She wriggled and fought but she could not escape. The monk half-flung her up the steps of the street. She threw herself sideways for one last look back.

"Mama!" she screamed. "Mama!"

CHAPTER TWO

APRIL HAD DRIFTED into May, and June was nearing. Though the sunshine was as bright as it had been in Lisboa, Lisboa lay a thousand leagues behind the caravel that bore Don Alvaro de Caminha southward.

Under the awning that had been spread for him on the after deck of the *Rio do Ouro*, Don Alvaro watched the little flock of ships trailing behind his own, and thought about his new position as donatario of São Tome. He did not particularly want to be the colonial administrator of an island a thousand leagues from anywhere and it would have been pleasant to blame his assignment on someone, but it was hard to decide whose fault it was. There were so many people to choose among: the king; the man Colon who had explored the western ocean; Don Alvaro's predecessor, who had died so inconveniently; the friar Frei Domingo; the Jews, for being available; and even, perhaps, himself.

He thought about the stormy day in early March — it seemed hardly credible that it had been little more than two months ago — that Colon, or Columbus, as the priest called him, had taken refuge in Lisboa harbor and been called to the king's presence. Standing with the other courtiers and fidalgos, Don Alvaro watched as the sailor, laden with gold, leading strange savages, bowed before His Majesty and affected not to notice the expression on His Majesty's face.

Years before, people said, this sailor had come begging King João for ships, and the king had refused him, looked at him with contempt in his heavy-lidded eyes and his coarse features, his thick lips hardly moving as he dismissed him. Don João was a king to be feared; he was not a likeable man.

So Colon had gone to Spain to beg for his ships.

But that day in March, Colon was back, and he had found the Indies, or something, at any rate. Don João gave one of the savages a bowl of beans and told him to make a map of the islands he lived among in the Indies. The native laid out bean after bean after bean. Leaning forward, his heavy sullen face dark with anger, the king saw an island empire laid out on the floor before him, a Spanish island empire he might have had, and he struck his fist against his chest and cried out with regret.

A little shiver trickled down Don Alvaro's back. From the faces around him he knew the others felt the same. Then the man was gone with his savages and his gold, and someone kicked the beans aside, but the king sat still and brooding.

Don Alvaro recalled turning to the man next to him to say, "Well, and Portugal has islands, too, doesn't it?" Though he kept his voice low, it was very clear in the silent room. He should not have spoken. The king did not like Don Alvaro's family — there had been some court intrigue a decade earlier that Don Alvaro's father had been involved in, as well as the Jew Abarbanel — but the king knew Don Alvaro to be capable and did not want to discard a useful man.

At Don Alvaro's words, the king's head flew up. "Islands? We do, indeed," he said. "But we have done little with them. We have been remiss." His eyes met Don Alvaro's. "But no longer, I think."

From that moment Don Alvaro de Caminha knew he was marked by the king, for good or ill; and when news came, only a few days later, of João de Paiva's death on São Tome, he knew without being told that he was the next donatario of the island.

But this madness of sending children as colonists — he had Frei Domingo to thank for that. "The refugees," murmured the friar to the king: "aren't there more than you agreed to admit? Will there actually be enough ships for them at the end of the month?" He paused briefly. "I wonder what will happen to those who stay illegally."

King João looked at the cleric with interest. "They will become the property of the Crown, of course; they should make useful slaves." He did not need to add that the revenue from their sale would be equally useful to the royal treasury.

"The adults, of course," agreed Frei Domingo. "But the children — the little children can still be molded. To take hundreds of these Jewish children and raise them as Christians — to save hundreds of souls from the torments of Hell — to swell the multitude of the faithful! Think of it! What an act of faith! What glory to the Church!" He gazed raptly heavenwards.

Slouched on his throne, Don João looked at the friar with an appraising eye. It was not always easy to tell if Frei Domingo believed his speeches or if he was only trying to take for the Church what the king had wanted, as a test of power. There are limits, however, to even a priest's power when it means a loss to the Crown of hundreds of potentially profitable slaves. To the courtiers it appeared that Frei Domingo had overreached himself. Yet Don João could not refuse the Church those children without making himself look like a heretic, now that Frei Domingo had laid claim to them. Don Alvaro was interested to see how the king could resolve the difficulty in his own favor.

"As you know, Frei Domingo," began Don João, "we have an island empire scattered in the reaches of the ocean and along the coast of Africa. To hold these islands for Portugal we must have colonists to inhabit them. Now, as Don Alvaro knows, no doubt — " his voice held dry humor — "there is a place called São Tome, in need of just such colonists. What better way, I ask you, Frei Domingo, to provide hundreds of loyal Portuguese settlers than by giving these children of yours a new home there? I put these innocents in your charge, Frei Domingo. You have the vision, the idealism to make these children a credit to their Church and to their king. You must be the one to see their spiritual growth on São Tome. No doubt your superior will agree with me."

The smile he gave the friar was not a friendly one; and the smile he received in return was thin. The mission pleased the friar very little.

So the children had been taken, from two years to ten, or so Don Alvaro was told, though when he went to inspect them he was sure some were older and thanked heaven for it. But two-year-olds! Scarcely weaned, and certainly not even clean, yet; he couldn't build a colony with babies! The discovery that many of the rest were not healthy disquieted him further. He had been given two thousand children. It sounded impressive until he discounted the infants and the sickly ones. The real number, the number of children he was willing to take to the island, he judged to be nearly eight hundred.

Trying to persuade the king to let him have his way had been risky: it could have meant the end of his political life. But Don Alvaro put it to him that sending sickly children to populate the island, to pass on their infection to the rest, would not only be unsuccessful but would reflect badly on the land: that the place was so unhealthy that men could not live there. Further, Don Alvaro pointed out, if his career were to be blighted by such a signal failure, he might as well blight it himself by refusing to go, and live in comfortable obscurity in civilized Lisboa. Perhaps the humor pleased the king. At any rate, he had agreed at last to the eight hundred, all healthy and none under three.

It was those eight hundred he had now in the dozen ships in his little fleet, as well as sixscore degredados out of the prisons: convicts who were glad enough to labor on an island in the middle of nowhere in return for a pardon. Still, Don Alvaro could hardly blame his friends who insisted on calling his new dominion "Nursemaid's Island." The place had other names, anyway: he had heard the seamen call it and its neighbors the "ilhas perdidas", the lost islands; and to São Tome they gave another name, "ilha dos lagartos" — island of crocodiles.

"Is it really so terrible?" A cheerful reedy voice broke into his reflections: Frei Bartolomeu.

Don Alvaro glanced behind him to see the friar coming up the ladder to join him. "Oh, I daresay it won't be so bad when things are organized, but it wasn't what I had in mind when I dreamed of advancement. I can't see that His Majesty will be satisfied with whatever I accomplish on São Tome; it's not going to be grand enough to boast about."

"What are you planning?" As he stood there, a small man in the white habit, his cowl thrown back so that above the reddish-mouse fringe of hair his tonsured head gleamed in the sun like polished marble, he seemed so full of optimism that Don Alvaro's gloomy mood lifted.

"To start with," the donatario began, "we'll need at least a thousand acres under cultivation just for our own needs; but after that, I was thinking of sugar cane. The profits go to the Crown, you know, so I thought it would please Don João. The older children could be useful there, too. I'm told the cane would do well."

"It would, yes." A shy smile lit the friar's face. "I was on São Tome for a few days on the way back from the Kongo — the ship I was on provisioned there and I looked around a bit."

"Did you? Then what's this business about 'island of crocodiles'? Are there really any?"

Frei Bartolomeu hesitated a moment before he nodded. "A great many. At first they used to roam all over the island — they ate most of the children of the Kongolese slaves that de Paiva brought in for field work — but eventually they were driven out of the interior. You only see them on the shore at the edge of the sea, now."

"Lovely."

"But wait until you see the island, Don Alvaro!" protested the friar. "It's a paradise! The streams are alive with trout; the sea teems with all kinds of fish: sea perch, bonito, sea bream; sole and tuna, herring and sardine and giant mackerel. And the trees — ironwood and baobab and trumpetwood — and the fruit! Ripe fruits simply drop into your hands: coconut, breadfruit, mango, banana; and there's plenty of malagueta-pepper that they say keeps the fever away."

"But de Paiva died of the fever in spite of the malagueta," Don Alvaro objected.

"Well, when it comes to fevers, one can catch the same fever in Venezia in the summer." The little friar's optimism was unquenchable. "And I learned many native remedies while I was in the Kongo; we can pray that they help." He turned to go.

"We can indeed." Don Alvaro's gloom was returning. "Don't go yet, Padre. I want to know something: what do you think of this kidnapping?" He swung his arm to include the whole fleet of ships, toylike on the sparkling sea.

A small silence hung between them while Frei Bartolomeu considered the question. When he answered, he began thoughtfully, "I find I often have private disagreements with my prior, may Heaven forgive me. I'm only a peasant who took vows to escape serfdom; I have no business questioning my superiors." He took a deep breath and let it out again. "If it had been a question of taking these children and placing them with good Christian families to be raised in the Church, well, saving souls justifies many things. But sending them so far to populate an island which everybody knows has no climate for young children? It will be years before they're old enough to marry, and who knows how many will survive? To me it seems less a mission than a death sentence. It's not a decision I'd want to be remembered for."

"And how does Frei Domingo feel about it?"

"Now that — " the friar waggled a finger — "is a question I can't answer. I'm not Frei Domingo's confidant. He's a close man and a hard one. Sometimes I think I'm not ruthless enough in the interests of the Church. Frei Domingo is."

Don Alvaro nodded his thanks. His eyes wandered over the sails, the sky, the sea around him, the foamy wake of the *Rio do Ouro*. "You know," he said after a while, "I'll be sorry to see this journey end, to let the degredados out of this hold, to set the children among the fevers and the crocodiles, to have to start trying to make sense of what King João's landed me with. Just now, it's still only a discussion; in another couple of days it'll be real." He realized suddenly that he would miss the little friar's company, too; but Frei Bartolomeu was the closest to a physician that they had. He would be needed more with the children than serving as the donatario's private priest.

"I'm afraid it will be real tonight," said Frei Bartolomeu regretfully. Nodding at a blue smudge on the horizon ahead of them, he said, "That's São Tome."

"Amazing." Don Alvaro had seen the sailors using the astrolabe to navigate, had watched them hang it by its ring and sight along the pointer, but it was still a mystery and a wonder that one could sail for weeks with no landmarks and end up heading directly for a tiny spot only a score of miles across. Fascinated by the idea, he watched the blue smudge grow larger as they approached.

Crowned with lush forests, the island rose slowly out of the ocean. Even at a distance he could see cliffs falling sheer to the water, giving way to crescent beaches rimmed with shining sand. Behind them, steep hillsides quilted with luxuriant growth surged upwards to mountain peaks thrusting toward the sky, and countless rivers plunged down their flanks in waterfalls that gleamed white through the foliage, crashing noiselessly to the sea.

As Frei Bartolomeu had said, it was a very beautiful island. For a long time Don Alvaro gazed at it, half-hypnotized by the ever-changing views. Not until they were actually rounding the headland into the fine bay did he wake from his trance to prepare himself for landing and assuming the duties of his new office.

As donatario he had the privilege of disembarking first. Standing on the deck of the *Rio do Ouro* for the last time, he glanced sharply over the collection of hovels that passed for the town of São Tome.

From the ship Don Alvaro could see the population of the island drawn up in formal array near the wooden dock. As he stepped ashore, he examined them. The whites: a couple of dozen men, woven hats on their heads but otherwise half-dressed and slovenly. The negros, blacks: barefoot, rags tied skirtwise around their waists, bowing with forearms crossed on their chests, grinning broadly.

When Don Alvaro halted opposite the assemblage, one of the whites stepped forward, a trifle unsteadily, the donatario thought. He looked the man up and down, not much liking what he saw. The fellow was grossly fat, his stomach bulging under a loose shirt, his doublet long ago discarded. His trousers hung loose at the knees above bare legs, and although he wore shoes, they were obviously not worn often. In the steamy heat the man was sweating so heavily that there were little rivulets running down his fleshy face, shaded though it was by the palm-leaf hat.

With the wide offensive grin of the old hand for the newcomer, the man said, "Welcome to São Tome, Senhor. I've been in charge since Senhor de Paiva died. I am called Estevão."

Don Alvaro gave him a long stare of distaste. "You are drunk, Senhor," he snapped.

Wagging his head in foolish agreement, the man, Estevão,

replied, "That's how you keep off the fever, Senhor. The fever can't get in when you're filled up with liquor."

"Try the malagueta," advised Don Alvaro dryly. "I'm told it has the same effect." His eyes flicked over the rest of the men. "That's all; you can all get back to work. Consider me welcomed." His head already swimming with the insistently blazing sun, he strode up the slight rise to the only building worthy of the name: the donatario's ... palace ... without doubt. Glancing over his shoulder to tell Estevão he would be wanted shortly, Don Alvaro noticed that Frei Domingo was herding the children towards the sandy expanse at the edge of the sea. "And get those children off the beach!" he added.

Estevão shambled heavily from the dockside. Tapping Frei Domingo on the arm, he said politely, "Padre — "

"Yes?" asked the friar shortly. Pulling his arm free, he backed away from the fumes on the man's breath. "I'm busy; can't you see?"

Estevão leaned forward confidentially. "Donatario says — " he swayed and almost lost his balance — "says get the children off the beach."

"After they've had a quick swim."

Shaking his head, Estevão insisted, "No, Padre, now. Don't you see all them crocodiles? They don't get many children nowadays; they'd really appreciate a tasty little girl."

Eyes following the man's pointing finger, the friar understood the danger. Along the shining curve of the sand, where the wavelets lapped lazily in the sunlight, lay dark objects. At first glance Frei Domingo took them for rocks scattered over the beach. But rocks do not move in ponderous progress to splash their tails in the sea. He was looking at crocodiles basking in the heat. With a haste that was unusual in one so dignified, Frei Domingo shepherded his charges back to safety.

Estevão led the procession to a shady place under the trees some distance past the huddle of huts that was São Tome. "First thing you got to teach these kids is, never go near that beach," he informed the missionario. "Second thing, never go out in the sun without a hat. Third, don't work too hard; it's too hot. I'll send you a black boy to show you how to make the hats."

Realizing that Estevão was about to leave, Frei Domingo forgot his dignity as missionario and caught nervously at his shirt. "Where are the houses for the children?"

"Aren't none," shrugged Estevão. "It's the gravana now, anyway; hardly rains at all for the next couple of months." Shaking his shirt free of the priest's grasp, he gave an uncouth hitch to his trousers and made off.

In the donatario's house Don Alvaro was sifting through the accumulated paperwork. He mopped his face and loosened his shirt. He began to understand why the whites had discarded their doublets. Somewhere in the house he could hear his luggage being brought in — slowly. He looked up to see the missionario's stern face.

"Frei Domingo," the donatario greeted him frostily.

The missionario drew a deep, indignant breath. "Do you realize, Don Alvaro, that there are no houses for the children, no latrines, no provision for cooking, no — "

"Padre," returned Don Alvaro irritably, flicking at the report he did not want to write, "there are over a hundred degredados at your disposal. Tell that fellow Estevão what you want, on my authority, and he'll see that you get it. The supplies, by the way, are still being unloaded," he added. "I'm afraid everyone will just have to be patient for a bit."

With a cool nod of thanks the friar departed.

CHAPTER THREE

LUIS CREPT CLOSER to the building that had just been erected. Careful not to lean against the flimsy walls, he put his ear to one of the many cracks and listened. Under the mistaken impression that all the children were asleep — a mistake no parent would have made — Frei Domingo had summoned all the friars to hear his plans for organizing the colony. His nasal voice made Luis feel like a cat whose fur was being rubbed the wrong way.

"I assure you, Frei Pero, that we will celebrate a requiem mass for poor Frei Tome and for all the children who perished on the journey here."

Good, thought Luis. One priest less.

"We shall have all the children in attendance, so that they may see that we are not indifferent to the sufferings of their brethren."

Luis could hear some restless shifting inside the hall. Frei Domingo's pomposity did not go down well; the other friars wanted to get the business over with and go to bed. Luis could well imagine that the friars were tired. After the long confinement of the voyage, the children were explosive with pent-up emotions: they were homesick, longing for their parents; over-excited at being released; fractious with the torrid heat; consumed with an intense, burning hatred for their captors. The friars were not having an easy time of it. Luis smiled.

" … and the children will be divided into teams, ten younger ones under each of seventy-odd ten-year-olds. The remaining ten-year-olds will be expected to help in the fields, and as time goes by the rest of the older ones will join them. Meanwhile, these teams will be given such tasks as gathering fruit or fodder for the goats and mules, catching fish, cleaning the compound, and so on, according to the age of the group. Except for tasks, the children aged three, four, and five will be under the supervision of a friar at all times, being taught and indoctrinated and, I may add, protected from the older children's influence. At present the children are still divided by shipload; those of you who came with them may choose the heads of the teams as long as none of them are from the same shipload as the children they lead. We want these children to feel they know no one but us well enough to turn to.

"In the last two days I've been observing the older children. There are three potential leaders who should not be used in any official capacity: Luis Navarro, because the children find him too likable; Yosef d'Ortas, because he's too self-possessed; Nechama de Lamego, because she's too competent. Is — "

A diffident cough interrupted him. "I'm afraid I've already had to use her to organize the cooking."

"There was a cook among the degredados." Frei Domingo's tone was stern.

"He died on the way," explained the apologetic friar. "And this Nechama is from a large family and has been working since she was ten — she's nearly thirteen — as the assistant to the cook in a large house. And I don't know how to cook."

"Does anyone?" Clearly the answer was negative. "Well, don't let her take charge of too much. You organize the girls to help her; don't let her do that."

"She's done it already."

"Keep an eye on her, then; that's all," snapped Frei Domingo, vexed. "All of you should be aware of any other older ones who need caution. Of course I want to put effort into them, too: if we can win them over, they'll lead the rest. Watch for weaknesses.

"I'd like to confiscate all belt knives, but the children need them for eating; see to it that they're blunted.

"Now, for the compound: I envision the cooking and eating facilities at the center of a figure-eight layout. Frei João, you have the services of the degredados for one month before Don Alvaro wants them back; if you would choose two other friars to help you supervise and see me afterwards for the plans — Frei Bartolomeu, the infirmaries are your province; I have some suggestions ... "

You would, thought Luis with a grin, as he slipped away. It was good to know where they stood. He was looking forward to laying some plans of his own.

The next morning the children filed sullenly into the open space before the single dining hall in which the friars had met the previous night. An altar had been set up at its doorway. Unimpressed by Frei Domingo's assurance that the mass was to be said for the souls of the children who had died en route, the young audience fidgeted and grew restive as the chanting continued. At the front of the crowd of children there was a slight disturbance: Luis rose quietly, clambered over his neighbors to a point in full view of all the children, thumbed his nose at the priest, and calmly walked away. Minutes later, another boy did the same. In the girls' section an entire row removed itself piecemeal but quite quickly. One by one, more and more children rose and wandered off, rather as though they had been watching some not-very-good mummers and had lost interest. Required to respond to the service, taken by surprise, the friars in attendance tried feebly to halt the exodus but scarcely even slowed it. By the time mass was ended, Frei Domingo turned to view an empty clearing.

Because he had been officiating, Frei Domingo had had his back to the unwilling congregation; but the other friars had not. There was a little conference and a quiet stroll and a sudden tight, silent group of friars around Luis a few moments later. Luis was escorted to a secluded corner of the rough compound.

"We want to instruct you privately," explained Frei Domingo in a kindly way as another friar caned Luis with professional ease, "because the rest of the children understand that we are their friends, but they might misconstrue our brief discussion here."

The "discussion" was brief, indeed; but memorable.

In the afternoon the oldest boys, assigned to field work, were put to digging around tree stumps. The actual removal would be done by the men, but Estevão had decided that the boys were capable of loosening the stumps and tossing out the earth.

Luis used his spade gingerly — the beating had been thorough — but he still grinned from time to time as he thought back to the morning's success.

Between spadefuls he glanced at Yosef, working nearby. He was puzzled at the boy's energy. Thrust and heave, thrust and heave: Yosef threw himself into the activity. He dug as though he were in a race, as though he thought he could tunnel his way back to Portugal. Why? Luis asked himself. They were certainly not being paid for whatever they did. Why should Yosef work himself so hard?

The steadiness of Luis's regard made Yosef raise his head from the trench he was bending over. "Nice job, this morning," he complimented Luis. "I would have liked to think of something like that. Have you been to Frei Bartolomeu for those weals?"

Luis shook his head. "Not yet. They sent us out here too soon."

"You have to have them salved before you go to sleep or they'll stiffen rather badly. They beat me on the voyage for insolence."

One of the other boys picked his way across the cratered clearing with a water-skin. Neither wiry like Yosef nor stocky and tough like Luis, he had been pressed into service as a water-boy. "I hate this job," he complained cheerfully as he handed them each a tepid drink, "but the entertainment this morning helped a lot. What's next?"

"I think we'll recapture the little ones," said Yosef in a considering tone. "The girls will have to prepare for them, but they aren't so overloaded with housework that they'll have trouble coping. I'll tell that girl, the one who seems to be in charge — "

"Nechama, that is," Luis said, "but I wouldn't tell her, if I were you, I'd ask her. They say she can be pretty hard to handle if you don't get on her right side."

Yosef looked at Luis with interest. "Will you do it?"

"All right."

The water-boy looked from one to the other in delight. "May I spread the word?" he asked eagerly. "I've got the perfect job."

"Not yet," cautioned Yosef. "As soon as everything's set, I'll let you know."

As the boy made his way to the next laborers, Luis looked intently at Yosef. "Do you really think we can?" he asked.

"I've got most of it figured out already," Yosef said confidently. About to resume work, he hefted the spade.

"Are you going to keep on digging like a maniac?" Luis asked suddenly. "What for?"

Yosef shifted his grip on the handle. "I like it. I like the challenge of seeing how hard I can work, how long I can go on for, after I think I can't do any more. Also, if we can organize ourselves to be independent of the friars, I want to be able to set an example of self-discipline for everybody. Mostly, though, it's just the thrill of being completely alive, the blood pounding in my head, the pull of every muscle, hearing the birds and monkeys, smelling the earth. It's an exciting place, new and wild, and when I throw myself into working here something sings in me. Don't you feel it?"

Luis shook his head. "Not in the same way." Saadya was still teaching him, but it was no substitute for living in a proper kehilla. He could never look at the beauty of São Tome without longing for the alley in Lisboa. He bent to retrieve his own spade, wincing as he did so.

Noticing Luis's grimace, Yosef said casually, "Look, do you mind if I do a bit of digging in your hole? If Estevão sees a hole that size, he'll go for you; he's pretty bad-tempered since Don Alvaro raided all the liquor caches."

"'Help yourself." Luis grinned. "I'll take a couple of spoonfuls out of yours in return. No, I'll do something else as well. I'll tell you what I heard last night." He repeated as much of the friars' conference as he could recall.

"Nice to know they're afraid of us," said Yosef with satisfaction. "From now on, we'd better not be seen together often, so they don't suspect we're plotting. But I do want to put together a delegation, about ten of the other older boys."

"No problem. I know who we want."

"Good. I want to see them tonight, just outside the compound at the far end. They'll have to slip away when the friars aren't looking. Tonight I'll talk to the boys; after Shabath we'll go to Don Alvaro."

Don Alvaro? Luis looked curiously at Yosef, but he had already resumed work and showed no inclination to say more. After Shabath, he thought. Shabath would be interesting. He wondered if the friars could beat everyone who refused to work or whether they would let the children have their way. But there would be no resistance without a core of rebellion: he would have to bring up the subject at the meeting that night. The dozen older boys would have to form that nucleus, willing to be seen holding fast to Shabath, willing to be beaten for it. Luis sighed. It's going to hurt me more than anyone else, he thought. Today's beating is still fresh, and Shabath is tomorrow night.

Tomorrow night: their first Shabath since arriving. There had been so much confusion that any tefiloth had been sketchy, an individual affair. But when Friday evening came, the boys began to drift together because that was how it had always been; that was part of Shabath. When tefilloth were finished and they turned back towards the compound, flames were flickering all over in the darkness: Shabath lights that the girls had lit in anything they could find that would hold oil, because that, too, was how it had always been; that was part of Shabath, too. Even here.

Biding their time, the friars left the children alone. In the morning, however, trouble began when the friars tried to round up the work force.

"Sorry," said one of the boys, blank-faced. "I don't work on my Shabath."

"You were baptized. You are a Christian. Today is a workday like the rest."

"I don't work on my Shabath."

Whack! A length of bamboo struck the boy across the shoulders. Frei Domingo had not been unprepared. As the friar lifted the cane for another blow, the missionario said gently, "No, Frei Paulo; we must pull up his shirt so he appreciates our argument fully." Above the bared back the bamboo rose again.

"I don't work on my Shabath, either." Yosef was on his feet. "Will you beat me, too?"

"I don't work on my Shabath, either." Another of the twelve.

"Nor I." And that boy was not one of the group. One after another, the boys stood and repeated the same words: "I don't work on my Shabath."

Disconcerted, the friar lowered the bamboo. "Please continue, Frei Paulo," Frei Domingo said mildly; "we'll just deal with the ringleaders today." With a few nods, he indicated the boys he meant. Immediately they found themselves held captive.

His arms bent savagely behind him, Luis arched his back against the pain of the friar's grasp as he watched the bamboo rise and fall. Frei Paulo wielded it expertly, bringing it down quickly with a faint hum. The rhythm was unvarying: humm — whack; humm — whack. Leaderless, the children watched helplessly: they made no move against the friars though they outnumbered them. Yosef was taken next. He made no outcry, and when he was released he gave the friars a look of casual contempt as he was shoved aside. Someone pushed Luis forward. I'm not going to enjoy this at all, he thought.

Frei Paulo yanked the shirt upwards. Seeing the fresh marks on Luis's back, he looked questioningly at Frei Domingo.

"This one doesn't seem to learn very quickly," the missionario explained. "Perhaps whipping will be more effective."

Luis tensed. He had not expected that. Beating was for naughty boys; whipping was for criminals. It hurt. For a moment he considered giving in; and then the moment was past and the pain came, so sharp and sudden that it took him by surprise and he could not help crying out. Again he screamed: a second fiery line seared across his back. There was just time to take a deep breath and hold it before he heard the lash whining above him. But the third blow never fell.

"Come on!" he heard a boy yell. "Are we going to let them kill him?"

There was some confused shouting, and Luis felt himself released. Raising his head, he saw Frei Paulo swinging from side to side like a trapped animal as the mass of boys closed in on him. With the quickness of a weasel he turned and ran. Frei Domingo had vanished.

Luis let his breath out slowly.

"You all right, hero?"

Luis leaned gratefully against the boy who had spoken. Chanan, that was his name. Nice boy; tough. "It was only two lashes, after all," Luis said.

"Sure. Nothing at all. Just what you need to set you up for the day. Come lie down, hero; call it a Shabath nap."

Luis was more than willing to obey. But by the time Shabath ended he was as impatient as the other boys to visit Don Alvaro on the mysterious errand.

In silence the delegation of twelve boys filed into the donatario's office. The man glanced up in surprise.

Yosef took a pace forward. "Senhor," he said without preface, "we are living in conditions that no colonist would tolerate. We have no proper housing. We're forced to live where the climate is unhealthy. Your degredados harass our girls. We have to put up with twenty times the number of priests any other colony would carry. Senhor, we were kidnapped and transported here, children taken from our homes and families. Yet you show us less consideration than you would to a common degredado. Because we're only children you ignore our needs."

"Well, boys, what do you want, then?" asked the donatario, with an expression on his face that Luis guessed was meant to be fatherly.

"Defend us from the degredados. Move us to the hills where it's cooler. And get rid of the priests."

"Oh, come now." Senhor Caminha gave a little laugh. "The degredados have as much right as you to marry the girls; the presence of the friars is the business of the Church; and the inconvenience of moving all you children out of the town — it's just out of the question."

Yosef remained resolute. "Senhor, no matter what your priests do to us, we stay Jews. We'll die before we desert our faith. Our girls will die before they let themselves be taken by your men. You hold orders to populate São Tome. Shall I tell you how many of us have caught fevers in the last week? You can't afford to keep us here in lowlands. You can't afford to leave us to the mercy of the degredados. Because you can't afford to let us die.

"I grant you, we don't clearly understand what it is to die; but I can assure you that we'll do it anyway, whether from fever or by our own hands. Does the thought of eight hundred small corpses help to change your mind?"

The donatario gaped at Yosef. "I'll ... have to think about it."

"No," said Yosef. "We want your promise now that you'll let us move to the hills. In writing."

"Impossible!"

Yosef's face was inscrutable. With a nonchalant movement he took out his belt knife and examined the blade, turning it to and fro so the metal caught the lamplight. "The trouble is," he said conversationally, "that if you decide tomorrow to change your mind, you won't be able to. And the king ... "

"All right, all right." Don Alvaro reached for a piece of paper and dipped the quill into the ink. Scrawling a few words, he signed his name with an angry flourish and handed over the paper. "But if this ever comes to light I'll deny it and say it's a forgery."

"Of course." Yosef pocketed the document. "We'll wait outside for a few minutes to listen while you give Frei Domingo and Estevão their orders."

As silently as they had come, they filed out into the darkness and stood listening to the heated discussion that ensued. When it was over, and they were walking back to their compound, one of the boys said to Yosef, "Did you really mean it about us dying by our own hands? I go funny just seeing a cut thumb. Did you mean it?"

There was silence for a moment. "I don't know," Yosef said slowly. "I hope I never find out."

CHAPTER FOUR

DAYS OF WAITING became weeks. Driven uphill in the morning to dig latrines and build houses, the degredados cursed the children when they saw them in the evening, cursed them for giving them so much extra work, for being privileged, for being children, for being Jews.

The friars still had control of the smaller children.

"Yosef, when are we going to get the little ones back?" asked Luis urgently as he sidled nearer on the way back from the fields.

"When we move uphill. I think we'll be going day after tomorrow. Pass the word for a meeting tonight. Now you'd better move off."

Luis moved. They were under Frei Domingo's careful scrutiny more than usual. Clearly Yosef's guess was fairly accurate.

That night, Luis was one of the first to join Yosef at the fringes of the forest. "You're giving out the jobs?" he asked.

"Yes. The girls are set up already. Now I need boys for the kidnapping, boys to receive the children as they're stolen, scouts, and guards. And the boy for the liquor; without him we won't be able to do a thing."

"That's Chanan; he's just come." Luis realized that Yosef did not know the boys as well as he did.

Yosef turned to the skinny boy Luis indicated. "I need you to make sure Estevão is drunk out of his mind the morning we leave, and to get at least some of the degredados just drunk enough to be hard to handle but not too far gone to be useless. That means breaking into the storehouse where Don Alvaro put the confiscated liquor — I think it was mostly palm wine, it's pretty powerful — and gauging your amounts very finely. Do you think you can do it?"

"Sure. No problem," the boy said offhandedly.

Luis could feel Yosef's annoyance with Chanan's tone.

"You're positive?" Yosef persisted. "It's serious; the whole operation depends on your work."

"I said I could, didn't I?"

"Yes, but — "

"Look, I grew up in the streets. My parents both slaved but we never had enough of anything. I scrounged. I've been taking care of myself since I can remember. So I know what I can do. If I say it's no problem, it's no problem, all right?"

"All right, Chanan," Luis broke in."Yosef's just worrying. No reflection on you. We know we can depend on you." I hope, he thought.

Chanan subsided to a truculent silence.

When enough boys had assembled, Yosef explained his plans. "We want to keep the friars as busy as possible," he began. "With Estevão out of action, the friars themselves will have to handle the degredados who are supposed to move the baggage. The friars aren't that good at managing the men, and the degredados will have enough wine inside them to make them temperamental. They'll need extra friars: they'll have to take some away from the children. We'll take the places of those friars." He went on to describe the plan in detail.

It was fun setting up that mischief at the mass, Luis thought, but Yosef is an organizing genius. He's put so much effort into this that it can hardly help but work.

But it did not work. The move was delayed another week, and in that time Yosef's plan fell apart.

No one but Saadya was pleased with the delay. "It's the Nine Days right now," he explained to Luis. "It's not a good time for a fresh start. I'm glad we won't be moving until after Tisha b'Av."

"Tisha b'Av?" Luis shook his head. "Has it only been one year since we left Spain?"

"You mean it feels like ten?"

Luis nodded. A sudden thought struck him. "Saadya," he said sharply, "are you going to tell the rest when it's Tisha b'Av?"

"I don't know. I can't decide if they ought to have the day to mourn for their families or whether we should just try to keep our spirits up and ignore the date."

"What about fasting?"

"I can't tell you the halacha," Saadya said abruptly. Regretting his shortness, he added, "But I remember once when there was a plague in our town, my father didn't let his kehilla fast. There's a lot of fever here. And a lot of the children don't seem to be healthy."

"Too many," said Luis grimly.

During a break in digging the next day, Luis commented to Yosef, "Awful lot of children down with fever."

"I know." Yosef gave the ground an angry jab with his spade. "Every week another child dies. And we lost a lot of little ones on the voyage. This place is deadly. On the way to the fields, somebody collapses with fever or doubles up with cramps; you go to sleep and wake up, but the boy next to you doesn't; you catch a fever and think you've recovered until it comes back on you."

"You forgot the diarrhea."

"I wish I could."

"Some of us are still healthy," Luis offered.

"For how long?" Yosef demanded. "They've got to move us away before there aren't any of us left to move." Glancing around, he spotted Estevão. "Maybe if you're nasty enough you survive," he commented as they resumed digging. "He's lasted longer than anyone."

That night Luis woke, drenched in sweat, teeth chattering. Shivering his way to the rough shelter that housed the infirmary, he found Frei Bartolomeu already awake and busy with someone else. He looked more closely. The other new patient was Yosef, vomiting.

"Cleared out, now?" asked Frei Bartolomeu.

"Thought I was last time." Yosef raised his head to look at the friar, and saw Luis. His face fell.

Luis did not need to ask what he was thinking. What would happen on the move with both of them ill? "Chanan's still all right," he said. The room started to revolve slowly.

Frei Bartolomeu was talking to the boy in charge of the

infirmary at night. "Don't let him eat for the next full day, Shimon, and only a sip of water occasionally. Now — " Luis felt a bench come up under him without warning — "let's see about you."

What, exactly, the friar saw Luis did not know. The next thing Luis was aware of was that he was no longer in an open shed but in a proper house. Yosef appeared at his side some time later.

"We made a mess of things," he said, looking down at Luis.

"Huh?"

"We've moved already. Everything went beautifully — for the friars. No drunken degredados. No kidnapped children. I was so weak I had to ride in a cart, and Chanan was ill."

Luis said something he had learned in the streets of Sevilla and closed his eyes.

But when he was strong enough to sit outside, blinking in the sun like a frog by a puddle, Yosef came back. "I don't feel so upset about the plans that failed." he announced.

"No?"

"No. The friars and the children are doing it themselves."

"How do you mean?" Luis squinted up at him, shading his eyes with a hand that was too thin.

Sitting down beside him. Yosef explained, "They're a preaching order, you see, not a babysitting order. They don't really know that much about taking care of three- and four-year-olds. In Lisboa they had plenty of help; here, they've had to assign so many of our girls to take care of the little ones that the friars really aren't in charge any more. Our girls are teaching the babies Judaismo, of course, and the friars know it. But the friars also know that they can't cope alone. So Saadya's sure they're going to let the little ones mix with the rest of the children soon."

"The friars are just going to give up?" Luis was incredulous. "Don't be silly. They never give up. I know."

"No." Yosef prodded Luis lightly in the chest. "Saadya figures you're next. He's guessing they'll try to win over the ones they think are leaders. They can't lock us away from the rest because they don't have a nice stone monastery here, and anybody can get through the sort of walls they build in this place.

After the business on Shabath, the others have the idea of resistance, so if the friars try to isolate us, the rest not only won't give in, they'll probably rescue us as well.

"So Saadya thinks they'll work on the ones who are ill, while they're still weak. Or they might refuse treatment to any ringleader who gets hurt, as a lesson to the others."

"Or only give treatment if they're allowed to missionize."

Yosef gave Luis a troubled look. "I wish I knew what choice I'd make, if it came to that."

"I'd ask Saadya."

"Why?" Yosef asked. "For that matter, how does he know so much about what the friars are thinking?"

Luis laughed. "You've never heard of kehilla politics? His father's congregation was expert at it. He teethed on politics. He breathed politics. Any twelve-year-old raised that way knows how people work; he probably knows better than a lot of adults."

"Useful sort of person," Yosef commented.

"Very." Luis nodded emphatically. "He's also very grown-up for his age. Worth listening to."

Yosef sat on the edge of the bench, as if eager to be doing something more. "I wish we could organize ourselves. Just having our own leaders should give us a better chance against the friars. But we can't do it until we know about the little children."

During the next weeks, Saadya's assessment was proved accurate — in part. Some of the youngest were found wandering in the compound, explaining that the friars had told them to "go back to the others." But the friars had kept the number that they believed they could handle, and had dismissed the girls who had been helping.

Luis was well enough to attend the next gathering of the older boys.

"They've still got about a hundred," reported Chanan, "and they've strengthened the palisade, too."

"Can we make ladders?" Yosef asked.

A younger boy threw up his head. "I'll chew through if I have to. They have my little sister in there."

"It's not that easy," said Luis. "The girls who worked in there say the children sleep right in the center of the friars' compound, nowhere near the palisade."

Saadya shook his head. "Where they sleep doesn't matter. You can't wake little ones in the middle of the night and expect them to behave sensibly. It has to be by day. Why not Sunday? The friars will be in church."

Because of the older children's stubborn resistance, the friars had been forced to allow them to keep Shabath. On the other hand, although the children were willing to work on Sunday, the friars could not countenance it. In consequence, Sunday in the hillside compound became the day to clear land for the vegetable patches the girls demanded, and to take care of any tasks neglected the rest of the week.

"Sunday is better for us, but it doesn't make much difference to them," interposed Luis. "Friars don't have to show up for every service. You can bet some will be on guard."

"However," said Yosef thoughtfully, "if we got over on ladders Motzaei Shabath and hid until morning ... "

The plans were laid.

Crouching behind a storage building, Luis shifted his cramped position slightly. There were so many boys hiding within the friars' enclosure that Yosef had been worried they would not all be able to hide well enough. But as the sun rose and they heard the children marshalled to attend church, none of them had yet been discovered. Luis could hear the sound of Frei Domingo's voice, a nasal drone. The words were clear enough; Luis remembered them better than he wished. Unwittingly, Frei Domingo himself gave the signal the boys waited for: the word "paternoster".

With a wild howl scores of boys launched themselves at the friars. At the same time Luis' party collected the little children as calmly as they could and hurried them to the gate, dodging stray clerics, fighting off those friars who realized what was happening. Chanan and a few others scoured the rest of the compound in search of further children, who might be ill or hiding. Not one Jewish child was to be left behind.

Robe flapping, a friar lunged at Luis. Luis grappled with him, trying to throw him off: he knew that other friars would be trying to steal back the children. All around the group of disputed captives there were scuffles, boys yelling, grunting men. We're not going to make it, Luis thought desperately; it only needs one child recaptured to make this a failure. We should have brought more boys.

As if in answer, there was a sudden long call, not from within the enclosure but from the palisade. All along the wall boys were leaping down into the fray, shouting with the joy of battle, swarming up the ladders of the night before and plunging into the compound. For a minute they milled around in confusion, but almost at once they discovered Luis's battle near the gate. A dozen of the boys overpowered the guards beside the doors, pushed aside the bar, and threw the gate wide. With a rush Luis bore the rescued children through as the reinforcements flew at his attackers.

The older girls were waiting to receive the little ones. As usual, the chestnut-haired one, Nechama, was in charge. Almost immediately the captives melted into the group and disappeared. Concerned for Chanan, Luis turned to go back and help him, passing Nechama as she herded the last tiny girl into someone's arms. Nechama glanced up at him.

"You're lucky," she said, a wild light in her eyes. "I wouldn't have minded getting in a crack or two myself!"

Luis grinned and plowed back into the fighting. I like her, he thought; she'd be good to work with. What a shame she's not a boy.

Ahead of him he heard Yosef shout. Somewhere there was the mad clanging of a cooking pot being beaten: the signal to withdraw. Boys streamed out of the gates and up the ladders. Before long the gates slowly swung shut.

"Head count," Yosef ordered tersely. He looked them over as he counted: plenty of bruised faces and black eyes, a broken arm, a dislocated shoulder, some teeth out. And every boy was smiling. "Two missing."

One of them was found almost immediately: a dreamer who had forgotten to report. It was a few minutes before Yosef realized the other was Chanan. "I don't think I need to worry," he said, glancing at Luis. "We'll see if he turns up by the end of the day."

"And if he doesn't?" asked one of the boys.

Yosef shrugged. "Let's wait, for a while."

The wait was only a short one. Chanan appeared an hour later, sauntering cockily over to Yosef. "Sorry I missed roll call," he said.

Standing nearby, Luis could see Yosef coming rapidly to the boil.

"You heard the signal and you ignored it?" Yosef demanded.

"I was busy." Chanan gave him a jaunty grin.

"You disobeyed orders! I've made myself responsible for every single child here. I can't do that job without everybody's cooperation. Don't you see that? If you start a vogue for disobedience, the whole colony will collapse. What you did wasn't just dangerous for yourself, it affected everybody. You — "

"I've got the idea, thanks."

"But you don't appreciate — "

"I said I've got the idea," Chanan interrupted. "You don't have to go on with the lecture. You've made your point. You can stop, get it?"

"He gets it. You both get it," Luis broke in. "No single combat, today, all right?" He led Chanan off, his arm across his shoulders.

Out of the corner of his eye, Luis noticed a party of friars making their way purposefully toward the track downhill, Frei Domingo's erect figure in the lead. Any delegation of friars, Luis reasoned, could mean only trouble for the children. With a peaceable word, he left Chanan and followed the men.

Only a little while later, Luis watched the friars enter the donatario's palace. Pushing through the rank growth at the side of the building, Luis pressed against the rough wall and picked a small hole through the rotten wood. Inside, Frei Domingo was reporting the children's raid while Don Alvaro sat absently tearing shreds of feather off a quill pen that lay on his desk.

Frei Domingo concluded his description, adding, "And I want your support and the presence of your men-at-arms to enforce my authority."

"What? Against ten-year-old children? Against infants?"

"You know as well as I do that there are any number of them over ten."

"Oh, no, Frei Domingo!" exclaimed Don Alvaro with mock concern. "I was assured they were all little ones. Definitely under ten."

"Whatever the ages," snapped Frei Domingo impatiently, "I have over seven hundred of them, all rebellious. I want those men-at-arms."

"I have only a dozen armed men to control a hundred unruly degredados," Don Alvaro said grimly. "I can't spare any of them except for an emergency. Your children aren't one."

The priest drew himself up. "I have a mandate from the Church to take charge of the spiritual welfare of these children."

"And I have a commission to populate the island, Frei Domingo." The donatario leaned forward slightly. "So I give you my warning now, Padre, that I will not make war on children. May I remind you as well, Padre, that if any of them die, it will not be you but our Lord who sees to their spiritual welfare?"

"May I remind *you*, Senhor de Caminha — " the priest's lean face was expressionless — "that the Church has claims as well as the Crown?"

Don Alvaro glanced down at the quill between his long fingers: every vestige of feather was gone. With a snap he broke the shaft. "Politics," he said shortly. "You tried to play politics between Church and Crown in Lisboa, Frei Domingo, and you lost. That's why you're here. My father tried to play politics, and he lost. That's why I'm here. You know — " with one smooth motion he swept his desk clear of feathers — "São Tome — it's only a little island, maybe twenty by thirty miles. It won't hold the king's interest for long, not if he finds something more promising, as likely he will. Your superiors have probably forgotten about you already. We'll do the jobs we were assigned here, but nobody really cares. Why shouldn't we try to get along, you and I?" With the ghost of a smile, he held out his hand.

"What is our compact to be?" asked Frei Domingo stonily. "That each of us may do as he sees fit as long as neither interferes with the other's commission?"

"Just that."

The priest gazed thoughtfully at the extended hand for some moments until, suddenly decisive, he grasped it.

"I've heard São Tome described as a Garden of Eden," said the donatario in a conversational tone; "but in the Garden of Eden there was a serpent."

Frei Domingo nodded. "Now the serpent was subtle beyond any beast of the field," he quoted. "As we must be subtle. And may our subtlety bring these children to ultimate salvation."

Luis slipped away.

That Sunday night Yosef laid the foundations for his dream of organizing the children. He explained Saadya's theories about the friars' next moves, and went on, "Luckily, Moshe and Shimon can handle most medical emergencies by now, but if something major arises and we do need Frei Bartolomeu, let's make sure only a few of us risk going without his treatment. We need scapegoats for the friars. Make your choices — but give each one a chance to refuse without being ashamed."

Luis. Yosef. Some votes for Chanan. Small batches of votes for one boy or another of the rest. In the end, most of the boys chose Luis and Yosef.

Rising and waving a hand for silence, Luis looked at the faces clustered in front of him. "I'll accept the risk willingly," he told them, "but I'm not the one to be 'parnes'. Let Yosef have the job and let me be his assistant. Will you?"

The arrangement was accepted. Luis sat down with a sigh of relief. Yosef was a good choice, not only because he was capable and determined but because he was such a born organizer. That's what we need right now, Luis thought, someone to whip us into shape, to get rid of slackness, to set an example. Yosef's been prepared for the job since we came. And he looks the part. We need someone who looks like him, someone we can look at and feel proud of. I don't mind being shabby and disreputable; but it doesn't do for the parnes.

Yosef had proceeded to the next point. "As a Jewish colony, we have to have someone who knows halacha. Just because we don't have a posek doesn't mean we can simply give up. We have to do the best we can with what we have. The only ones over bar-mitzva are Luis, Chanan, and I. None of us have learned. Is there anybody who's twelve who was still sitting and learning when we were taken away?'' Into the silence he added, ''You won't be one of the 'scapegoats', by the way.''

Luis saw a boy nudge Saadya. Saadya gave him a glance that seemed frightened and hunched down.

'' ... eleven-year-olds?'' Yosef scanned the gathering. One or two hands rose unsurely.

But Saadya has learned, Luis said to himself. He's twelve; his father is a rav; he's good at teaching. He taught me so much. ''Saadya,'' he said into the hush, ''how old are you?''

Saadya turned white. ''I hardly know anything!'' he protested.

''Even in the alley in Lisboa, you were still learning with your father, even though it was mostly from memory,'' Luis went on inexorably. ''You know more than I do; more than Yosef does; more than every boy here.''

''I don't know enough halacha,'' Saadya said desperately. ''I could be leading you all into one aveira after another and none of us would ever know it.''

''You can have the eleven-year-olds for aides, if you like.'' To Yosef, Saadya's appointment was already firm.

''I can't do it! It's a crazy notion!''

''You'll be lamdan, not rav, if that makes you feel better,'' said Yosef. ''But there isn't anybody else. The job is yours.''

Luis saw Saadya sink slowly into himself, like a burning brand in the fire. It's true, he thought, there isn't anyone else, but it's awful for him to have the responsibility if he doesn't want it.

All during the next day, as he worked in the fields, the picture of Saadya's white face and of the slow, frightened shrinking kept coming back to him. Luis had to know how he was. By the time they had climbed the long zigzag trail back uphill it was close to sunset and most of the boys settled gratefully to supper. Luis was not hungry and went in search of Saadya.

He found him, after some trouble, leaning against a tree outside the compound, staring somberly before him into the recesses of the forest.

''It's not that bad, is it?'' asked Luis.

''If you don't mind burning in Gehinom, no, it isn't.''

"But if you don't know an answer, can't you just say so? We only expect you to give a psak when you're sure."

"That's what you say." Saadya's tone was bitter. "But when I don't know, you'll press me to give you an opinion, or an idea of how I feel. It'll be the same thing, in the end."

Luis could see that he was right. An educated guess, they would insist, is better than an ignorant one.

"Just to make things really rotten," Saadya went on, "it means that I have to give up all my own plans, too."

"Plans?" Luis echoed. Other than escape, what kind of plans could a twelve-year-old have on a lost island a thousand leagues from anywhere?

Abruptly Saadya moved away from the tree. "Come on; I want to show you something," he said. "You're probably the only one who can understand how I feel."

Luis was silent as Saadya led him away from the compound, past the beginnings of the girls' vegetable plots and through a thicket of palms, fronds rustling in a soft breeze. They climbed a steep slope, pressing through the forest and occasionally through an open glade where a tree had fallen and the young growth had not yet shot up to blot out the light. Somewhere not far off they could hear a bird calling, the sound a liquid gurgle like a wine flask emptying.

They walked slowly, making so little noise that they heard the tiny dry rustle in a fan of branches which Saadya was reaching out to push aside. Winding through the foliage was a sinuous green snake only about a foot long, gracefully twining itself in and out of the leaves. Saadya froze.

"It's beautiful," said Luis, not understanding.

"Yes," agreed Saadya, stepping delicately backwards. "Also deadly."

A careful detour brought them out further along the upper part of the hillside. In the sudden way the ground had on São Tome, a valley opened before them, an unexpected hollow thickly overgrown with small trees whose branches were festooned with tangles of convolvulus.

Descending a short distance into the valley, they found that the light breeze no longer reached them: the air was still. Around them the slope held the warmth of the day, and the heavy sweet scents of flowers and leaves hung over the boys. Bright blue bees blundered into ivory-colored convolvulus blossoms, droning like tiny pepper-grinders.

Saying nothing, Saadya gestured to Luis to sit down. For a little while they waited in the sleepy late-afternoon sun, unmoving, half-dreaming. Suddenly Saadya touched Luis' arm. "Look," he whispered, "they're here."

Luis saw a small creature alight on a narrow branch, its long delicate fingers clutching the bark. It gazed about with huge golden eyes that overwhelmed its face and gave it an expression of amazed friendliness. Rising from its greenish-gray fur, its large, delicate ears moved constantly as it sat chirruping softly to itself. Luis stared entranced at the little animal until Saadya touched his arm once more. Without warning the trees were full of the creatures, creatures of every age and size from babies as big as a large locust, to the adults a little longer than Luis' hand. Their slender orange-brown tails undulated behind them as they sprang airily from branch to branch, twittering sociably, sitting occasionally with their graceful pink hands held up in delighted astonishment.

Signalling at last that it was time to go, Saadya crept softly away from their hiding place, Luis close behind him. When they had reached the crest of the slope they had followed from the compound, Luis was finally ready to ask, "Saadya, what are they?"

"On the African coast the natives call them 'shilling'. There's another kind here, with very dark fur and an altogether different expression on their faces, desperately apologetic. But I love these."

"So do I." As they walked back, faster than they had come, in order not to miss mincha, Luis added, "You know so much about this place."

"Only the beginnings." Saadya kicked a rotten log aside with more energy than he needed. "One of the friars was teaching me. He'd spent time in the Kongo, preaching to the natives. He learned a tremendous amount about the plants and wildlife. On the ship he taught me to use an astrolabe, and he promised me that when we arrived he'd tell me all he knew about São Tome."

Luis said nothing.

"It's a whole new world," Saadya went on, "with such a wealth of things to explore and understand. I'd planned to learn so much — he was an excellent teacher. Now I have to give it all up, just for marath ayin. I can't let the children see their 'lamdan' hanging around with a friar; there's too great a risk that they might decide its safe to do it themselves."

"Isn't 'hanging around with a friar' too great a risk for you, too?" Luis asked. "He was only teaching you so he could find a chink in your armor; then he'd have worked it open till he could shovel in all his saints and saviors and fill you up with Christianity."

"I know that." Saadya was unperturbed. "My weakness is my thirst for knowledge, any knowledge. I feel I want to learn about everything I see. I've always been that way. I used to skimp the time I gave to Torah — " He stopped and gave Luis a rueful glance. "Though if I'd known I'd get stuck with this job, I'd have learned day and night and then some. But I knew that Frei Martinho would concentrate on that weakness. I don't think I needed to worry."

Luis made no comment on that statement. He only said, "You enjoyed his company, too?"

"Of course. He has such an alert, inquiring mind; it's wonderful to be with him."

"You know," Luis said in a quiet voice, "when we first moved out of the port town, I was going around asking some of the little ones what their names were, the little ones we took from the friars and the ones they let out. Do you know what names they told me? Pero. Vicente. Tome. João. All Christian names. All Portuguese names."

Luis did not shout when he was angry. He became very calm and spoke softly. His voice now almost a whisper. "When we were on the ships," he went on, "don't you remember there were no children under five with us? They weren't with anybody — except the friars.

"From the start, they separated the very small ones from the rest of us. They baptized them, as they did us, and gave them

Christian names. From then on, the priests used only the new names. If the children didn't respond, they were locked away or beaten or starved. Three-year-olds. Four-year-olds. How long do you think they held out, such tiny ones? How long do you think the friars had complete charge of them? Close to three months since the children were kidnapped?"

Saadya looked at him with a quiet unblinking gaze and did not answer.

"Saadya, when I asked them their real names, almost none of them could remember. Do you realize what those priests did to our children? It wasn't enough to take away their homes and their families. They took even their names from them. The lucky ones have sisters or brothers who recognize them; a few might remember their names or where they came from; but there are some who will never, ever, know who they are. You think about that, Saadya; you think about that and then tell me if you ever want to learn anything from any priest again, your whole life long."

CHAPTER FIVE

ATE IN ELUL Luis was feeling downhearted, thinking about the Yomim Noraim. I was going to learn so much, he reminded himself; Saadya and his father were both teaching me and by the next Rosh Hashana, they said, I'd be almost an expert. Next Rosh Hashana is nearly here, and what do I know? Still almost nothing.

"Luis, look at this!" Saadya was standing over him, holding something out.

"What?" Shading his eyes from the sun, Luis peered up at him.

"Two siddurim and a Chumash, that's what! Three of the children managed to smuggle them out of Lisboa. We'll have proper tfilloth yet!" He was grinning so widely he could hardly speak.

"Fan-tastic." Luis could not work up any enthusiasm.

"It is, you know." Sitting down beside Luis, Saadya went on, "So what's bothering you?"

"This. What else?" Luis swung his arm around to include everything in sight. "São Tome."

"Nobody asked to come here."

"I know. But I'd barely begun to understand what Judaismo was supposed to be like when I was snatched away from it. It's even harder for me to resign myself to being here."

Yosef, walking past, stopped in mid-stroll. "São Tome isn't so bad that we can't adjust to it. It's just deciding that you're going to accept it and deal with it. You have to have bitachon, be able to say 'gam zu l'tova'."

"Gam zu l'tova? This, too, is for the good? What's so good about São Tome?" Luis flashed.

"It's good because it came from Hashem Yithbarach," broke in Saadya. "Look, having bitachon doesn't mean expecting everything to turn out the way you'd like it to. It means accepting that everything that happens is good and right because it comes from Hashem, even if you can't see that goodness and rightness at the time."

"So why are we here?" asked Luis stubbornly.

"How should I know? All I can see is that it's such a crazy notion, sending children to colonize any place, let alone one like this, that no sane person would think of it without the Ribono shel Olam's direction. So there must be something to be gained from living here, lessons to learn. We have to see São Tome as a challenge."

"I like that," Yosef said.

"I don't." Luis frowned. "I see what you're saying, Saadya, but I don't want to accept São Tome without any reservations. Maybe one day I'll be resigned to it, but I never want to forget that things were better once."

"Nothing wrong with that, if that's what you want." Saadya stood up. "Except, of course, that it hurts more."

Maybe, Luis thought, I prefer it that way.

On Rosh Hashana Saadya drew him aside. "It's so unlike you to be moody, Luis," he said. "Can't you try to throw it off? After all, it's a new year, a fresh start. Come on; set an example for the rest."

"What should I do? Walk around with a silly grin on my face? What good is that? It won't change the way anybody feels.'

Taken aback, Saadya stared at him. "You're right," he admitted at last. "That's my job: changing the way they feel."

"Can you?"

Saadya shrugged. "I have to try." He sighed. "But I wish it didn't mean speaking publicly; I hate it."

By the time Yom Kippur arrived, Saadya's speech was prepared. Luis watched him rise and go forward just before starting mincha. He did not look timid or unsure or unhappy; there was nothing at all in his manner or bearing out of the ordinary. Only to Luis he looked very young to be carrying the responsibility for guiding seven hundred children in their faith

"Are you hungry today?" Saadya asked. "Are you thirsty? Why only today? Why aren't you hungry and thirsty the rest of the year? You ought to be. Do you know what it says in the *Menorath Hamaor?* 'The people of our times are hungry for food and thirsty for wine; they do not hunger or thirst for the word of Hashem.'

"My father said too many of us were like that in Spain. Of course, we had a lot of gedolim. But look at the easy parnassa we had there. We could have been a nation of lamdanim. You could all have known as much as I do; more. But what did we do? We hungered for food and nibbled at the Torah. Yes," he added, "I did, too.

"Now we're living in a place where fruit falls off the trees into our hands, where crops shoot out of the ground as soon as we sow the seeds, a place — a place where parnassa is easy. Maybe we should look on it as a kind of second chance. Today, now, while we're thinking about tshuva, maybe we should consider what matters, what we ought to be hungry and thirsty for. Because even here, we can be zocheh ... "

Ribono shel Olam, Luis said silently, give me the strength to live here or perhaps to die here, because no matter what Saadya says, this galuth is very, very hard for me.

And then Yom Kippur was over and it was practically Sukoth. With a start of surprise the children realized that they actually had lulavim at hand, they could build sukoth: some of this holiday's mitzvoth were within reach. *Zman simchatheinu!* Luis laughed with sheer delight of anticipation as he slithered carefully down a palm tree he had stripped of lulavim.

"Yosef! " he shouted, "Yosef, let's go somewhere Chol haMoed!"

His enthusiasm was contagious. Yosef's rare smile flashed suddenly, quickly, like lightning. "Who shall we visit?" he mocked, laughing.

Luis threw his arms wide. "We'll have a day off — fool around — just be children for a while! If we do it on Sunday we'll have no trouble with Estevão."

Yosef considered the proposal. "It sounds reasonable. Why not? We can send everyone in the usual work parties. You and I can be substitutes in case one of the leaders can't go."

"And we'll choose several locations, shall we?" Luis added. "So not everybody goes to the same place?"

And so I can keep Chanan away from you, he thought. The two of you are like flint and steel, striking sparks whenever you meet. He knew Chanan would not have been easy for anyone to handle. Independent, contrary, unreliable; capable and levelheaded: he was all of these. Did one give him responsibility because he was one of the oldest and because he was so competent? Or did one withhold it because he was undependable? Or did one give him the responsibility and try to supervise him? Yosef had tried that, and another skirmish had followed. But, of course, Yosef was not that easy to deal with, either.

Planning. Organizing. Those were Yosef's strong points: working with ideas. But when it came to working with people — Luis groaned inwardly. Why couldn't he understand that people might think differently from him or need things he didn't find necessary? Why hadn't it occurred to him that people have feelings? It was more than — as Yosef openly admitted — not particularly liking children or knowing how to deal with them. The problem was that Yosef dealt with people as though they were objects. Of course they resented it.

They were even coming to resent Yosef's forte: his organizing ability. He could organize, Luis thought, but he could never bring himself to let go. He assigned jobs, and then hung over the people doing them to make sure they did the jobs the right way. He was just too heavy-handed, but he certainly could be aggravating, and it was exactly that sort of nagging supervision that Chanan found unbearable.

More and more Luis found himself acting as a buffer, his easy-going personality tempering Yosef's compulsive conscientiousness. He hoped Yosef would not be needed to lead a group on the outing.

That Motzaei Shabath they reviewed their plans, detail by detail. With relief Luis saw that only he would be needed as a substitute leader. Turning to Yosef, he asked, "Is it all right if I shuffle a couple of leaders around? I'd rather look after ten-year-olds with Chanan and shift someone else to these six-year-olds who need the substitute."

The idea of someone trustworthy paired with Chanan appealed to Yosef. "It'll be fine," he said. "And I'll be free to keep an eye on the rest of the groups."

More nagging supervision, Luis thought. Chanan's well out of it. I can just imagine his reaction if Yosef comes all the way down the hill to interfere. After they finished the last arrangement and went to bed, Luis fell asleep satisfied that he had avoided trouble for the next day, at least.

The site they had chosen for the older boys lay well down the track to São Tome town. There was a clearing they had found that looked as if someone had once thought to wrest a plantation from the forest. Perhaps it had proved to be unworkable; perhaps the man had died. At any rate, there was only the open space now, lying at the foot of a crashing waterfall, the last before the river flowed to the sea. The pool there was full of trout, leaping wet and shining in the sun, their scales silvery-iridescent like living rainbows in the waterfall's mist.

Before sunrise Luis and Chanan assembled their groups, aides helping each team leader to keep his party together. Luis distributed equipment for building sukoth and catching fish: they would take turns carrying the tools along the way.

As they walked down the road, Luis looked up at the majestic trees that guarded their path, encouraged to reach greater heights by the rush of sunlight that the road let in. Other than the dazzling blue pygmy kingfishers flashing among the leaves, Luis saw few birds, but he heard many more: the high piercing cries of one bird, the muted coughing calls of another, monotonous clinking and knocking sounds, and a chorus of other notes too mixed to distinguish. Although the sun was barely showing over the horizon, unseen hosts of cicadas droned incessantly: the day would be hot.

Through a break in the trees to his right, Luis caught a glimpse of a view stretching across a valley to the heavy forest that clothed the feet of the mountains clustered in the center of the island. The peaks barely showed above a blanket of mist, but as Luis watched, the mist began to flow down the steep hillsides like a liquid, covering the low forest and filling the valley. As the sun rose higher, bathing the mountains in an ever-changing wash of opalescent colors, the mist rolled and eddied, smoking upwards in plumes and streamers that drifted into wonderful dreamlike forms: birds and dragons, trees and flowers like unspun wool palaces of mystery.

Captured by the beauty, Luis did not realize he had halted until a loud, indignant "Chuck-chuck!" woke him from his trance: on a branch above him a striped squirrel glared challenge at him. Luis laughed and looked around. The boys waited restlessly, looking at him with faint curiosity, as though he had stopped them to tell them something. Most of them had hardly noticed the sight that had held him spellbound; still, it seemed to Luis that this was a good place to pause for shacharith before continuing.

In the further hour it took them to reach the clearing, the sun climbed well above the sapphire ocean and the day's heat began to beat into them. When they reached the clearing they were grateful for the shade of the wild-mango trees that spread their branches wide at the edge of the open space. Tall grass had rushed in to take the place of the trees that had been cut, forming a meadow. As the boys walked through it, the grass rippled like a golden sea and a cloud of bright-colored butterflies rose about them.

In the center of the glade wild guineafowl pecked inattentively while a flock of red-faced parakeets spread brilliant green wings in restless flight from bush to bush. A few pinky-brown doves floated down from the trees, disturbed by a hornbill's careless landing. The heaving branches and wild rustling sent a troop of monkeys into a brief screaming fit.

It was not that the boys of both parties did not appreciate these novel experiences; but the heat left them only one interest: following the waterfall's sound to the banks of the stream. Standing on the begonia-covered rocks that framed the pool, they gazed wistfully at the water. Further on, the river swirled and foamed along its stony bed, geese and herons picking their way across the overgrown banks.

Through spreading branches they could glimpse the sea, the gentle curve of the beach followed by a fringe of bamboo-palms. Gleaming in the brightness, the white sand swept down to meet the water licking its edge; the few torpid crocodiles sunning themselves were hardly noticeable. Against the deep blue vault of the sky, kites and an eagle hunted in slow, sweeping, flight.

Chanan glanced at Luis. "Are you sure we can't let them go in?"

With a shrug Luis spread his arms wide. " 'No swimming' is Rule Number One."

"But that was on the beach, when we were in the town."

Luis gestured at the view through the trees. "The beach isn't that far. But if they stay on the bank they can splash each other. They should enjoy that."

Chanan made a disgusted face and went to deliver the message. Returning, he asked Luis, "How many sukoth are we planning to put up? Only you and I are old enough, really, to need one."

"I know," Luis replied, "but without reminders it's too easy for us to forget what the Yom Tov is supposed to be like. I'd prefer to have everybody eat under s'chach if we can manage it."

"All right. My boys dig and clear; you can do the cutting. Posts at the corners as well as s'chach. What did you bring for walls?"

Luis grinned. "You'll see."

Giving his boys a little longer at the stream, Luis led them beneath the great canopy of leafage into a strange green-tinted world. Filtering downwards uncertainly, the sun touched the forest floor with pale smears like pools of water. While they worked among the trees they could not even tell that the sun was rising steadily higher other than by the changing angles of the slanting shafts of light.

After some time Luis returned to the meadow to see if Chanan's group were ready for his boys to bring the posts they had cut. He was surprised at how oppressive the heat had become, away from the shade. Hardly a bird called in the stillness; even the cicadas sounded drowsy. The air was heavy with scents: the sharp tang of the ocean, the heady rankness of thick undergrowth, the dark warm odor of freshly dug soil. Wiping his forehead with the back of his hand, Luis could smell the sweetness of his skin mingling with the pungency of sweat.

Waiting a moment until his eyes adjusted to the brightness, he looked around for Chanan's team. He could not see them, but he could hear their voices. He could hear, as well, a great deal of splashing. A suspicion began to form in his mind. He started for the river.

A distant movement caught his eye. Turning his head for a better look, he saw Yosef striding briskly down the road, perhaps coming to see how Chanan was doing, after all. Yosef looked happy and strong and full of life, as close to being easy and relaxed as Luis had ever seen him. With a sigh for the unpleasantness that he suspected would follow, Luis moved to intercept him.

"Hot?" he greeted Yosef.

"Not too bad." Yosef shrugged. "I suppose I'll get used to it over the years. São Tome's not so bad otherwise."

Luis reeled mentally at Yosef's answer. He himself had but one goal: to return to a normal Jewish community, to leave São Tome the instant he could to rejoin the stream of living Judaismo. But to Yosef, São Tome had become as good a place as any to plow and plant, cook and do laundry, to perform the domestic labors that occupy people everywhere. To Yosef it was a place to build homes and be content. Perhaps it was the most realistic view to take; but Luis did not believe it was the right one.

"Not so bad," he said, "except for Jews."

Yosef half-smiled noncommittally and dismissed the topic. "Where's Chanan?"

"I left him digging holes with the boys," Luis answered evasively.

The clearing was empty. As Yosef walked towards the river his pace increased. Luis moved more quickly to keep up with him. Yosef caught sight of Chanan standing on the rocks by the river.

"Chanan!" Yosef's tone was peremptory.

With an expression of angry disbelief, Chanan turned to face him. Simultaneously there was another shout of "Chanan!" from the direction of the stream. He turned back.

"Yitzchak's cut his foot!" The boy who shouted was frightened: his voice was shaking.

"Bring him here and let me look at it!" His cool voice calmed the other boy as he climbed over the rocks and reached out a hand to the younger child.

Yosef was not calmed, however. As soon as the boy was safely out of the water Yosef rounded on Chanan and clamped a hand on his arm. "What the blazes do you mean, letting those kids in the river? You know it's not allowed! What makes you so irresponsible?" Without waiting for an answer, Yosef strode to the river bank. "All of you!" he shouted. "Come out now!"

Calling and laughing, splashing in the water, the children were too far to hear him. No one responded to his order. Yosef stripped off his shoes and hose and waded in after them.

"That's the end, now!" he shouted when he was closer. "Everybody out of the water; let's go!"

Luis was not surprised that they had not heard him. Even standing where he was, downstream of them, Luis found Yosef's voice hard to hear against the rushing of the waterfall above the children.

Slowly, regretfully, the boys began to edge toward the bank. The day was so hot; the water was so wonderfully cool. It seemed a pity to leave it. Yosef chivvied them along, but a few determined stragglers remained in the middle of the pool. His annoyance obvious, Yosef retraced his steps to force the last boys out of the river.

Afterwards Luis wondered why it was that no one else had seen the small disturbance in the water. Had it been the angle he was looking from? He took a step forward, curious as to what made it. Only then did he see the huge dark shape arrowing through the clear water.

"Crocodile!"

The last three boys leapt to the safety of the rocks, running with water as they clung to the stones. But Yosef was too far from shore. The water he stood in was not deep, only up to his knees; but he move against it with nightmare slowness.

The great body swept past him, the armored back breaking the surface in a tumult of spray, ten feet, twenty feet. Twenty feet: longer than three beds end to end. Twenty feet; one ton of massive reptile after blood. Luis caught his breath.

Snatching a stick, he began to run. He saw the crocodile give

a flick of its huge tail, a flick so casual it seemed almost an afterthought. But when a creature weighs a ton, there is nothing casual about a flick of its tail. Yosef was knocked entirely out of the water and flung onto the rocks. Luis could hear the dull ugly thud of his head striking the stone.

Instantly the monster pivoted and shot across the short stretch of water, its jaws opening to expose the glistening membranes and leech-infested gums. Luis raced forward. He had to reach Yosef in time. The crocodile would kill him, not all at once, for crocodiles like their meat alive; but Yosef would be dead more or less horribly, all the same.

Chanan stood frozen with horror. Luis hit him as he ran past. "Come on!" he cried. For a moment Chanan stared, dazed, before he woke to action. He caught up a splintered branch and dashed after Luis.

Already the creature was upon Yosef. Luis saw Yosef's head roll limply, his body sliding inch by inch into the water. Impatient, the crocodile heaved itself upwards, its claw raking the side of Yosef's face. The jaws reached for an arm.

With all his strength Luis rammed his stake down the dreadful throat. Beside him Chanan jabbed with his branch. The crocodile gave a grunting bellow of pain. Leaving Yosef, it wrenched around to find its attacker.

The other boys had come, now, beating off the reptile with spades while Luis dragged Yosef away from the river. A hail of rocks thundered down on the monster, driving it into the water, back to the sea. Vainly trying to dislodge the stake, it let the current bear it downstream. As the boys crowded to the edge of the stream to be sure it would not return, the birds on the banks rose in a flurry of alarm. On the beach the crocodiles were gathering at the river mouth, jaws wide, to devour their comrade.

Laying Yosef down in the long grass, Luis squatted beside him. Yosef was breathing, but unconscious. The gashes in his face were bleeding badly, because any head wound bleeds badly; the bleeding looked far worse than it was because Yosef's face was wet and the water made the blood run down onto his shirt. Luis glanced up. Chanan was standing near him; his face had no color in it.

"You'd better get Frei Bartolomeu," Luis said quietly.

Chanan's lips moved but he did not say anything. He turned and ran toward the uphill track, slipping and stumbling as though he could not see clearly where he was going.

Breathless, he reached the compound. Frei Bartolomeu was talking with Frei Domingo. Tugging urgently at Frei Bartolomeu's sleeve, Chanan said, "Could you come, Padre? There's been an accident."

Both friars were suddenly attentive. "What happened?" asked Frei Bartolomeu.

"A crocodile went for Yosef d'Ortas."

"Madre — !" The small man lifted his cassock to run more freely. "I'll come — "

"I think not," Frei Domingo's cold voice cut in smoothly. "After all, he's one of your leaders, is he not? One of those so determined to do without those very inconvenient priests? Independence — it is a wonderful thing to be independent. I think, for once, he should be allowed to be independent without opposition. Frei Bartolomeu is busy with certain commissions of mine." Turning, he began to walk away.

"You'd just leave him?" Chanan's eyes swung from one to the other.

The tall, spare friar stopped and faced Chanan. "One reaps what one sows."

"But Frei Domingo — " Frei Bartolomeu spoke humbly — "he is, after all, only a child. If by treating him I could make him see reason — ?"

The missionario looked searchingly at Frei Bartolomeu; then he transferred his intent gaze to Chanan. He inclined his head in a thoughtful nod. "Frei Bartolomeu is persuasive. I might consider allowing him to attend this Yosef — but only on condition that he do so with the Cross in his hand and the words of Our Lord on his lips." Frei Domingo drew himself up to his full height. "Do you agree?" he demanded.

Chanan looked from Frei Bartolomeu, obedient to his prior, to Frei Domingo, impassive, inflexible. They offered him a choice that was no choice. How could he tell whether this decision was necessary? He did not know how badly Yosef was hurt. Perhaps

Yosef was hardly injured at all: then Chanan would be wrong to allow the friars this foothold in the children's frail fortress. But what if Yosef were seriously hurt? Might he die without the friar's treatment? Chanan stared in front of him, wanting to wait, to think the thing through, knowing he did not have that time. He saw again the still, bloodied figure in the long grass.

He raised his eyes to meet Frei Domingo's. "I agree," he said.

CHAPTER SIX

ESTLING AGAINST THE SPONGY trunk of a kapok tree, Esperansa could see most of the compound from her seat high above the ground on one of the great, leaping roots. Past the girls' area, past the cooking and eating houses that divided the boys from the girls, she could just glimpse the boys' infirmary with the new room built on at one end. In that place lay the boy the crocodile had attacked.

She did not know Yosef. Only nine years old, and a girl, she had nothing to do with a boy so old as to be nearly grown up, and the holder of an exalted office as well. Even Nechama, who ruled the girls, was too important for her to be friendly with. Then, too, except for the littlest ones that the girls mothered, the boys were kept so strictly separate from the girls that she hardly saw any of them at all, other than as a vague impression of movement beyond the dining houses. All the same, Esperansa wondered about Yosef.

How badly had he been hurt? There were so many rumors that she did not know what was truth. She thought he must be very ill because his sister Reina went to sit beside him every day, though only briefly. Before the accident he had hardly seen his sister at all, he had been so busy, even on Shabath afternoons. That was the one time brothers and sisters were allowed to visit with each other.

It must be pleasant for them, Esperansa thought. It must be pleasant to have sisters and brothers near your own age. She let herself recall her own family, her sisters and brothers so much older than herself that they had not even been taken by the monks. Nearly all grown and married, they were so tall and good-looking that she could not help feeling small and plain and unimportant next to them. They did not mean to make her feel that way, but she did, nonetheless.

Esperansa had only seen Yosef from a distance, but she had thought then that he was handsome. She liked looking at him, as she liked to look at a beautiful sunset. Reina was pleasant to look at, but Esperansa did not want to stand and stare as she did with Yosef. She thought that Reina was nicer, though.

Reina was the right sort of person to be in charge of the girls' infirmary at night; Esperansa felt better knowing that she was there. But she did not like thinking about the place altogether: she had seen children who had died being taken out of the building. Vivid and unforgettable, there was a picture in her mind of one time they had brought a dead girl out. The girl did not seem like a person any more. Esperansa wondered if Yosef might die and be like that.

Shivering momentarily, she dragged her gaze away from the compound to stare instead into the deep calm of the forest. Within the compound they had left trees to shade the houses, but it was nothing like the feeling of being in another world that she had under the thick leafy canopy. In some places there were palms in scattered groups, or occasional thickets of bamboo. Elsewhere you had to be careful of heavy ripe breadfruits thudding down onto carpet of foot-wide leaves underneath. Where Esperansa sat, there were a number of massive Kino trees like the one she sat on. Some had roots that sprang from the earth to meet the parent tree like flying buttresses; others, like her own, sent their roots writhing for yards through the forest like arboreal octopi. Trees of various sorts mingled with them, but the kapok trees were almost like living creatures.

It was the quiet Esperansa appreciated most. In São Tome there had been the inescapable heat, the constant threat of the rough men, the swarms of flies and mosquitos, the temptation of the forbidden beach; but most of all there had been noise. Too many people around her made Esperansa uncomfortable; she needed solitude, peace from the incessant noise of humanity.

She drew a deep, grateful breath. It was quieter here in the uplands; it was cooler. Everyone felt better. Even the chickens seemed to feel better, Esperansa thought, as she watched them pecking industriously between the stumps in the compound that there had not yet been time to clear. As she watched the birds she saw a girl running through the compound, scattering the chickens. They fluttered away in mock alarm and returned to their pecking, unperturbed, a few feet farther on. Esperansa waved.

"Paloma!" Standing up so that the girl could see her, she called, "Up here!"

Paloma and Esperansa had met and comforted each other in the black strangeness of the hold of the ship that had brought them to São Tome. During the journey Paloma had recovered quickly, had kept the children entertained with her laughter and high spirits and exasperated their friar with her mischief.

Paloma had huge, liquid eyes full of innocence — like a cow's, as she described them — and a fine-boned, delicate face; but the fragile features were misleading. Paloma was an imp who ran wild, a clown who reduced everyone to giggles, a chatterer who would not be stilled. Yet at times she could subside to a deep, contemplative silence. Answering Esperansa's wave, she came to sit companionably beside her.

For Esperansa it was a new experience to have a friend her own age. Her home had been her world, sheltered and restricted. She had been permitted to play only with one little girl whom she did not like; apart from this child, all of the people around her had been adults. She had become staid, almost elderly, more thoughtful than people suspected. So accustomed was she to playing by herself that if a stranger had asked her if she were lonely — the thought had not occurred to her family — she would have found the question puzzling.

Until she met Paloma, Esperansa had not known what it was to share yourself with someone, to talk over your thoughts together, to giggle under the blankets at night when you should have been asleep. Paloma showed her all these; Paloma taught her to laugh. It was not in Paloma's nature to be serious for long, while Esperansa was inclined to be too solemn. Through her friendship with Paloma, Esperansa discovered the lacks there had been before: she began to discover childhood.

It was very pleasant to sit side by side, doing nothing. The little free time they had was precious. Mornings were devoted to lessons: for part of the time the under-tens who could read taught those who could not; for the rest of the morning the oldest ones taught various ages to meldar, or about the sedra or dinim. Occassionally, there was an arithmetic lesson, as well. For some of the children, the education they were receiving was more complete than they would have had in Spain.

Much of every afternoon was taken up with tasks. Besides the ordinary domestic occupations — and multiplied by the vastly greater number of children than any family had, they were not quite ordinary any more — Nechama was planning vegetable plots and places to grow flax. Vegetables would give greater variety to their diet of bread, fish, and fruit, she had told the girls.

They knew already that flax was a necessity. Forgetting that children grow, the donatario had not thought to bring much cloth. What there was, Nechama discovered, was the coarse, poor-quality woolen goods that Portugal produced. She did not know if Don Alvaro would send for the cottons she wanted; but at least flax seeds were no bother to import, many of the girls had learned how to ret the stalks and make linen thread, and linen did not bother your skin the way rough wool did. Esperansa liked the way Nechama had explained it all to them. It was not as hard to take your turn at clearing a bit of ground if you knew what it was for. And it was even nicer if you had your best friend working beside you.

Esperansa glanced at Paloma. Her silence was lasting longer than usual. "Are you all right?" asked Esperansa.

"I don't know; I feel funny."

Saying nothing in return, Esperansa nevertheless kept a wary eye on Paloma until they went to sleep. During the night Esperansa woke. Next to her Paloma was tossing and trying to cry soundlessly.

"What is it?" Esperansa whispered, unwilling to wake the other eight lying in the sleeping-house with them.

"My head hurts — I feel awful."

Before even touching her friend's face Esperansa could feel the heat. "You've got a fever," she accused. "You should have gone to the infirmary this afternoon. I'll take you now."

Paloma nodded miserably. Hand in hand they crept outside. Across the compound they could see a single light: the lamp Reina insisted on burning all night at the infirmary. Esperansa led Paloma toward it and saw her received and put to bed.

"You'd better trot off," Reina said kindly to Esperansa. "I don't want you taking the fever yourself."

"But Paloma — will she — will she be all right?" She was so frightened for Paloma. Behind her night lay on the compound, dark and comfortless.

Trying to return to Paloma and her other patients, Reina sighed. "I don't even know yet what she has." She gave Esperansa a brisk pat on the shoulder. "Off you go."

Obediently, Esperansa wandered away through the compound, a maze of starlight and shadow. Sleep was impossible. She went to the dining houses to see if there was any fruit lying conveniently to hand. Eating seemed a way to fill the empty space inside her. There had been some fruit, she found, but the fruit bats had been at it first and she did not much want the squashed sticky mess they had left her. Somewhere nearby an owl was calling, a lonely questioning note that made her feel exposed and unprotected. She did not know why its cry had that effect — it was only another bird, after all — but it made her want Paloma beside her so badly that she laid her head on a table and wept until she fell asleep.

"Do you want to make yourself ill, child?" demanded someone who shook her awake. The morning sun, slanting in through the doorway, showed Esperansa who was scolding her: Nechama, up early to organize breakfast.

Nechama organized everything, assigned jobs, gave advice. Some of the girls, Esperansa knew, thought she was in charge of too much — Paloma called her bossy but good-hearted, in a tolerant voice — but when everything was disorganized or in the hands of the friars, it seemed to Esperansa that a little bossiness was not out of place. She liked Nechama: her responsible air, her unruly chestnut hair trying to escape her braids, the way she seemed to look right through you in a way that made you feel uncomfortable until you were used to it, and then you didn't mind.

"I couldn't sleep; my friend had a fever," explained Esperansa.

"You slept fine on the table," remarked Nechama. "Don't make it a habit if you don't want to join her in the infirmary. Can you teach your group this morning? It'll keep your mind off your friend."

Esperansa nodded.

About to begin work, Nechama turned back to her. "Who is it, anyway?" She knew almost all of the girls by name.

"Paloma. She's my age."

"I'll drop by later and see how she is, shall I?" offered the older girl.

"Oh, please, yes," Esperansa said thankfully. "They won't let me in. Will they let you?"

"I think so."

Esperansa went to her own responsibilities, but the day passed slowly. All during the afternoon she watched to catch Nechama, but not until evening did the older girl come to her. With an arm around her shoulders Nechama drew her away to a quiet place.

"How is she?" asked Esperansa, with an anxious edge to her voice.

"She really is very ill. If you know any Tehillim, I think you should say them."

Esperansa caught her breath. "Will she die?"

Nechama went very white. "I hope not," she said. Abruptly she left Esperansa and hurried away.

Through the days that followed, Esperansa haunted the compound near the infirmary. Lonely and fearful, she found that no one had any answers for her. She did not know how ill Paloma was. She did not know if she was growing better or worse. She did not know if they expected Paloma to recover. It did not seem fair that they would not let her in to visit Paloma. Nechama came and went as she pleased.

Well into the second week of Paloma's illness, Esperansa stole out of her bed, past the sleeping girls, and slipped across the compound to find her friend.

Somewhere Reina was sleeping, lightly as always, but she

did not wake as Esperansa stepped silently along the row of beds. In the fourth one lay Paloma, stirring slightly. She was so thin that for a moment Esperansa thought she was mistaken, that the girl was someone else; but when she whispered Paloma's name and the eyes opened, Esperansa knew her.

At first Paloma mumbled things that had no meaning; then she seemed to waken fully and smiled up at Esperansa. "I'm glad they let you come at last; I missed you."

She spoke very softly, not as though she did not want to wake the others but faintly, as if all the strength had been sucked out of her.

With the flickering light of the small lamp, shadows went racing up and down the walls and across the hollows in Paloma's face. "I was remembering," she said, "or maybe I was dreaming, about home, about the big old fig tree we used to have." She paused to breathe carefully. "We watered it and fertilized it and made sure the earth around it was nice and loose. We took such good care of it. But it hardly had any figs." Her eyes closed and her head rolled to one side, as though speaking cost her too much effort.

After a time she roused herself and went on, "The last year, that summer we left, we hardly ever remembered to do anything for the fig tree; we were so busy with packing. But just that year it had so many figs — so many!" Her eyes opened wide. "Enough for all of us to have a whole one, Esperansa, not just a scrap. They tasted wonderful ... And Papa had two ... "

Her voice faded. Esperansa reached out and took her hand. Paloma's gaze seemed to see something far beyond Esperansa.

"Papa said they had the taste of Gan Eden," she whispered, "to give us strength for what lay ahead." She let her hand rest confidingly in Esperansa's. "The taste of Gan Eden ... " She smiled slowly and closed her eyes.

Esperansa stayed with her, still holding her hand. She did not know when it was that Paloma slipped from her world to the next, but at length she sensed that Paloma was not there any more, so she eased her hand out of Paloma's and went away.

In the morning Esperansa got up and ate something, she was not sure what; she took her class and sat through her own lessons.

In the afternoon she drifted away from whichever job it was that she had been given and went and sat alone on the leaping root of the Kino tree. There was nobody to look for in the compound any more so she did not look at anything. She did not think about what had happened; she felt that a part of her had gone and she felt too lost and empty to think.

Gradually she became aware that there was someone beside her. She did not want to see who it was. She did not want anybody to sit there beside her: that had been Paloma's place and it was not for anyone else to take. There were no other children nearby; they had all gone away. The sun had sunk behind the mountains and it was growing dark in the forest. Overhead, birds were finishing their end-of-day chorus; from time to time monkeys screamed ill-bred cries. Through a gap in the leaves she watched a hawk-eagle circle briefly before flying westward for the night.

"Come have supper, Esperansa." The voice was Nechama's.

Even though she admired Nechama, Esperansa did not want her. She turned her face away.

"You can't be like this," Nechama said gently. "You have to just pick up and go on."

Esperansa stared in front of her, "She was my friend. I never had a friend like that before. I'll probably never have anyone like her again. You can't miss her the way I do."

"No, I can't." Nechama's voice was soft. "I have to miss her in my own way. She was my little sister."

"I didn't know that." Turning towards Nechama, Esperansa noticed how ragged the neck of her dress had become. "Your dress is torn," she said.

"Yes." Glancing down, Nechama fingered the ripped fabric. "We were such a large, happy family." She touched one rent after another. "Chaim, and Miriam; Chana and Asher, and this — " she held the edges of the new rip, a raw wound in the material — "this is for Paloma. There won't be any more." She started to climb down. "I have to go sit shiva now."

Esperansa shrugged. She let Nechama go, but after a while she drifted aimlessly after her, absent and alone: one small, silent child.

CHAPTER SEVEN

JOSEF REACHED UP to feel his cheek. Very dimly he could recall having tried to do that before, when there was searing pain in his face and the smell of scorching. Someone had caught his hand before he could lift it very far. Now his hand was free. Touching the bandages on his face, he discovered that it still hurt a great deal underneath them. But he could not remember why this should be.

Overhead he heard a pattering, and after a time he realized that it was raining. There was no other sound in the room save his own breathing. Why was he alone? The infirmary was never empty. The rain on the thatch told him nothing. With an effort he opened his eyes.

He could not see anything.

His eyes were not bandaged — he lifted his hand to them to make sure. But there was only darkness. Yosef let his hand fall to his side and lay rigid, terrified.

Terrified. Afraid. He had never been so completely overcome by fear. What would it be like not to see, to be blinded? He thought of shadows falling purple on a whitewashed wall in Spain, an orange moon, sunsets and sunrises, the veins of a leaf. He knew he was being foolish: what mattered was far more prosaic. Not getting lost in his own room. Finding the food in front of him on a table. Always remembering where he was and how he had gotten there. Falling over things people had left lying about. He'd be little use in the fields, he thought: if they put a shovel in his hands he could dig, but never with the same confident energy as before.

He strained into the blackness that surrounded him. He had

heard it called suffocating, and it was. It pressed in on him like a softly smothering cushion. But at the same time it was a void, an absence of everything familiar, that made his breath emptiness.

Outside there was a soft splash, as though somebody had stepped into a puddle. A mild exclamation of annoyance followed. Suddenly Yosef thought he could see a faint glimmer through a chink in the boards of one rough wall. The glimmer grew stronger; he knew it was not imagination. A door opened, and into the room stepped a small friar holding a candle that guttered wildly in the draft and sputtered for the instant that a raindrop fell onto it. Yosef knew the man: Frei Bartolomeu.

As though he had done it many times, the friar pressed the candle into a holder that stood empty on a small table. He moved closer to Yosef. Seeing that Yosef's eyes were open, he did not exclaim but said only, "Good evening." From his tone one might have thought that he had met an acquaintance on a street corner.

Yosef found it wonderfully reassuring. Everything was quite normal after all. He had been hurt. Eventually he would remember how, and after a while he would get better and work again. The rain clouds had shut out the sunlight so that night had come earlier, and the friar had perhaps been a little late coming in with the candle. There was nothing to be frightened about.

He was wrong, of course; but he did not learn that until the next day. This night, he fell asleep almost at once, relaxed and at peace.

When he woke in the morning, Reina was sitting by his bed. Because the bandaging covered so much of the right side of his face, Yosef could not see her properly without rolling his head to the right, toward her; but as soon as he tried, he found that it hurt too much. "Reina," he said, stretching out his hand to take hers.

Catching his hand, she bent over him. "Yosef," She was smiling, but a little tremulously. "I was so sure you wouldn't die, but then I kept thinking that, if it had happened to so many others, there was no reason it shouldn't happen to us."

"Was I hurt so badly?"

"The cuts in your face were infected. Frei Bartolomeu washed them out with wine but it didn't help. You know how it is here when your hurt yourself — it always festers. You had a blazing fever and your face — " She broke off. "In the end Frei Bartolomeu had to cauterize all the wounds."

"You saw him?" Had Reina had the courage to watch?

"No, but I was coming every day. Now and then I saw the dressings changed."

"It's bad?" Yosef asked.

She did not answer.

"It's a mess," he answered himself, his voice grim.

"I didn't say that," Reina exclaimed quickly. Too quickly.

"You didn't need to." He turned his face away from her and pulled his hand out of hers. Inside his head thoughts tumbled in confused heaps. When he looked back at her, she had gone. He lay quietly, trying not to think. He was glad to see Frei Bartolomeu enter.

In his hand the friar held a bowl of something that steamed and smelled good. "Do you think you can eat anything?" he asked. "It's been a while since you did anything but drink."

"I'm starving."

"Good." With his free hand the friar pulled a stool next to Yosef's bed and sat down. Lifting the spoon, he was about to begin when Yosef shook his head slightly. "Is it the food?" asked Frei Bartolomeu. "You don't have to worry. The big girl Nechama does all the cooking herself for the infirmaries."

Yosef had not even thought of that. "I've been asleep," he explained. "I have to wash my hands. It's the halacha — Jewish law."

"Of course. I should have remembered." As he fetched a jug and bowl, the friar continued, "You'd be surprised at what I've noticed just supervising the medical facilities." Moving the bowl of food to the table, he set the water for washing on the stool. "I'll help you sit up; you're less likely to spill it over yourself, then."

Yosef was weaker than he knew. Without Frei Bartolomeu's arm he could not have raised himself. He rested his right hand over the bowl and reached out with his left to take the container of water.

Nothing happened.

For what seemed a moment of eternity Yosef held his breath. Leaning against the friar's shoulder, Yosef let his eyes move to the coarse blanket that covered him. He saw the fingers of his left hand lying oddly crumpled against the rough wool and did not at first understand why this was so. Gradually he realized that he could not move his fingers, or his hand, and that his arm hung heavily against his side. Under the blanket his left leg lay still.

Yosef's gaze was fixed on his hand. He did not seem to be able to look anywhere else. His mind was numb.

Gently Frei Bartolomeu reached across him and took his hand to rest it on the edge of the bowl next to the other one. Yosef's eyes followed his hand, his body turning a little because the bowl had been left on the stool and he had to lean to that side. He watched the well-trained friar pour water over his hands as he should, alternately six times; but none of it was real. As if in a dream, he saw his hands dried and the bowl removed.

Seating himself, Frei Bartolomeu picked up the food once more, but Yosef turned his face from it. "Just a bit; it will do you good," the friar cajoled him.

"Getting better would do me more good."

Frei Bartolomeu did not answer.

Like a trickle of flood water seeping under a door, the suspicion crept into Yosef's mind that there was something very large and very frightening so near that no more than a word or a gesture would bring it rushing in upon him. He let a minute pass; and another; and then he asked, "What is it?" His voice was tense.

The friar did not reply at once. He hesitated, avoiding Yosef's eyes. At last he said, "I saw an old man once who had been kicked in the forehead by a horse many years before. He was much as you are."

It was not the flood outside the door after all, Yosef decided. It was instead an incredible, crushing weight that bore him down. His shoulders ached and he felt as though he could not breathe. If he had not always been proud of his self-discipline he would have cried out; but that pride kept him silent.

Afterwards, when he remembered that day, it was not the friar's voice or the insistent smell of the untasted food that he recalled. What stayed in his mind was the exact weave of the unbleached woolen blanket where his hand lay on it, the way the threads were spun unevenly and slubbed, how they crossed each other, over two and under one, over two and under one, each row one thread further over so that it formed a slanting pattern. Climbing delicately across the blanket was a lithe pale-pink gecko, its large dark eyes intent on an ant that wandered through the forest of stray fibers on the surface of the cloth.

That the gecko had made a sudden rush and snap, and had paused, blinking and gulping, before disappearing over the edge of the bed, Yosef remembered; but it was not part of the picture that remained with him. Only the blanket, and the gecko, and the ant; and he saw them every time he was brought back to that moment when he had known that he would never do anything easily again.

Papa would have said "gam zu l'tova" immediately, Yosef thought. He would have said it unhesitatingly and he would have meant it. He stared down at the crooked fingers. But I'm not Papa, he wanted to cry, I can say it until I'm hoarse and I still can't mean it. He had failed his father. He had tried so hard to be like him and he had believed he had done well until the test came and he found he had not done it at all. I ought to say "gam zu l'tova" anyway, he thought dispiritedly; maybe just saying it will make me feel better. So he said it, but he felt nothing, except that afterwards he felt guilty for feeling nothing.

Hearing Yosef speak, the friar asked, "What did you say?"

"It doesn't matter," Yosef said heavily. "You wouldn't understand."

"I think perhaps I might," ventured Frei Bartolomeu, "but never mind." He rose and walked to the door. "I'll call Chanan back now," he went on. "He's been at your side ever since the accident, but I thought it was better for me to be with you when you — " In mid-sentence, he went out.

The accident. It had not come back to Yosef yet; maybe it never would. And why Chanan? They had been at each other's throats most of the time. Briefly both questions bothered him; then he was suddenly too tired to care any more. All he wanted to do was lie down, and that he managed, carefully, by himself.

As the days passed it was, indeed, Chanan who took care of him and helped him and did what was necessary for someone who had not yet learned to manage with half as much as he had had before. But it was not the brash, rebellious Chanan that Yosef remembered. Abruptly Chanan had become quiet, obedient, as though he were a horse broken overnight to the saddle.

When Yosef was ready to try to manage the few yards to the conveniences, it was Chanan who eased him off the bed and helped him stand. It was Chanan's arm that held him firmly, Chanan's shoulder that Yosef gripped so tightly that, although he did not know it, he left five purple bruises there. Without complaint, Chanan bore him humbly, as compliant as a beast of burden.

Much of the time Yosef was occupied with mastering the petty demands of everyday life that now loomed like a never-ending range of mountain peaks, each one of which he had to conquer. From the absurdity of not being able to tie his own hose-cords to the horror of the slow, dragging progress that had replaced walking, every action was a challenge to be overcome. But with each success came no thrill of achievement. Yosef felt like a rich man suddenly reduced to penury, making shift and cutting corners, cheapened and degraded.

So much of Yosef's concentration was devoted to these tasks that it was only incidentally that he recalled he wanted to ask Chanan about something. And Chanan was so sparing of words that there never seemed to be an opportunity to bring up the subject of the accident. When the chance came, Frei Bartolomeu's cross was to blame.

Until the day he left his bed for the first time, Yosef had not seen the wall above his head. There was no reason to twist around to look at it; it was a wall like the rest, flimsy and bare. But when he faced towards the bed that first time, Yosef saw that Frei Bartolomeu had hung a cross there. It was a depressing object, with the figure of a dead man carved on it: not an encouraging omen for anyone who was ill.

In view of Frei Bartolomeu's presence, it was perhaps not wholly surprising to find that he had installed the crucifix. But why had he put it above Yosef's head? If he wanted Yosef to see it, he should have hung it on the opposite wall. For the friar himself, there were crosses enough in his own quarters, and he wore one as well; there was no need for another in a patient's room. Besides, no crosses hung in the infirmaries, so why did Yosef have to put up with it?

He had worked his way outside to sit as an old man might, in the shade with the sun reaching in toward him under the overhang of the roof. Leaning on Chanan, as always, he rose to go back indoors after only a short while: the sun was too hot. As he entered the dim room his attention was caught by the cross, still hanging at the head of his bed.

"Why is that thing hanging on the wall?" he asked Chanan sharply. "Frei Bartolomeu won't take it down." His hand held Chanan's shoulder, and under his fingers he felt him grow tense.

"I agreed to it." Chanan did not look at Yosef's face. "Frei Domingo wouldn't let Frei Bartolomeu treat you unless I did. There was nobody to ask; Luis was down in the meadow with you, trying to stop the bleeding."

There was a pause. At last Yosef said, "Chanan, what happened? I don't remember any of it."

There was a small, stifled sound from the other boy. "Luis knows as well as I do," he said after a time.

"Luis isn't here right now."

"Isn't it enough that I've done tshuva?" cried Chanan. "Do I have to strip myself bare for you, too?"

Yosef's fingers bit into Chanan's shoulder. "Tell me!"

"All right, then!" Shaking off Yosef's hand, Chanan confronted him, his face flushed and angry. "It was my fault: is that what you want to hear? *I* decided that the no-swimming rule was only for the beaches. *I* let the boys play in the river. You came down and caught me at it. You had to go into the water yourself to chase the boys out, and a crocodile came up from the beach and knocked you onto the rocks with its tail."

Yosef glared at him. "Now tell me the truth."

"It is! One of the boys cut his foot and the blood in the water attracted the crocodile." He stopped for breath. "Of course I'm sorry, but that's too late for you, isn't it? I never expected anything like this to happen, but I'll carry the guilt for it for the rest of my life.

"It was your fault, too, but you'll never understand that, will you? You'll never see how you goaded me, how you gave me jobs and hung over me as if I were a five-year-old, how you let everybody know that you didn't trust me to be responsible. Didn't it ever enter your mind that people have feelings? Just because you're so terribly self-disciplined, does everybody have to be?"

Hands clenched, blazing with resentment, he glared at Yosef. Then, suddenly, his anger was pinched out like a snuffed candle. Almost as if nohing had happened, he returned to his place at Yosef's side. Quietly he asked, "Did you want to lie down or sit at the table?"

Yosef hardly knew what he answered. Chanan's unexpected attack had left him disoriented. Often enough Yosef had thought about himself, had explored how he felt. His pride, his self-discipline, his reactions to people: he was acutely conscious of all of these. But he had never thought to analyze anyone else: the idea of people reacting to him as he did to them had not occurred to him. He had never suspected it mattered.

CHAPTER EIGHT

T THE BEGINNING of the last week in Cheshvan Frei
Bartolomeu changed the dressing on Yosef's face for the last time:
the wounds were finally healed. There was no longer pain when
Yosef touched the area. Slowly his fingers followed the new
contours, traveled over ridges and down crevasses where the
burnt-out wounds had pulled into themselves. A scar ran through
his eyebrow, he knew; another one near his eye pulled at the
eyelid; one of the other scars by his mouth drew up his lip in a
small involuntary grimace. He did not ask for a mirror; there was
no need. He looked at Chanan, and Chanan looked away. No
word passed between them.

Clearing his supplies away for the final time, Frei
Bartolomeu looked from one boy to the other. "It's a funny
thing," he remarked; "I was always told that yours was a deity of
vengeance, yet you treat each other with kindness; and ours is
supposed to be a god of love, and we show each other cruelty.
Our gods seem to have gotten mixed up. I look at you children,
half-brought up in your Jewish ways, and I can't get over the way
you behave. I'd have expected Yosef to be cursing you, Chanan,
with every word he knows, but he says nothing."

Stretching up, he removed the crucifix from the wall with a
casual hand. "There's no need for this any more," he observed.
The cross with the dead man carved on it lay in his palm. His
thumb rubbed the smooth, polished wood; he seemed hypnotized
by the motion. The silence was stretched tight among them.

The friar broke into the tautness. "I suppose you think I'm
more trustworthy — or less untrustworthy — than the other
friars," he said, "because I persuaded Frei Domingo to let me treat
you."

Yosef looked at him curiously, his head cocked to one side; but Chanan nodded.

Frei Bartolomeu half-smiled. "Thank you for the compliment. It was all play-acting between Frei Domingo and me; we had arranged it in advance, in case an opportunity arose. We wanted a chance to worm our way into your confidence. It was easy to paint Frei Domingo, whom you didn't like anyway, as the villain; and I — I ran the infirmaries, so you could easily see me as the concerned fatherly friar full of Christian love.

"I was going to hang the cross where you would see it all the time and remember by whose kindness you were cared for. While you were weak and receptive, I was going to speak of our savior and our religion." He glanced down at the cross and shook his head regretfully.

"But you didn't do any of that," objected Yosef. "Why are you telling us all this?"

"Because of what you said in Hebrew that first day." The friar spoke hesitantly, as if the words made him feel guilty. "Chanan told me what it meant: 'this, too, is for good.' To say it when you did was a triumph of faith. After that — " he lowered his gaze to the cross in his hand and sighed — "after that, I simply didn't feel I had anything to offer. I kept my pledge to Frei Domingo: I hung the cross on the wall soon after you were conscious. But by then, of course, it didn't matter." He shrugged. "And why am I telling you? Because faith is precious to me, even your faith, and we friars are not to be trusted. I once said to Don Alvaro that I didn't think I was ruthless enough in the interests of the Church." He gave them a rueful smile. "You see? I was right."

After they had watched Frei Bartolomeu walk away, Yosef said to Chanan, "But I didn't mean it."

"Didn't mean what?" asked Chanan.

"*Gam zu l'tova.* I still don't mean it. It hurts too much."

Chanan flinched and went out.

Yosef did not care. There was a second time the friar had misjudged him: if Frei Bartolomeu had not spoken into the silence, when Yosef was exploring the scars on his face, Yosef would certainly have said something unpleasant to Chanan. It would not have been cursing; Yosef did not use such language. Instead he would have said something hard and cutting, because Yosef wanted Chanan to know how he felt. To Yosef's mind, Chanan did not seem nearly sorry enough, yet.

Late in the afternoon, after he had dozed briefly in the heat, Yosef noticed a new item in the room. Leaning against the wall near his bed was a crutch. Someone had spent a good deal of effort on it. Well-made, with neat, tight joints, it had a look of strength without heaviness. The maker had thought about the humid heat of São Tome, had seen a sweaty hand slipping down the smooth upright; he had attached a small crosspiece, a handhold. In the sunlight the dark wood of the crutch seemed to have a warm glow to it that was brought out by the silken oiled surface.

Yosef had always appreciated beautiful woods and he knew fine craftsmanship when he saw it. As an object, the crutch had the rightness of being well suited to its task, as well as the beauty of its making. But it repelled Yosef.

Looking at the crutch, Yosef was seized with the conviction that he dared not touch it. As long as he leaned on Chanan, as long as he depended on someone's help, he did not have to think of himself as permanently crippled. If he were only temporarily disabled, he would not be changing his life to adapt to it: he was entitled to expect help in coping until he could manage again. But once he touched that crutch, he admitted that there had been a change in him, a permanent change. Once his hand rested on that wood, the fact of being crippled was inescapable. Frei Bartolomeu's cross had been made of the same dark wood as the crutch; but to Yosef the crutch was infinitely more threatening.

Yosef ignored the object, making no mention of its presence. On Chanan's shoulder his hand pressed heavily. As each day passed, Yosef found fresh demands to make on Chanan's obedient service, as though by increasing his dependence on Chanan he was proving to himself that he did not need the permanence of the crutch.

Yosef received few visitors. Once the initial danger had passed, Reina came less often, unsure of her welcome and busy with her own tasks. Saadya and Luis called infrequently. During the week, laboring in the fields, they were tired at the end of the day, weary from the long trek uphill, ready only for supper and sleep. Only on Shabath they came, or perhaps stole a few minutes from the busy Sunday hours.

On the Shabath at the end of that week in Cheshvan, Saadya tapped on the door to Yosef's room.

"Come," said Yosef, tense, watching to see Saadya's reaction to his mutilated face.

Saadya's expression did not change. Seating himself, he nodded at Yosef. "Shabath shalom." Elbows resting on his knees, he leaned forward, one hand grasping the other wrist. There was an air of maturity about him that was so convincing that Yosef had the disquieting impression that he was talking to an older brother. Did it come from Saadya's position in the colony? he wondered. Or was it just Saadya?

"This isn't just a social call," Yosef said.

"No."

"Well?" Yosef hated the preamble of social chitchat that began most exchanges, the conventional rubbish of "Nice day" and "How are you?" that delayed the actual message of a conversation.

"While you're ill and Luis is acting parnes," Saadya asked cautiously, "do you submit to his authority or he to yours?"

"I think he's in complete charge."

"That's what he thought, too," said Saadya. "He's going to order Chanan back to normal working."

Yosef felt as though he had been punched. "I need Chanan."

"You don't, really." Saadya straightened. "But he needs to get away from you. I've never seen him so miserable."

"Shouldn't he be? Look at what he did to me."

"You know, Yosef, sometimes I can't get over the way you behave," Saadya said, unconsciously repeating the friar's words. "You act as if you never heard of the word 'n'kama' or 'destino' or 'ahavath Yisrael'. Don't you think about your Judaismo?"

If he had answered, Yosef would have had to admit that he did not think about it, particularly. He thought a great deal about what being crippled meant in terms of doing without; he fanned the coals of resentment and bitterness; but he did not see in Torah a way to deal with his problems.

"Look," Saadya went on, "to begin with, it was destino that you were crippled. You can see that, right? Because everything is the will of the Ribono shel Olam."

Saadya was taking him step by step, as though he were just learning these concepts, as though he assumed that because Yosef did not discipline his thinking according to these ideas he knew nothing of them.

"If the accident happened through Chanan, that's Chanan's problem — that he deserved to be the trigger on the crossbow. But it doesn't affect you. You would have been hurt anyhow. It isn't even sensible for you to take n'kama on Chanan."

"I'm not taking n'kama," Yosef protested. "I know revenge isn't allowed."

"You take your feelings out on him. You want to make him feel miserable. You want to use him as a slave. What do you call that? What happened to ahavath Yisrael? Don't you have any concern for him? Do you have any idea how he feels? Every time he looks at you, he says, it's like somebody stabbing him. He told me he had promised himself that you would never lack for anything as long as he was alive. Do you understand what that means for him? It means making himself a slave to someone he can't stand, for the rest of his life. He's done tshuva. You have no right to treat him the way you do."

Rising suddenly, Saadya strode to the corner where the crutch stood, unused. He snatched it up and thrust it at Yosef. "Stop leaning on Chanan. Use this."

"No!" Yosef shrank back so slightly that if Saadya had not been staring at him he would not have noticed the trace of movement.

Something warned Saadya that there was more to Yosef's clinging to Chanan than malice. Laying the crutch across the foot of the bed, he resumed his seat in silence.

Some while later Saadya asked suddenly, "Have you gone anywhere since you were hurt?"

"Where can I go? I've been to the conveniences."

"Not even to the dining houses?" In Saadya's tone there was a note of disbelief. "Why not?"

Why not? Because I know my face is hideous, Yosef thought. Because the way I move is awkward and grotesque. Because I'm ashamed to be seen, to be stared at, to feel as though I've been caught half-undressed. But he would not say any of that to Saadya. All at once he knew how Chanan had felt when he insisted that he tell him about the accident. "Because I — don't want to," he said at last.

Saadya considered the answer. "Is it that you don't trust us? We're all your friends, all the children. Like family."

"No. They're your friends. They're Luis' friends. But they aren't mine. Except for you and Luis and Reina, I have no visitors. When I was parnes I concentrated on getting the job done, not on being popular. I think that's how a leader ought to be, and when I'm parnes again I'll be the same. But it didn't make me friends."

"I see." Saadya was not hearing anything new. "But don't you feel oppressed here, trapped inside these same walls all the time?"

"It's not the walls I'm trapped inside," said Yosef bitterly.

"Inside your body?" Saadya shook his head. "You can still learn to manage reasonably well with what you have. You're not trapped inside your body, Yosef; you're trapped inside your mind."

❧ ❧ ❧

Sunday morning Yosef wrestled himself into his clothes alone. Chanan hadn't even said goodbye, Yosef thought resentfully. But perhaps they hadn't given him a chance. They might at least have sent a little boy to help out for a bit. He'd have been no use for leaning on, but he might have carried things and run errands.

Yosef looked at the door. He needed the conveniences, and Chanan's shoulder was not by his hand any more. His eyes flicked to the crutch, lying on the floor where it had fallen during the night. Such a simple object it was, he thought, to be full of menace. He did not want to be tied to it, to a piece of wood. As soon as he used it he knew he would become so dependent on it that it would be the first thing he reached for in the morning.

He resented having his disability uppermost in his mind, so

that he was always conscious of it. One day, he thought, he would come to take it for granted, and he resented that still more: that he would cease to think of himself as he had once been and accept the maimed body he had now.

But he needed the conveniences.

It was too humiliating to be defeated by so prosaic a physical need; he had to salvage some scrap of self-respect. He stared down at the thing on the floor, hating it. He could no longer walk with dignity, the dignity that made him look like his father. He could not say *"gam zu l'tova"* sincerely, as his father had.

The words Luis had once said to Saadya came back to him: I never want to forget that things were better once. And Saadya's reply: ... except that it hurts more.

Yes, it hurts more, he thought savagely. Let it hurt. Luis was right. I will never forget, he promised himself, never forget that once I looked like a young grandee. And I will never accept myself as I am now.

Never.

He reached down for the object at his feet.

❧   ❧   ❧

Five days passed.

Sitting on the bench outside his door, Yosef picked at the tepid mess that was supposed to be his dinner. Chanan had always seen to it that his food was hot. Now, the boy who brought the meals to the infirmary delivered Yosef's as well. Ever since Chanan had been sent away, the bowl had been scarcely lukewarm when it arrived. The boy seemed to have a positive knack for leaving it when Yosef was not there. Perhaps he waited — that would explain why it was never hot. He never knocked. He never left it on the table, only on the bench outside. Yosef had not yet mastered the technique for carrying the food without spilling it: he had had to eat sitting on the bench.

Yosef did not want to complain to anybody. Surely the parnes ought to be able to solve so minor a problem himself. He would have to catch the boy and speak to him.

At the approach of the next mealtime, Yosef stationed himself just inside the door, leaving it ajar only a fraction. There was little activity outside; all the children would be at the dining houses. In the infirmary supper had already been served. Through the wall he shared with the main building Yosef could hear the clatter of spoons against wooden bowls. But the boy still had not come to him.

At length he saw a shadow gliding along the ground, reluctantly nearing him. Throwing open the door, he caught the boy as he put the food on the bench once again. Feet apart, balancing lightly, the child was obviously ready to dart away as soon as his hands left the container.

"I'm accustomed to eating at a table," Yosef said.

The boy jumped apprehensively, jerking back his hand too quickly, so that the dish tipped and fell, the cold meal sliding out in a slow dribble. He looked at the mess.

"And I'd be pleased to get it at the same time as the rest of the compound," Yosef added. "Is that clear?"

For the briefest instant the boy's gaze turned towards him, taking in Yosef's whole person in that glance. Just that moment he stared; then he whirled and ran.

Yosef swallowed hard. Kicking some earth over the spilled food to discourage the flies, he replaced the bowl on the bench and went inside. It did not matter that he was doing without supper; he had no appetite for it. He had seen the expression on the boy's face; he had seen it change as the boy looked at him. He had seen it change to fear.

When Luis visited on Shabath Yosef did not mention the incident, though his meals were still delivered in the same way and in the same condition. Yosef remembered the days in Lisboa when anything beyond a scrap of bread seemed a feast. He sat on the bench and ate. Not until Reina came in the following week did anyone else know.

Reina had eaten her supper quickly in order to have more time with Yosef before she was to go on duty. They had been talking for some time when Reina heard a noise outside. "What's that?" she asked.

"My supper, no doubt."

"Now?" Reina exclaimed. "But everyone must have finished long ago!" Opening the door, she saw the bowl on the bench and picked it up, meaning to bring it to the table. "Why, it's cold!"

"Never mind. At least I don't burn my thumb when I carry it."

"That's disgusting, that they don't even put in on the table. Who brings it?" Reina demanded, incensed.

"Some little boy," Yosef said tiredly. "It doesn't matter."

"Of course it does. Why doesn't he bring it in?"

Yosef looked steadily at Reina and said in an even tone, "Because the way I look frightens him. At first he left it there because he had never seen me; now he does it because he has."

Yosef watched Reina's eyes grow larger and larger.

"Oh, Yosef," she said. She came to him and put her arms around him. He knew she was crying because he could feel the tears soaking into his shirt.

He patted her back because that was what one was supposed to do. "You can't blame him. Anybody would be afraid of someone who looked like this."

"No, they wouldn't," she sobbed. "If Luis looked a hundred times worse, nobody could be afraid of him. Ahavath Yisrael is part of him: he loves people and they know it and love him back. You don't have any of it, not a speck. You have less idea than a baby of how to get along with people, and now you're dependent on them and there isn't anyone. And I don't think you even see how terribly, terribly alone you are." Her arms drew so tightly around him that he had to reach up and loosen her grip.

"I'm parnes, Reina," he said. "Leaders don't make friends that easily, anyway."

Reina sat on the bench and wiped her eyes. "Luis is acting parnes and he has loads of friends," she said stubbornly. "Who comes to visit you? Anyone?"

"Luis or Saadya, sometimes."

"Nobody else?" she persisted. "What do you do with all that time by yourself?"

"Mostly I work at doing all the things that used to be simple. I have to get to the point where I can be parnes again. I left things well organized, but I'm worried that Luis may be letting things slide, he's so easygoing. But I'm not ready yet." He made an impatient gesture with his good hand. "I'm so occupied with learning to tie knots one-handed that I can't do anything useful for anyone else."

"For the colony, you mean? There must be something you can do even now," Reina mused. "You ought to ask Saadya,"

"Why not Luis?"

"Luis runs muscle work; Saadya's in charge of brain work." She rose. "I think I'm out of time; I have to go to the infirmary. Promise me you'll talk to Saadya."

Yosef shrugged. "All right." He watched her out of sight.

Watching the shadows lengthen into dusk, Yosef sat waiting for night. He had heard the working teams arrive a little while ago; he could have gone to Saadya by now. But he remembered the look on the boy's face and stayed where he was.

When it became dark enough, he sought out Saadya. He felt strange, venturing more than the few yards from his room, as though he were Binyamin of Tudela exploring an unknown Jewish community.

Sitting cross-legged on the ground outside the house he slept in, Saadya was reading aloud and translating the parshath hashavua. His crude little lamp made an island of light around him and lured gullible moths away from the moon. As Yosef approached, Saadya broke off his learning to slap a mosquito. He glanced up and saw his visitor. "Sit down," he invited.

Yosef shook his head. Sitting down was little problem, but getting up again was too complicated to bother with. "I just came to ask if you had any work I could do until I'm a working parnes again."

"You know how badly we need more copies of the Chumashim and the siddurim," Saadya answered readily. "But you might prefer teaching."

"The children wouldn't. I'd scare them all away."

The bitterness in Yosef's voice pulled Saadya to his feet. "Of course they'd be shy at first," he said matter-of-factly, "but after that they'd be willing to see what you were like. As long as you treat them like reasonable little people, with thoughts and feelings like anybody else, you ought to get on fine." He smiled. "You won't have any trouble controlling them, at any rate; discipline is your strong point."

Yosef shook his head. "I'm not up to it. From the way Reina talks, I'm not much at getting on with people of any age. She seems to think of me as a sort of dancing bear in need of a keeper. I'll work with a siddur, thank you."

With Saadya's help the table in Yosef's room was organized for the new task, and Yosef began work. As day after day crept by, however, Yosef learned that copying a siddur was not an inspiring experience or a pleasurable occupation for him. While he was saying tfilloth, it would sometimes happen that a word or pasuk would leap out, suddenly full of meaning; but copying the tfilloth did not have the same effect. Letter by letter, word by word: there was only one careful, tedious stroke after another, each painstaking page legible and correct and empty.

CHAPTER NINE

HVAT BROUGHT A SUNDAY afternoon that was too hot for any exertion. The still, humid air felt too warm and thick to breathe, and the children wanted only to take turns fanning each other. The temperature inside and out was inescapably oppressive.

Their shirts sweated dark against their backs, Luis and Saadya sat with Yosef on the bench outside his room, too lethargic to do more than flick a hand at the odd inquisitive fly.

"I wish we'd have some cooler weather," Yosef remarked.

"We're lucky to be up here," said Luis in reply. "At least it'll be a little cooler tonight for the meeting."

"Meeting?" Yosef asked.

"Didn't they tell you? I thought everybody was meant to attend."

Yosef shook his head. "No, but they must know that I wouldn't come, anyhow. They probably thought it wasn't worth bothering."

Saadya leaned forward to see around Luis. "I think you ought to come, Yosef. I have a funny feeling."

Luis glanced at Saadya. "Do you know something I don't?"

"Just my suspicious nature, maybe. General meetings do that to me." Although Saadya's tone was bantering, Yosef had the feeling that he was trying to warn him without alerting Luis. But there was no way to ask anything further.

That night, about an hour after sunset, all of the voting boys — seven and up — and a good many of the rest settled themselves in an open space between two dining houses. There were too many of them to fit into any of the buildings, so they sat outside, with a few bonfires for light.

Within his room Yosef sat for a long time trying to decide whether or not to attend. It had been so long since he had been among people that he felt shy even about standing at the edge of the group. In the end it was the mystery of Saadya's apparent warning that prodded him out the door towards the glow in the center of the compound. As he neared the meeting he moved more quietly until he found a place in shadow where he could hear. Unseen in the darkness, Yosef listened to the discussion.

Chanan's voice cut sharply into the murmur. "If you'd done it straightforwardly instead of behind his back, I'd probably have voted in favor, but this sneaky way of having a meeting without him — well, it makes me wonder if there isn't something wrong with the whole idea."

"There is." Luis's voice, low and controlled, was hard to hear. It was not loud: Luis must be angry. "I don't want the job. I don't want it permanently and I don't want to take it from someone like this. Besides, you won't give him credit for doing it well. Whatever you say, he was a good parnes."

There was a pause. "Anybody else before we vote?" someone asked.

"Yes." That was Saadya. "You're not voting 'good' or 'bad'; you're talking about different styles of leadership. If you hadn't had Yosef's strong discipline and good organization, you wouldn't have been able to elbow the friars out. You like Luis's style better because it's more relaxed. But he's in charge right now, anyway. I don't see anything wrong with wanting to make the change official, but I think out of decency you ought to wait until Yosef is back on his feet. To do it now is kind of hitting him when he's down. It's not acting with chesed."

"Will he ever be back on his feet?" It was less a question than a challenge.

"Very possibly not." Yosef started forward, moving among the boys, running a gauntlet of curious stares. Almost no one had seen him since the accident: every eye was drawn towards him. He felt exposed, conspicuous, bizarre. Every detail of the distorted face, the useless arm, the dragging foot — every detail was being sucked into an awed, silent sea of eyes. By the time he reached the front he felt as though he had been stripped bare right down to his bones.

Turning to face the meeting, Yosef held himself as proudly erect as always. "I'll never be able to be parnes in the same way I used to. I won't be working harder or longer than all of you in the fields; I'm no use in the fields any more. I can still organize and direct, but that isn't what you want. The kind of leader I am won't change; you don't want that, either.

"When I was parnes I may have done things you didn't like, but I know I did one thing right: I put myself second and the colony first. Luis is a good, competent parnes. You all like him and work well with him. If you feel you need him, you ought to have him. Maybe you made a mistake when you chose me for parnes. It would be a much greater mistake, for your own sakes, to leave me in a position you feel I'm no longer fit for."

There was no reason for him to remain. Yosef began to work his way through the crowd. As he passed, he was surprised to see the boys all around him rising to their feet. Puzzled, he stopped and glanced back. On every side there were eyes, still; but the eyes spoke friendship and respect.

He had never known anyone to look at him in this way. He did not understand why his words had made the boys regard him as they did. All he knew was that they understood that he had sacrificed something that meant a great deal to him — being parnes — and they appreciated the gesture. They were standing now in wordless tribute to him.

The gesture was unexpected. Yosef hardly knew what to make of it, though by the time he reached the darkness outside the splash of firelight, he found he had to rub his sleeve roughly across his face. He was angry with himself for being so affected. What did it matter, he told himself, that they appreciated his sacrifice? Could they even imagine how much being parnes had meant to him? They had not wanted him, anyway, had been so impatient for someone else that they could not bear to wait even a few months to see if he was going to recover.

I don't want your respect, he thought at them in bitter anger. I don't want your sympathy, I don't want your respect, I don't want your honor. You were going to vote me out of office. What did it matter to you that I surrendered my position five minutes before you would have stripped it from me? Did you think I did it to make myself look noble? I did it to keep my self-respect, not to impress you.

He thought of the faces again, turning toward him with something that was not awe, not so much respect, though that was there, too. What had it been? Kindness? Gratitude? That was it. Gratitude. They had known they could and would replace Yosef, but even as they were convinced it was necessary, they felt guilty for the way it had come about. Even for the good of the majority they did not want to publicly reject him. They did not believe in building a successful society by tossing aside one boy whose personality blocked their way. Yosef had resigned of his own accord. He had saved them from wondering, with every future achievement, if it really had been necessary to hurt someone for it.

They could not have told him they were relieved without shaming him, but they had been grateful nonetheless. So I did do something for them that they appreciated, Yosef thought. All the time I was parnes I tried so hard and they didn't appreciate anything; now I resigned selfishly, to keep my pride, and they were grateful. And their respect mattered to me; it mattered because I had the good of the colony at heart, their good, and I wanted them, just once, to understand that. He almost sighed. People were so unpredictable.

He would have liked to discuss it with Reina, but it was not until two days later that he saw her, and it was not the right time to mention it. Seated near the door, at his table, Yosef was beginning a second copy of the siddur when he heard Reina's voice close by.

"He's a bit sharpish, sometimes, but you mustn't mind; that's just his way. He doesn't really mean it."

Leaving his work, Yosef went outside to meet her. "You're too kind," he said sarcastically, as she appeared around the corner of the building. Behind her trailed a child who hung back warily.

"Be good, Yosef," pleaded Reina. "Don't frighten Esperansa. She's been terribly ill with the fever, and she needed to get out, so I brought her along; but if you're going to upset her I'll have to leave." She was obviously worried about the child.

"I'll try; but I'm not used to children. You know I don't like them the way Luis does."

It was not much of a promise. Reina shrugged, resigned. Turning to the little girl, she said, "Come and be introduced, Esperansa."

Eyes on the ground, the child approached and executed a formal curtsy. "Don Yosef," she said, stiffly polite.

"She has very courtly manners," explained Reina with an affectionate smile. "Sit in the shade, Esperansa, and amuse yourself."

Choosing not the shade of the overhanging roof, as Yosef would have expected, but the shadow of a nearby tree, the child settled herself on the ground and began an investigation of the earth in front of her.

"I didn't come at once," Reina said as she sat down next to her brother on the bench standing outside. "When I heard about the meeting I thought you might want a couple of days to get used to the change and you might not like company."

Yosef shrugged. In his hand he held his small belt knife. Hardly noticing what he was doing, he was gouging holes in the bench with the point of the blade. "I kept busy."

"With what? Teaching?"

"No; I don't know how to handle children." He nodded toward the table, strewn with writing materials. "For the last month or so Saadya's had me copying a siddur. I labor in holiness." There was a caustic edge to the words.

"You don't like it?"

"I'm bored sick." The knife flicked a few splinters. "This copying — anybody can do it. If I stopped somebody would take over and there would be no difference. I want to do something that's as special as being parnes was. I'm restless. I'm used to working hard in the fields and falling into bed at night. Oh, I suppose I should be grateful it was my left side and not my right. At least there's one job left that I can do. But not being parnes — I can't get used to being just ordinary. There doesn't seem to be a place for me on São Tome any longer, but I can't go anywhere else."

"I know." Reina said nothing more.

Yosef shifted his attention from destroying the bench to watching the child Reina had brought with her. Still occupied with whatever it was that she had discovered, the child was unaware of his scrutiny. He wondered how old she was. From her manner alone, he would have put her age at close to eighty, but from her appearance he thought she must be about six or seven. She was very thin — that would be because of the fever — but he guessed she would have been slender, almost fragile, before that. The fever accounted as well for her short hair, very dark, that scrambled over her small head in a tangle of curls: they would have cut off her plaits while she was ill to relieve her of their weight. Bent over as she was, the haze of curls hid her face. Yosef wondered what it looked like.

He did not realize how intently he had been regarding the child until she sat up straight, looked at him with a direct gaze, and said primly, "I was taught that it was impolite to stare at people, especially if they are ugly."

Yosef flushed. "I didn't notice you staring at me at all."

"I didn't," she said. "But you stared at me."

He could see her face now, a small olive-skinned oval with a pointed chin, a face in which there was not much beauty but a great deal of character. Of Reina's sort of prettiness there was little; instead the features were sensitive and mobile with an alertness that made the child's face vividly, intensely aware. It was a face that appealed to him.

As Yosef wondered what its usual expression was — just now the expression was one of offended dignity — the child exclaimed crossly, "And you're *still* staring!"

"But you're not ugly," he said, startled.

"Of course I am." Her tone was matter-of-fact.

"Don't call yourself ugly!" Yosef threw himself to his feet and swung towards her.

Rising to meet him, the child said calmly, "Why not? We do have mirrors, you know; I've seen myself. I know quite well I'm ugly."

"Don't you ever say that!" Yosef blazed down at her. "If I ever hear you say that again, I'll beat you! Do you hear me?"

Puzzled by his vehemence, the child gazed up at him. She

was remarkably self-possessed, he thought. Almost as if she had decided that she had to be tolerant of older people's oddities, she shrugged. "All right."

It was a superficial surrender. Yosef knew that, and liked the child's stubbornness even as he wanted to make her see reason.

"I think we ought to go now." Reina's strained voice came from just behind him.

Looking at both of them, the child said, "I'm not afraid."

With a smile Reina held out her hand. "I know you're not. But we'll go, anyway."

When they had gone, Yosef remained where he was, reluctant to return to the copying. He could not understand what had happened. Why had he been so upset with the child? What did it matter how she saw herself? He did not like children, anyway. Luis was the emotional one, Luis was the one who liked children swarming around him.

But Luis would have known instinctively what to say; he always did. Children confided in him. He did not need to understand how people worked inside: he had some inner sense that told him without words. He felt for everyone.

To Yosef people were incomprehensible. He had no sensitivity, he concluded; that was why he had shouted at the child. He wanted to explain to her. He wanted to apologize. But Reina would never bring her back again. Discouraged, he returned to the siddur. He was safe working with things.

Between the end of Shvat, when Luis had become parnes, and the middle of Adar, Yosef kept himself working steadily at the copying. He would have a change, soon, he knew: Saadya wanted another Chumash next. That meant that Yosef would have it by day, and Saadya would fetch it to learn from at night. It would be an inconvenient arrangement, but it meant that Yosef would have a regular visitor, and he was looking forward to it.

He had not yet finished the siddur, however, when he ran out of paper just before Purim. Saadya had persuaded Don Alvaro to sacrifice a large portion of his stock of paper. There would be no more until the next ship arrived from Portugal some weeks later. For the time being, Yosef had nothing to do but think.

Idle and restless, he made his way to the western edge of the compound. Here the forest had been pushed back little by little, to give Nechama the gardens she wanted. There was a clear view, now, of the peaks jutting up in the center of the island. Until the accident, those mountains had been part of Yosef's dream of São Tome: one day, he would climb one of those peaks and stand on its summit among the eagles and falcons, swathed in rainclouds like the mountains themselves, triumphant.

This day he stood looking to the southwest at the mountains. Fitting the rest of São Tome's precipitous landscape, they were magnificent to look at, beautiful beyond words. But Yosef could not shut out their arrogant, ringing challenge. It sounded as clearly in his ears as it had when he had first seen them from the ship. He had accepted their challenge, and they had won. They had won without his having taken one single step on their lowest slopes.

Why should he torment himself? He turned and went back into the heart of the compound. Luis was there, busy with some minor task, undisturbed by the clusters of small boys that attached themselves to him like bunches of ripe fruit. What Reina had said was true: leader or not, Luis had friends.

Like Mordechai, Yosef thought suddenly, the ending of the Megilla coming to mind. He had only recently copied those words from the siddur: "popular with the majority of his brothers, seeking the good of his people, and teaching peace to all his offspring." He did not want to be like Luis, festooned with admiring children; yet he envied him.

Purim came quietly to Yosef. Evening and morning he listened dutifully to Megillath Esther, listened to the children racketing happily; but it was all outside him. Within him there was silence. He went back to his room and found a boy to deliver his shalach manoth: Reina, Luis, Saadya. He could not decide whether or not to send any to Chanan, so he waited to see if Chanan sent shalach manoth to him; and he did, so Yosef sent some back. As the morning wore on, Yosef stood in the doorway for a while, watching the clouds billow up into heavy, rolling featherbeds dark with rain. When the downpour began, sudden and pounding and short-lived as these tropical storms often were, he went inside and lay down. He had not intended to sleep, but by the time he woke the rain was gone and the sun had come out. When he went to stand outside he found the wet steaming up from the earth with the distinctive warm moist smell that rain leaves behind. Shutting his eyes, he concentrated on the scents that hung in the air.

"Don Yosef."

His eyes flew open. It was the child. Yosef had forgotten her name but the face was perfectly clear in his mind. Smiling up at him, she held out a package.

"Shalach manoth from Reina," she said. "Simchath Purim!"

Taken by surprise, Yosef thanked her with a faintly abstracted air. Stretching out his hand for the package, he was puzzled when the child held it back.

"Where would you like me to leave it?" she asked.

Yosef indicated the table. When she had deposited the basket, he said gravely, "That was very considerate of you." How had she known, he wondered, how hard it was for him to carry everything?

"Yosef, you really have to look at this." Reina appeared with another parcel. "Shalach manoth from Esperansa."

"From Esperansa?" Yosef was dumbfounded.

"But look," Reina went on, "she's made it in the shape of a bird, with the wings tied across the top. Isn't it sweet?" Snapping the string, she let the wings fly open.

Holding the small basket in his hand, Yosef examined it. The shape was crude, the weaving inexpert, but there was, indeed, something vaguely birdlike about it. The food inside was the same as everyone else's. She had worked on that basket. It was quite decent for a child's work.

"I wanted it to be a bird," Esperansa said, "because of flying." Seeing that Reina did not understand, she appealed to Yosef, "Do you know what I mean?"

"I know." He looked down at the basket and saw what she had seen: a falcon flying free, soaring aloft on the wind. He was touched by her thought. Standing a little straighter, he let his fingers close around the basket. She had seen the restless vitality, had seen a boy who sat like a wounded falcon with fierce bright eyes, had seen him bound with a cord that could not be snapped. Yosef looked at the little girl gratefully. "After I was so impolite to you last time?"

"You didn't mean to be." After considering briefly, she went on, "We used to have a cook who shouted, quite horribly. Mama explained to me that I didn't have to worry if she shouted because that was just her way of showing that she cared about you. She really was very kind." There was a pause. "She was a very good cook, too."

Beside him Reina was laughing gently, but Yosef regarded the child as seriously as before. The woven bird lay in the hollow of his hand. "Would you put your gift somewhere safe, please?" he asked Esperansa. "I don't want to damage it by accident."

Obediently she took it and placed it on the table. Turning back to Yosef, she smiled. "You needn't worry. It's much too strong for that."

Drawing Yosef down beside her, Reina settled on the outside bench. As brother and sister chatted, Esperansa curled up on the dry ground by the wall, and gave herself to her dreams.

Shifting position after a time, Yosef caught sight of the rapt expression on Esperansa's face. "What does she think of when she looks like that?" he asked Reina in a low tone.

Despite his care, the question recalled the little girl from wherever she had been. She gave Yosef a curiously searching look, as though to reassure herself that he could be trusted with her confidence.

"It was my very private dream," she said at last, "about when I leave this place and go back home, because I find my Mama and Papa again, and home is where they are. Mama puts her arms around me and I hear her skirts rustle, and then she brushes my hair so there isn't a single tangle in it any more. Papa comes home from work smelling of all sorts of sharp strange scents, because he's a spice merchant. And cook is shouting at everybody, and she gives me something sweet; she slips it into my mouth when nobody is looking.

"Then all my big brothers and sisters come to visit — they're so much older than I am that they're all married already — and we have such a lovely evening, and when it's time for them to go home, we stand outside in the summer night with the stars bright and listen to the nightjars calling as we watch everybody walk down the street."

She gave a little sigh. "I tell myself my dream every night after I say kriath-sh'ma."

"A lot of us do," Reina said softly.

"Do you have a dream, Don Yosef?" asked the little girl.

"Of sorts." It seemed only fair to return the confidence. "It isn't as pleasant as yours. I only dream that I may get back to a Jewish community one day, and make a place for myself."

Esperansa gazed at him with compassionate eyes. "It's very plain."

"Yes," he said heavily. "Grownups' dreams often are. Maybe they feel that if they only ask for a little, the Ribono shel Olam might let them have it."

"Should I ask for less, too?" Esperansa asked.

With a half-smile, Yosef shook his head. "No, you ask for everything you want. You be a child for as long as you can. There's time enough to be grown up when you can't avoid it any more."

"Are you so very unhappy here, Yosef?" Reina asked.

His eyes met hers. "Yes." That one word held everything he felt.

For some while Reina was silent. Esperansa had turned away from them and Yosef was about to ask what she was watching when Reina began to speak.

"There's a native canoe in the undergrowth near the river," she said. "Since the time we found it, nobody's used it. I think the man who made it must have died. You know ships call at São Tome now and then; they always go on to Portugal. If we took the canoe and went out to sea far enough to meet a ship as it came from the bay ... "

"We?" Yosef looked at her in astonishment. "Aren't you afraid?" It was inconceivable that the fearful little sister had overcome all her terrors so quickly.

"Yes, I am," she answered frankly. "But what happens to you matters more to me than being afraid. So I have to go with you anyway, no matter how I feel. Do you see?"

"No." He glanced at his right hand. "I'm sure I could manage to get the canoe just that short way by myself."

"It's not the canoe, it's afterwards. Yosef, you're setting out with nothing, no money at all. When you were handsome and proud, you had such a regal manner that people found themselves doing things for you simply because you expected it. I remember seeing it happen. You still have the same manner, but you don't look the same. It doesn't work any more. You have to know how to get on the right side of people in order to get what you need. I know how; you don't. That's why I have to go with you."

"I see." Yosef was playing with the belt-knife again, turning it over and over on his knee. Suddenly he exploded. "I'm sick of being crippled! I hate it!"

Without warning he drove the knife violently into the bench. Startled, Reina cried out involuntarily. Hearing the cry, Esperansa swung around. Reina saw that her face was blotchy and her cheeks were wet.

Forgetting her own shock, Reina exclaimed, "Esperansa! What is it?" She held the child in her arms, trying to soothe her.

"After Paloma died, I was alone," Esperansa sobbed. "And then I had you and Don Yosef, I had someone I belonged to. But now you're going away. I'll be alone again. Don't leave me alone! Don't leave me!" Her fingers twisted so tightly into the fabric of Reina's dress that the worn material started to tear.

"Sh! Esperansa, don't cry. Listen to me." Reina was rocking her gently back and forth. "I won't leave you alone. If I have to go away, I'll make sure you have somebody who cares for you. You know Nechama does, anyway; remember how kind she was to you after Paloma died?"

Esperansa nodded. "But she's too important to belong to."

"She isn't too important to need a little sister," Reina said firmly. "Wait and see." Giving Esperansa a no-nonsense pat on the back, Reina released herself from the child's grip. "Now, try to be happy," she added, "especially since it's Purim."

Yosef examined the idea of escape that day and for many days afterward, weighing his chances of success against the risks. When he was convinced he had thought the idea through, he sought out the new parnes late one afternoon, In the same dining-house he himself had used as an office, he found Luis and Saadya, heads together, discussing something with such absorption that they did not notice his approach.

Yosef did not know what they were discussing — very likely it did not even affect him — but seeing the two of them so engrossed in plans for the colony made him feel shut out. They did not mean to make him feel that way; they did not even know he was there. But for the first time Yosef was forcibly reminded that he was no longer parnes. Others were planning for the future he had expected to build.

Yosef sat down on a bench near the door to wait until they had finished. They were planning Pesach. It had not yet been a year since they had come to São Tome.

"So how much maror do we need altogether?" Luis was saying. "For that matter, what do we use?"

"This stuff." Saadya laid some withered leaves on the table. "It's bitter but not poisonous."

"How do you know?" Luis looked at him curiously. "You keep coming up with these bits of information. Not still what the friar taught you in the beginning?"

Saadya grinned. "Of course. 'Hashem prepares the cure before he sends the malady.' You want to hear something else? That friar, Frei Martinho, fell ill of fever and died two weeks after I stopped studying with him. Tidy, isn't it?"

Luis grinned back. "Very neat." Returning to the matter they had been considering, he went on, "So how much of this — " He noticed Yosef. "Shalom aleichem! Visiting?" He got up and went to share the bench with him. "Nice to see you out."

Looking at the friendly face, Yosef could not bring himself to be resentful. Luis was capable and conscientious and impossible to dislike. Saadya nodded cordially but stayed where he was.

"I want to try to escape from São Tome," said Yosef bluntly, "but I can't do it without help."

Luis stared. "Alone?" he croaked when he found his voice.

"Of course not. With Reina. Give me credit for a little sense."

"But you can't! It's too dangerous!" protested Luis. "Besides, you can't even get near the sea; the beach is absolutely forbidden."

"*Swimming* from the beach is. Fortunately," Yosef said dryly, "we forgot to forbid escaping by canoe when we wrote the rules."

"Who has a canoe? Is Reina going to paddle it all the way to Portugal?" demanded Luis. He was thoroughly upset by the whole idea of such a perilous venture. "I can't allow it. It's totally mad. It's almost suicide." He was trying to speak calmly.

"No, it's not!" Yosef slammed his hand down on the table. "If you'd let me explain, I'd show you. Look, Reina says there's a dugout canoe on the rocks by the stream higher up. She banged it with a stick a couple of times and it didn't fall apart, so the termites haven't found it yet. We want to get out to meet the ships bound for Portugal as they come around from the bay, and try to talk our way on board. Do you see? Only I can't get the canoe to the beach myself, and I don't even think I can get me to the beach without help."

Luis spent a long while considering the proposal. "I can't think of a single thing here in the colony that you could use to pay your passage," he objected.

"The Portuguese Jews would probably ransom us if necessary."

"Possibly." Luis thought some more. "No, it's just too risky. I can't let you go. I don't like it."

"Neither do I," interposed Saadya unexpectedly. "But not for any logical reason. It bothers me, that's all. It sounds too much like the Jews who left Egypt before the right time had come, and met an unhappy end. Yosef, every galuth has its purpose, even a little one like ours. Can't you find some understanding of it that will make it bearable?"

"You don't know how it feels to have no place, no job I can do — "

"I thought you were making copies of seforim."

"Don't you think I know busy-work when I see it? If those siddurim were so urgent you would have had a team doing the job the same way they gather fruit and clean the compound.

"I can't contribute to the colony any longer. I'm useless. Luis — " he turned to the boy next to him — "I was parnes once and now I'm useless. I can't stand the way it makes me feel, to have slipped in an instant from complete power to none at all. Let me go, Luis."

"You can't get through the crocodiles. There's no beach — "

"There is, Luis," Saadya said. "There's a rather small one with trees right down to the water. It's shady and the bottom drops off underwater very sharply. The crocodiles don't favor the beach because they can't bask in the sun at the edge of the water as they like to."

"Others will want to try it."

"I don't know," Yosef said. "You can make them wait, at least, until you know if I was successful. If I get back to civilization, my idea is that I can tell people about you so they can send ships. If the ships come, you'll know I reached safety. The ships will take you all off São Tome, so there won't be any problem with escaping. And if I haven't made it to safety, the ships won't come, and it'll be obvious to everybody that it's too dangerous to try again."

"I'm parnes," said Luis after a silence. "I'm responsible for you as much as for the others."

"It's the only thing left that I can do for the colony." There was such desperation in Yosef's eyes that Luis glanced away. "There's nothing for me here."

Luis went to stand by the door, gazing out at the compound.

"How long have you been thinking about this, Yosef?" Saadya asked suddenly.

"Since Purim."

Saadya sighed. "Luis, he's been thinking of arguments for weeks. He'll keep at you until you agree; you might as well give in now. All we can do is to say Tehillim that he survives the journey."

The journey? Yosef asked himself. I hope I survive the walk down to the beach. It'll be grueling; I've hardly walked the length of the compound since the accident. But I don't want to have to be carried.

Luis turned around. "I suppose I'll have to allow you to do it. But you'll have to wait until after Pesach; we're too busy now, preparing, and we can't spare anybody. And when you do go, it will be very, very quiet — just Saadya and Chanan and me, and the girls who are closest to Reina, on the beach to see you off."

And maybe I'll reconsider between now and then, thought Yosef, that's what he hopes. But there's no chance of that, no chance at all.

He rose carefully and went toward the door. Worried and unhappy, Luis still stood facing him. He gave Luis' shoulder a quick, grateful squeeze, said, "Thank you, Luis," and went away.

CHAPTER TEN

EANING BACK in the stern, Yosef felt like a fool. In front of him Reina dipped the paddle regularly and cleanly into the shining sea. He felt as though he were playing a part in some foolish mummery, a prince being rowed in a royal barge, a great concourse of people in escort. But the barge was only a crude dugout canoe, and there was no escort: the others were on the beach. He twisted around to look at them, the ones who had been kind to him and to Reina: Luis, Saadya, Chanan, and standing a little apart from them, Nechama. They were already very small figures and could not tell that he had turned to look at them. He saw the boys clustered together slightly as though they might be talking. They might have said something to Nechama, for she moved nearer, revealing Esperansa who had been hovering behind her. Slowly they walked away from the beach. One of them, Luis, Yosef thought, stopped for one last wave, although he could not really have been able to see Yosef properly.

Watching them, Yosef felt a queer sense of regret that he had not expected. Leaving had seemed the right decision at the time. He had thought for so long about it and it had appeared so appropriate: the rejected leader retiring nobly from the field. But perhaps he was just running away? The people he was leaving behind on the sand were friends. He had not regarded them as friends until now, only as people he liked who were there when he wanted them. As they receded, he realized that they were too precious to be taken for granted. A sense of loss grew inside him: he did not think he would find friends like these again.

After they left the beach, Yosef reluctantly turned around. Before him sat Reina, apparently relaxed and confident, absorbed in the rhythmic motion of the paddle, up and down, up and down, flicking drops of water in quicksilver showers from the blades. In a way Yosef did not understand, Reina seemed to have grown older since she had decided to go with him; she appeared to be quiet and competent and undaunted. Did she have regrets? He had never thought to ask. It was only because of him that she was leaving São Tome. Did she think he would have been more adult to stay and do whatever jobs were left to him?

Glancing around, Reina said, "You're very quiet."

"I was wondering if I should have left."

"Do you want to go back? It's not too late."

"Do you?" For the first time, he really wanted to know how she felt, but she shook her head and smiled.

"I'll do whatever you do," she said.

Letting the paddle rest across the thwarts of the canoe, she waited for his answer, not looking at him but at the expanse of water ahead, ripples glinting in the sunlight. Far above them, a hawk eagle hung motionless; below them, in the depths their tiny craft hardly dented, huge dark shadows passed: tuna or shark or sea turtle or giant ray.

"I still want to go on," Yosef said at last, not because he was eager for the journey but because there was nothing to go back to.

Reina lifted the paddle. "It's just as well. Somebody would have wanted to try it, and it might as well be us as anyone."

For a little longer they glided on; then they stopped, waiting for the ship they knew would be leaving the harbor about now. Some while passed. Heat blazed from the cloudless sky. Yosef could feel sweat trickle down his face and under his shirt.

"The *São Vicente*, its name is?"

"There's only the one," Reina assured him comfortably. "We won't miss it."

And then they saw it, the ship rounding the distant headland, setting her course for Portugal. She would be under full sail soon; they wanted to catch her before the mainsails were set. Noticing that they were not yet far enough out, Reina set to work again, more quickly than before, moving them toward the ship's path.

When they were close enough to be seen, Reina waved the

paddle above her head, the wet blade gleaming mirrorlike. Together Yosef and Reina shouted, and shouted again. For a despairing moment they thought the ship would pass them by, but its progress had slowed. Someone was hailing them from the deck. Reina brought them nearer.

"What do you want?"

Cupping her hands around her mouth, Reina called, "To come aboard — passage to Portugal!"

"Do you have the fever?"

"No!" They were almost beside the ship now. "My brother had an accident. He's no use to the colony. We want to go back to Portugal. We have an uncle in Porto — he's very rich — he'd pay well if you brought us home." The uncle in Porto was imaginary.

There was a heated discussion on board between the two men whom Yosef guessed were the captain and mate. Although the noise was audible, the words were not clear. At length Yosef and Reina were hauled on board, roughly spilled onto the deck like a pair of not very desirable fish. As they were pushed along the planking, they heard the end of the conversation.

"Either way, we have to keep them in decent condition. If the uncle is real, he'll pay more if they arrive in good shape. If he isn't, we'll want to keep the girl saleable. She should be worth something."

"And the boy?"

"You never know; might find a Jew to ransom him. Otherwise, toss him over the side. No bother at all." Not even a glance was spared for the captives as the two men resumed their tasks.

Reina squeezed Yosef's hand. He saw that her jaw was set and she was trying very hard not to cry. Her mission of appealing to the good side of the people they encountered was not a simple one.

They stumbled throught a narrow way between the cabins under the lower sterncastle. The passage was so dark it was like a tunnel. A door was slammed open and they found their cabin in front of them: a small cubicle on the port side with four bare walls and a single square porthole that admitted some air and less light. From the hold the strong spicy odor of malagueta-pepper pervaded the room. Yosef sniffed gratefully. It might as easily have been a cargo of Kongo slaves, and the odor the overwhelming, nauseating smell of human misery. He wondered how the crew of such a ship could endure six weeks of it.

As the days went by, they were permitted on deck as long as they stayed out of the way. Now and then a tolerant seaman addressed a few words to them, but no friendships developed: they learned to keep to themselves. They watched the sailors at work, watched the cook at his fire near the sterncastle cooking food they could not eat, while they softened their stale bread in cold water.

As the favorable winds held, they drew closer to Portugal, heading out away from the African coast to catch the trade winds, then following them eastward again. At about the latitude of Arzila, however, the *São Vicente* ran into a storm that kept Reina and Yosef in their cabin through Shavuoth. The cooking fire on deck had to be put out and the crew had nothing but cold food until the storm blew itself out. The ship had been driven far to the east. Now, forced to beat up the coast with uncertain winds, the ship was in far greater danger than in the open Atlantic. It was not only the peril of the coastal waters; piracy was an ever-present threat.

They had almost reached a point opposite the Straits of Gibraltar when the wind dropped. Slack and empty, the sails sagged with a dismal air. The sounds that accompany every sailing ship in motion had almost ceased, the creaking and straining of the rigging, the rubbing groan of the timbers. Around the ship the water lay flat as oiled silk.

Pacing urgently back and forth, the captain muttered to himself and set the men to gun drill, running out the twelve cannon that had too short a range to be effective against any up-to-date arms. Men ran as orders were barked. They needed practice.

From the lookout in the rigging there was a sudden shout. Standing in the doorway of their cabin, Yosef and Reina could not hear the words, but the captain exclaimed, "Madre de —!" They did not need to be told more. There was still no breeze, not a breath to ruffle the sails; yet the lookout had sighted a ship, a ship that was a threat, because the captain was worried. Only a galley needed no wind. Only a pirate galley was a threat.

The gun drill was no longer practice but in earnest. Every man of the crew would be fighting for his life. If the pirates won, there would be only two choices: to die fighting or to die on the galley's rowing benches. Dropping to their knees for a brief prayer, the crew rose to face the oncoming battle.

The minutes crept by so slowly that time seemed almost at a standstill. At their stations, the men remained alert, unmoving. Distantly, over the water, a soft regular beat reached them: the sound of the drum that set the rhythm for the galley's rowers.

Looking down at Reina, Yosef saw her set face, the way she bit her lip, her hands clutching at the fabric of her dress. The sound of the drum set the blood pounding in his veins; he wanted to see the galley, the banks of oars crashing into the water, the human gutter-sweepings of a dozen ports lining the rails ready to leap on board the *São Vicente*. But Reina was afraid. She had come with him because she worried about him. He owed her something for that. He reached out and let the door fall to.

The galley was much nearer. Even closed in, Yosef could hear the drum. Without a pause the pace of the beat increased. The galley was breaking into the attack, coming up on the *São Vicente*. The drumbeats grew louder. He heard a sudden long rushing noise that he thought must be the oars biting into the water as the galley passed very close to the Portuguese ship. He felt the ship roll clumsily in the galley's wake. An overpowering stench crept into the cabin, the smell of sweating, stinking human bodies, the reek of human filth: the distinctive odor of a galley.

Finally they could bring the guns to bear on the pirate: there was a thunderous roar of the guns being fired. The ship rolled again, but purposefully this time, in recoil. Something rumbled viciously across the planking and a man screamed. Likely one of the guns had broken loose, Yosef thought, and it had crushed one of the sailors.

There was a brief pause. Yosef could picture the galley coming about for the final run now, while the cannon were being reloaded. Drumbeats signaled the approach. Moments later the galley rammed against the Portuguese ship with a rending crash.

From the harsh scraping of the two vessels Yosef guessed that grappling hooks held them together. Almost instantly there were thumps and running feet on the deck: the pirates plunging on their prey,harquebuses firing, cutlasses clashing. The screams of dying men punctuated the fighting. Yosef listened tensely to the sounds. The battle raged on and on.

Momentarily there was a lull. Inside the cabin Reina sat huddled in a corner, her eyes shut, her hands pressed tightly over her ears. Yosef was about to touch her shoulder to let her know that the conflict had ended when it began again. Perhaps the pirates had found a few last Portuguese in a hold somewhere. Yosef was certain that the pirates would win in the end. He could hear fighting in the corridor outside the cabin. Someone thudded into the door. The door crashed open. Into the tiny room a body slid slowly, blood spilling out of it.

Reina's eyes flew wide at the slam of the door. She saw the body and leapt to her feet and pressed back against the bulkhead, screaming. Yosef went to her and put his arm around her. Holding Reina against himself while she quieted, he glanced at the open doorway.

In the space outside the cabin stood a man, bare-chested and hard-muscled; he wore Turkish trousers with a smeared scimitar stuffed casually in the sash. Seeing Yosef, the man tossed some coarse joke over his shoulder to the rest of the pirates nearby, then beckoned the two children out and pushed them in the direction of his chief.

Standing erect, with a touch of arrogance that was more pathetic than offensive,Yosef faced his captor. Beside him he could feel Reina trembling, vibrating like a plucked string.

Rather than the pointed helmet some of his men wore, the captain had a turban; he was just finishing rewinding it. Dressed after the Moorish fashion in a white robe that was still tucked up for battle, he had deeply tanned skin that showed very dark against the cloth. What his nationality was, however, Yosef could not tell: there were not enough clues in the delicate brows, the finely chiselled nose, the rich, curling black beard.

The pirate captain looked Yosef up and down, his deep-set eyes taking in every defect of his new property. The black brows drew together in a scowl, ruining the effect of the handsome face. A handsome face, Yosef thought, but ruthless.

The appraising gaze moved on to Reina. Now a half-smile quirked the corners of the mouth.

"You speak Spanish?" The question came abruptly.

Yosef nodded. "We're Spanish Jews, refugees."

An eyebrow was raised. "The supply seems to be inexhaustible. Your people will pay for you?"

"Maybe, maybe not. Except for my sister, I have no family left."

"She's a different matter entirely. I can sell her. You, I can't."

At a gesture from the captain, one of the men herded Yosef and Reina back to the cabin. The body had been removed.

Once the cargo had been examined and its contents noted, the captain returned to his galley, leaving a prize crew on board the *São Vicente* to bring her into port. In command was the man they had seen before, the man in Turkish trousers, Ismail.

It was this pirate lieutenant who would dispose of them, Yosef learned; he was to bring the ship and its cargo to Alger for sale. For most of the journey Ismail ignored the children, but when they neared Alger he came to inspect them.

"What's wrong with her?" he demanded, with a finger jabbed in Reina's direction. The girl was huddled on the floor. Near her there was a bowl of water.

"She has a fever," Yosef admitted uneasily. He did not want Ismail to see how ill Reina was. If he thought she could not be sold, he was likely to throw the two of them overboard at once. There had been no further mention of ransom.

The pirate squatted by Reina and pulled at her dress.

"Take your hands off her!"

"Shut up," growled the man contemptuously. "I'm only looking to see if she has a rash." He released the dress. "And she does. Ship's fever. How long has she had it?" His voice held an accusing note, as if Yosef had infected her deliberately.

"She's been ill for a week."

"So she'll just be over it as we come into Alger." The man spat. "They say children usually survive it. You better grow up very, very slowly for the next week."

Seven days. Their last seven days of freedom, perhaps. It seemed unfair to Yosef that they were too hungry and ill to appreciate them, unfair, too, that the days sped by so quickly that the port of Alger seemed to rush up on them overnight. Reina's fever passed, but she was still very weak.

Yosef expected that they would be taken off immediately when the ship arrived, but he and Reina were left on board under guard for some hours after they had docked. Ismail had gone ashore at once and had not yet reappeared.

"I wish he'd come back soon," Reina said wearily. "I hate not knowing what's going to happen to us."

"It shouldn't be much longer." Yosef did not tell her that if he were not ransomed, he did not think he would be sold; that after she was bought and he was left, somebody would take him into an alley and knife him quietly. He hoped that when it happened, he would die quickly. He felt sorry that his life had to end so shabbily; it seemed such a waste after all he had endured. Strangely, he was not afraid.

When Ismail returned, he regarded the two of them with disapproval before he spoke. "Your Jewish rabbi can't afford you," he announced bluntly. "He says he ransomed fifty Jews only last week for seven hundred ducats and they're out of money. And I'm not waiting for him to send elsewhere for more. Sooo ... " He stuck his thumbs in his sash and rocked thoughtfully on the balls of his feet. "I doubt I'll get more than a few crescents for her, and you — " He let the words hang. With a few brisk movements he had tied Reina's wrists with a length of rope. "Just to remind you not to run away," he said casually. He did not bother with Yosef.

Chivvied towards the slave-dealers' souk, Yosef moved slowly. All the time he had been on the ship he had hardly walked more than a few paces at a time. His muscles jerked and ached with the unaccustomed strain. Again and again Ismail jabbed his fingertips into Yosef's back to force him to walk faster.

As the walk stretched on, Reina's hands grew numb. The knots that had been so hastily tied had shifted slightly so that the rope was very tight around her wrists, with a short length hanging loose between her hands. She tried to relieve the pressure, but the cord was too stiff.

Near the market Ismail stopped them in a dingy side street to try to make them more presentable. As he stood back to look at them an expression that was both thoughtful and calculating crossed his face.

Yosef suspected that the pirate was thinking about the face of the slave dealer when he offered him the two prisoners, the girl colorless and weak, the boy disfigured and crippled. He could almost see the dealer's face as he looked from one to the other in disbelief. "Joke, eh?" he would ask; and Ismail would have to agree or become a laughingstock.

While the pirate was considering them, Reina leaned against a wall.

Concerned, Yosef asked her, "Are you all right?"

"Only a little dizzy and tired." She closed her eyes.

Standing next to her, Yosef realized with a pang that in half an hour or so, he would not need to be concerned about her any more: she would be gone to someone who would be concerned for her himself, as for any animal he owned. Raising his hand to touch her cheek, he turned further in her direction.

"Get away from her!" the pirate ordered roughly. "How can I see what's salvageable if you're crowding each other?" He strode to Yosef and shoved him away from Reina, standing between the two children himself. "Can't you straighten your own tunic, boy?" His back to Reina, he moved closer to Yosef to adjust the clothing, bending to grasp the hem. He rested his hand on the haft of the knife in his sash, pushing it to one side to keep it from jabbing into his belly.

Reina looked down at the rope between her wrists. Now. It had to be now. There would not be another time. Raising her hands as high as she could reach, she stretched out and brought her tied hands over Ismail's head. The short length of slack rope tightened. With a sudden pull backwards she hung her whole weight on the cord. The pirate's head snapped back. The rope slipped from the neck over the chin, scraped across the face, and came free. Reina fell heavily. A moment later, the pirate collapsed, slowly, in sections, as though someone were folding him up.

Reina saw Yosef leaning forward a little. She did not notice the knife in his hand until he began to cut the thong that held the pirate's money-pouch with it. There was blood on the blade.

"Hurry, before he comes to," she urged.

Yosef gave her a strange look. "He won't come to. We've killed him."

After a first disbelieving look, Reina squeezed her eyes shut. "I only meant to cut off his air — " She shuddered violently.

"Don't feel too guilty. He was going to knife me." He took the purse and slipped it into his doublet. "Let's get away from here."

Through one back street after another they wandered. Neither could move quickly, which worried Yosef until he remembered that neither of them looked capable of killing a man, either. Along the way Yosef called a halt to free Reina's hands and count the money in the stolen purse. It took longer than he expected to saw through the rope: it was new and tough, out of the *São Vicente's* stores. By the time he finished, Reina's wrists were chafed raw.

While sensation returned to her hands, he took out the pouch and spilled its contents onto the ground. They did not know the coins, but it did not seem to be a great deal. Gold and silver look like gold and silver everywhere. Their eyes met in disappointment. They had hoped for so much more. But Ismail was — had been — only a subordinate, after all. Scooping up the coins, Yosef replaced them in the pouch and tucked it away again.

"Never mind; it'll get us somewhere."

When they worked their way through the back alleys to the harbor, they found themselves far away from where the *São Vicente* was moored. Around them was noise and bustle, shouted orders, brawls, dockhands unloading, ships taking on cargo. Porters elbowed them out of the way, impatient to press on through the confusion.

"Which ship shall we take?" Yosef asked Reina.

"Oh ... I don't care. The nearest." He saw that she was swaying slightly.

Her choice was not a bad one, Yosef decided. Before them there was a smallish carrack, a European ship. It was on the old side, but still solid. Its rounded sides gave it an air of comfortable ordinariness, a cozy dumpy housewife of a vessel.

Yosef hailed the master. Glancing sharply over the side at the two waifs, the man asked, "What is it?" He spoke ungraciously, in rough dockside Italian, but it was understandable.

"Where are you bound?" Yosef's pure Castilian made him sound superior and condescending.

"Tunis, then Genova." The voice was no friendlier.

"Can you take two passengers?"

The master regarded Yosef suspiciously. "Who? You? What'll you pay me with, fleas?"

"We were given money." Yosef held out half of what he had taken from Ismail. "I don't know how much the voyage costs. Is this enough?"

The master leaned over the side to eye the pieces in Yosef's hand. "Just about," he admitted grudgingly, which Yosef took to mean that it was more than enough. "If they're good." When he let them on board at last, he made sure to bite two or three coins to test them, and seemed almost disappointed when they passed.

The quarters he gave them were an insult to paying customers: dirty, cramped, furnished with filthy sleeping mats. But once the ship was under sail he showed no inclination to lay hands on his passengers to see if they had more money, or to maroon them on a deserted islet, or to sell them for slaves. There were other captains who had; during the months in Lisboa horrifying tales had been told. They were grateful to be ignored.

Nearly a week after they had left Alger, Yosef and Reina stood on the little forecastle as the ship waddled into the harbor at Tunis. Under a late spring sun and a light breeze, the busy, prosperous port spread itself out before them as though in welcome.

"It looks almost as if it wanted us to settle here, doesn't it?" Reina said wistfully.

Yosef thought back to the days when they had had a home. Only a couple of years — was that all it had been? It had faded until it was like a memory of a visit to someone else's house. "Settle?" he asked. "I've forgotten what it feels like."

While the carrack filled up the last spaces in her hold with sugar and dried fruit, Yosef went in search of the Jewish quarter. Once within the mellah, it was not long before he found the Chacham of the local community. At Yosef's inquiry, the Chacham shook his head.

"I would have no rachmanut for you if I encouraged you to stay," he explained. "You have to understand that when the Sicilian Jews were expelled two years ago, nearly all of them came to Tunis. Our little kehilla could not possibly cope with so many. Some of the Spanish refugees found their way here as well. We feel we are beginning to make some headway, but even now, they live in the most dreadful conditions. Many still beg in the streets. I could not offer you anything better."

Yosef's heart sank, "So we should go on?"

The Chacham spread his hands helplessly.

When Yosef rejoined her Reina saw from his face that they had not yet finished wandering. She accepted the disappointment quietly. Watching the tears straggle down her face, Yosef was shocked by the hollows in her cheeks and the way her cheekbones jutted out sharply. In the mellah he had used some of their money to buy decent food for her, but he had not realized how much she needed it. He had known that bread and water and an occasional onion was not enough; he could tell that Reina was not getting her strength back; but he had not actually seen how thin she was. Inside him he found a cold knot of fear that she might not survive the journey.

Genova. Italy. So many refugees had gone to Italy. Surely he and Reina would find the end of their traveling in Genova. Surely a city that was at the hub of so many trade routes would have Jews who could take them in? And if not Genova, what then? Milano, perhaps; Yosef had heard that it was a growing financial center, the gateway to the northern markets. Markets and trade and banks and Jews: they all went together.

At the end of a peaceful passage, the carrack brought them into Genova: yet another port, yet another quay. Climbing out of the carrack's little boat, Reina and Yosef slowly made their way up the harbor steps. Yosef had to mount the steps one by one, like a small child; Reina was too dispirited to do more than climb beside him, holding her skirts out of the way. The torn hem of her dress caught Yosef's eye. He glanced at the rest of her garment. Threadbare, stained, too tight to be decent: it was a disgrace for Reina to be seen like this. Looking at his own clothing Yosef reddened. The picture of Luis flashed into his mind, Luis in the alley corner in Lisboa: "Being poor is having to look ugly and ridiculous." Dirty, outgrown velvets, seams half-split, rubbed bare of the nap like a mangy dog, threads trailing from frayed edges: he looked ridiculous; he was ugly. Under his clothes he could feel insects crawling on his skin. He wondered why he had been so afraid of being poor; he hardly thought to notice it.

There was a man coming out of a chandler's shop. Ashamed of his appearance, Yosef hesitated a moment before accosting the man. But they still had not found an end to their journey. He moved into the man's path.

"Jews?" exclaimed the man in reply to Yosef's question. "Of course not! They aren't allowed to stay in Genova for more than three days!" Before turning away, he gave them a look so contemptuous of their poverty, their homelessness, their vulnerability, that it seemed to Yosef a compendium of humiliation.

He tensed with anger; but a touch from Reina restrained him until the man had gone. "You must never do that," she said. "You must learn to let people insult you and take advantage of you, because you can't do anything about it."

Unwilling to admit that she was right, Yosef shrugged. Reina curved her fingers around the hand Yosef could not use. "Shall we go?" she invited him, as lightly as the little sister of the past asking for an afternoon stroll.

They did not know how difficult it would be to find a cart that was willing to take two people as disreputable as they looked. Most of the carters merely turned away; a few spat and said what they thought; one or two were willing but were only going as far as Tortona. At last it was Reina who charmed someone into letting them perch atop his assortment of boxes and bales.

Smiling down at the driver from her high seat, she said, "The further we go, the nicer people get."

"Don't bother sweet-talking me," growled the man; but he helped Yosef climb up.

The carter claimed it would take three days to Pavia, four to Milano. Morning of the fourth day saw them just passing through Pavia, however.

Yosef and Reina glanced at each other. "Maybe there are Jews in Pavia?" Yosef suggested.

"I'll ask." Clambering over the jouncing load, Reina shouted over the rumble of wagon wheels, "What's in Pavia?"

The carter did not take his eyes from the road. "University. Cathedral, maybe. I don't know."

"Are there any Jews?"

The man shrugged.

Returning to Yosef, Reina said, "He doesn't know."

"Better not risk stopping, then. It was too hard getting this ride."

It was not until they had passed too far beyond Pavia to turn back that Yosef remembered that it was Friday. He squinted up at the sun, high in the sky; but he did not know how much further it was to Milano.

Again Reina made her precarious way to the front of the wagon. "Will we reach Milano by sunset, please? We can't travel after that," she called.

The carter twisted around for a moment. "We'll be in Milano in plenty of time. It's — "

A sudden jolt rocked the wagon. Yosef heard a heavy creaking a fraction of a second before the whole cart tipped to one side with a splintering crash. Boxes and bales slid down the slope and tumbled into the road. Cursing, the carter jumped out to survey the damage.

Reina crept silently back to Yosef.

"What happened?" Yosef was already working his way off the back of the ruined vehicle.

Reina came after him. "When he turned to talk to me, the mules went to one side and pulled the cart half out of the wheel ruts. The strain popped a wheel right off the axle."

"That's all we need," Yosef said grimly. "He's sure to blame us. We'd better get away from the cart."

"Couldn't we — couldn't I just apologize? Or — at least thank him for the ride?" Reina offered hesitantly.

"And get his hand across your face?"

"He wouldn't —"

"Yes, he would. Come on."

Edging around the side of the cart furthest from the driver, they began to walk towards Milano. Yosef's handicap made their progress so slow that only a few miles lay behind them when they had to stop to make Shabath. They spent the day of rest in a quiet corner of someone's orchard, screened from the road by a low stone wall. For every seuda they had bread and a few scraps of dried fish. At the end of Shabath their food was finished.

Yosef counted over their remaining money. "It'll take us who knows how long to reach Milano by foot," he said. "We won't get another ride. I'm not sure we can buy enough bread to last us." The moonlight glinted dully on the coins he held.

Reina regarded the dark orchard. "Like Rabbi Akiva," she said. "No donkey, no cock, no lamp. And *gam zu l'tova.*"

Gam zu l'tova. A wave of bitterness flooded through Yosef. Rabbi Akiva had been lucky; he had seen that losing the donkey, the cock, and the lamp had saved his life. But things like that didn't happen any more. If they starved to death on the road to Milano, whatever good there was would not be in a form they would recognize. They would just be dead. They would see where the good lay when they were in Gan Eden, but that was not quite the same.

And for this I'm expected to say *"gam zu l'tova"*? he asked himself resentfully. Why?

"You're thinking?" Reina asked.

"Nothing special. Just that life isn't very fair."

"Of course not." Reina's tone was practical, down-to-earth. "Really," she went on, "we ought to be grateful for having such a horrid time, knowing that we'll have nicer places in Gan Eden, but it's very hard to be grateful when it's happening to you."

"Yes," Yosef agreed, "very hard." But Papa, he thought, Papa would have accepted it. What's wrong with me, that I can't?

❀   ❀   ❀

From Pavia to Milano it is only a little over twenty miles. A strong walker can cover the distance in about six hours. It took

Yosef and Reina three days of concentrated effort. Trudging along the side of the summer-hard road, they coughed as each conveyance rumbled by, muffled in its cloud of choking dust. At night they were so tired that heaps of flints would have felt like featherbeds.

The first night was pleasant, cool but not chilly; but the second, as they neared Milano, held a dampness in the air that made them want to draw cloaks close about them. But they had no cloaks. They felt as dreary as the weather. All day they had gone without eating, for they had almost no food left. Before lying down they ate what remained, because although they could walk on empty stomachs, they had found that it was much harder to try to go to sleep that way. Reina was too tired to notice that Yosef had given her some of his portion: he had seen that she felt the lack of food.

All during the next morning they followed the road through a thin, persistent rain, slipping on a slick veneer of mud. As the road dragged on endlessly, they felt as though the strength had drained out of them. Yosef's leg was as heavy as a millstone; under his arm, where the crutch chafed, it burned like fire. He saw that Reina was beginning to stumble.

"Are you all right?" he asked.

"It's nothing." She forced a smile. "Just a stone."

Step by step, they followed the roadway around a bend,and on for another hour. Yosef was feeling light-headed from hunger. He began to think that they would not reach Milano after all, that they would keep on plodding as if in a dream, their goal never any nearer. Raising his head, he gazed blankly into the distance.

And there was the city spread out before him behind its walls, large and prosperous, crowded with fine buildings jostling each other for pride of place. Directly ahead he saw the massive round towers buttressing a city gate that was dwarfed between them. "Baruch Hashem," he said softly. "Baruch Hashem."

It was not long before they found themselves in a marketplace so dizzyingly hectic that their only thought was to find a way out of it. Easing through the crush of carts laden with everything from ironwork to bolts of silks, they came upon a street that led them to a peaceful piazza with a fountain in its center. Sinking down onto the stone coping of the basin, they listened to a nearby beggar reciting Dante loudly.

"Nel mezzo del cammin di nostra vita, Mi ritrovai per una selva oscura ... " he intoned, flinging his arms aloft in gestures that had nothing to do with the words. Passers-by gave him money anyway.

The drizzle tapered off and a watery sun threatened to break through the overcast, briefly turning the fountain's spray into a shower of crystal. Reina and Yosef felt that they could not possibly walk any further. Around them the piazza was sprinkled with placid pigeons cooing throatily. Behind them water splashed gently into the pool. Reluctant to move away, they lingered, dabbling their hands in the water and feeling the grime float off their fingers.

Abruptly the beggar rose and approached them with an aggressive air. "See here," he snapped, "this is my territory. You be off."

Drawing himself up, Yosef felt Reina's warning hand again.

"I'm so sorry," Reina said quietly. "We're very tired; we've walked ever so far. Do you know where we might find a Jewish banker?" She could hardly stand.

For answer the beggar held out a hand. Yosef dropped the empty purse into it.

"We can't give you anything," Reina said. She forced a tired smile. "Perhaps you'd take us just to be rid of us?"

There was a short surprised silence. The man seemed startled to hear himself say, "All right then, come on." Yosef heard him mutter under his breath something about getting soft in his old age. He led them a short way, growing impatient because they had difficulty in keeping up with him. He left them at a short flight of steps leading up to a pair of plain, solid oaken doors.

Confronting the anonymous entrance, Yosef wondered if it was the right one, and then decided that if it was not, it did not matter. Reina was swaying on her feet and he did not think he could last much longer himself. Every so often he was having a swimming sensation somewhere between his eyes and the center of his brain.

"Just up the steps," he said to Reina.

He really was feeling very fuzzy about the head, he concluded as he stumbled up the few steps. It was odd how quickly doing without food affected you. But of course, hiking along roadsides wasn't how you expected to spend a taanith. He could feel himself striding forward and was puzzled to discover that he was only entering the grand reception room just inside the doors. He tried to stand erect, tried to lift his head, but his head persisted in hanging. His eyes wandered like sleepwalkers, following the maze of veins in the marble at his feet. Beside him Reina leaned against him more heavily with each passing minute.

"Che vuole? What do you want?" a voice asked.

With a tremendous effort, Yosef dragged his head upwards. In Spanish, he said, "The Jewish bank." He could not think of anything else to say. The face in front of him was indistinct; he could not force his eyes to focus on it. The vague mouth was opening to say something when Reina cut through the formalities by fainting, sinking gradually and quite gracefully to the marble floor. Yosef let his head fall forward.

Somewhere there were running feet. There was an exclamation in a deeper voice than the one that had questioned him. He saw Reina lifted and carried away. When it was his turn, he was dragged up a flight of stairs, through two doorways, or perhaps it was three. He was helped onto something soft and yielding. The relief was agonizing: the sudden release of aching bone and muscle was as sharply painful as the tension. The places the crutch had rubbed raw throbbed like a drumbeat. A bitter mixture was put to his lips and pressed into him, but he was glad for it, for it floated him away from the pain. With a sigh he relaxed and slept.

CHAPTER ELEVEN

ONSCIOUSNESS TRICKLED BACK a little at a time. Yosef first realized he was awake when he noticed that his right hand lay on a silken coverlet. He let his fingers explore the smoothness and marvelled at the feel of luxury. It was remarkable how quickly he had become unused to comforts he had taken for granted; scarcely two years had passed since he had gone to sleep on such fabrics without giving them a second thought.

Most of the room was hidden from view by thick expensive draperies that hung around him, but to his left they were partly drawn back. He could see a doorway and a massive chest, deeply carved and so highly polished that he could see a window reflected in the flat areas of its surface. The door hinges were on the inner side of the jamb: was there a mezuza there or not? Had he and Reina found the Jewish bank? He could not tell.

He saw the door open. Into the room stepped a man with an air of neatness about him. His trimmed gray beard, his black scholar's robes, the precise movements of his hands said "physician" to Yosef even before the man's actions made it clear.

"Bruno," said the man shortly, introducing himself.

Throwing open the curtain on the window side of the bed, Ser Bruno turned Yosef's face so the light fell on the scarred cheek. For some minutes he examined it, moving Yosef's head slightly. Eventually he grunted "mmp" and walked around to Yosef's left. In complete silence he moved the useless arm and leg, flexing and straightening them, looking more closely at the hand and foot. "Ah," he said, and proceeded to a more routine examination.

When he had finished, he gave Yosef a keen look. "For this — " he touched Yosef's face with great gentleness — "I can do nothing; it is too late. But here — " he jabbed Yosef's left shoulder

— "there may be possibilities. If I give you exercises, will you do them?" He snapped the question harshly.

"Yes." Yosef's voice was firm, and his eyes, meeting the physician's, held such longing that the man winced.

"Don't look at me like that, boy," he said roughly. "I'm not promising you anything, do you hear? There's a chance you may have a little more use of that arm and leg, that's all. A little!"

"Will you show me, Signor?" Yosef's gaze did not waver.

As though to impress Yosef with the importance of the undertaking, the physician regarded him intently before agreeing to work with him. For a few minutes he showed Yosef what to do; then he said "mmp" again, and departed without another word.

Alone once more, Yosef became acutely aware of his hunger. He could see no food in the room, so he tried to get up, meaning to go and find some.

"Stay there!" ordered a deep voice.

Now Yosef could see the person behind the voice he remembered from his arrival: a big, barrel-chested man dressed in a long, full-sleeved robe as thickly padded as the short doublets in fashion, and a good deal more decent. Below a high forehead, deep-set eyes viewed him with humor and sympathy; next came a slightly bulbous nose, then a mouth that looked as if it knew how to be sensitive but had learned to be harsh. Sprawling untidily over much of the face and a quantity of the chest was a most impressive beard, the more interesting for being in the process of changing from gray to white in an odd, striped fashion.

"So how are you?" he asked. Surprisingly, his Spanish was not hopeless but almost tolerable.

Yosef was rested and relaxed; he lay enfolded in luxury; he was attended by an obviously expensive physician. But the greatest pleasure of all was being free of the insects creeping over his body. "The insects are gone," he said gratefully.

"I should think so. They scrubbed you like a dirty tablecloth." The big man laughed and pushed something back and forth on his head.

"La gorita!" Yosef exclaimed with relief. "I couldn't tell if we had come to the right place. But you're Jewish — you wear la gorita."

"A who? Ah! The kappl. And I am Herr Salzmann — or Ser Hirsch, or whatever. It's confusing, this being a German Jewish banker in an Italian city."

"Baruch Hashem," Yosef murmured.

"And your name?" Herr Salzmann encouraged him.

"Yosef d'Ortas."

"Baruch haboh, Yosef d'Ortas," smiled the banker. "And the young lady with you who is still asleep?"

"My sister."

Yosef's stomach rumbled impatiently. Herr Salzmann heaved himself to his feet. "Food! We must see to it at once!"

More than food was seen to. The children's decaying rags had been burnt at once, of course. Herr and Frau Salzmann provided new wardrobes for both Yosef and Reina, choosing clothing as fine as they might have received from their own parents.

Reina recovered gradually from the effects of her weakness and the journey, Frau Salzmann hovering beside her bed. In many ways Frau Salzmann was an undistinguished person. Of medium height, she was neither good-looking nor plain, although she had no doubt been moderately attractive in her youth. She dressed well, but simply, by Italian standards. Her manner and her voice were comfortable and pleasant, with nothing to mark them as anything out of the ordinary. Only Frau Salzmann's chesed was outstanding: in this she was so accomplished that Reina felt an almost physical touch of comfort when Frau Salzmann entered her room.

All of the Salzmann children were grown and married. The parents had come to Milano without the concern for chinuch and shiduchim that would have made life in Milano's tiny community difficult. Finding her house strange when it was empty of children, Frau Salzmann welcomed Reina as another daughter. She was delighted to find Reina impatient with her slow recovery.

"Not one of my daughters enjoyed lacemaking, though I love it," she confided. "Would you let me teach you?"

"I thought it was terribly complicated."

"It is and it isn't." She bustled off.

Shortly Reina found herself pushing ivory-headed pins into

a firmly stuffed cushion in an intricate pattern. Frau Salzmann's experienced hands guided her own, leading the different threads in and out of the forest of pins. Ivory bobbins, their threads anchored at various points, dangled over the sides of the lace-making pillow. By the time the first lesson was over, the intertwined cords looked, if not yet like lace, as if they had every intention of becoming lace in time.

Reina regarded her work with satisfaction. "It's ever so pretty," she said. "Could one earn money doing it?"

"Oh, yes," the lady assured her. "So many people find it tedious that you don't have as much competition as you might expect."

Herr Salzmann was no less kind to Yosef. Perceiving at once that Yosef saw himself as a beggar, the banker set his mind at ease. "Very convenient, this arrival of yours," he remarked. "One of my clerks is leaving in a couple of months, after the Yomim Noraim, and it's not so easy to find someone competent. I take it your handwriting is legible?"

"It is, Signor." Yosef thought of the copied siddur he had labored over.

"Then perhaps after the Yomim Noraim you'll begin at my office. Would that suit you?"

"Only if it's not invented."

"Ach, you Spanish Jews and your Spanish pride! I see you want to earn your own way; my clerk is about to desert me; I offer you his place. Must I beg?"

"No, Signor; you have an employee. Grazie."

Yosef was grasping Italian quickly enough to be able to cope with paperwork in that language very soon. But Italian was less useful than he expected. The Salzmanns were part of the Jewish loan-banking community that had only recently been invited to establish itself in Milano. Unexpectedly, the Norsas and da Pisas had not elected to open branches there; instead, it was the German Jews who extended their financial network southward. Among the Jews in Milano it was not Italian that was spoken, it was the mixture of German dialect and familiar Hebrew expressions that they called, simply, Jüdisch.

Standing beside Herr Salzmann as he chatted with his

colleagues, Yosef could not tell whether they discussed business or someone's latest grandchild. Knowing Spanish had made Italian easy for him: the words were often the same, only pronounced a little differently. But this Jüdisch! Even the Hebrew he should have recognized sounded foreign.

"Kennst du Berl Handler?"

"Der was hat die zway dochter, in Augspurg?"

A nod. "Eine grosse simcha — er macht chasane."

"Mazel-tov! Wer ist der choson?"

"Ich waiss nicht."

"Nu, sol sein a binjan olom, das ist genuog."

Forgetting the language barrier, Herr Salzmann insisted on bringing Yosef with him on social calls. All too often, Yosef stood silent and alone as the conversation flowed around him, too ill at ease to move closer than the fringe of the group, too mannerly to leave. He felt keenly that his appearance made him conspicuous; he shrank from the stares of pity or curiosity that he came to expect. Increasingly he kept to his room when visitors arrived; often he refused Herr Salzmann's invitations to accompany him. A reputation for moodiness began to attach to him.

Reina, on the other hand, had become a great favorite. More perceptive than her husband, Frau Salzmann had made sure that Reina picked up enough Jüdisch to fumble through a conversation. Making an entertainment of her efforts to speak the language, Reina made a friend with each mistake. Where Yosef was solemn, Reina laughed; people liked her for it, liked the young girl who had lost home and family but could remain cheerful. As soon as she was well enough, Reina was invited to many homes, not as the Salzmanns' ward but for herself.

Although they lived in the same house, Reina and Yosef saw as little of each other as they had on São Tome before the accident. Reina was busied with household tasks. She was starting to learn to play the lute. Acquaintances begged for her company. Every minute seemed to be accounted for: Frau Salzmann swept her away in a rush of activity.

In the midst of a morning practice session Reina struck a discord on her lute and set the instrument down. Raising her head from her lace-making, Frau Salzmann gave her a surprised look.

Reina's answering look was guilty. "I shouldn't be idling like this. I hardly see Yosef any more. I know I've been neglecting him."

Laying the lace aside, Frau Salzmann leaned forward a little. "Reina, my dear, it's what I've intended. You came here trying to help him live his life. It's not good for either of you. I'm sure he does find you useful — too useful. He has to learn to manage on his own. After all, one day you'll be married and he'll have to do without you. And you have to learn to be yourself."

"But Yosef is all the family I have left."

Frau Salzmann patted Reina's arm. "You'll still be very close, but in a different way: as two people, not as one person and a shadow."

Reina thought of Yosef alone too much in his room, wary of strangers, aimless, restless. He needed her. But perhaps, she reflected, having her to turn to encouraged him in his brooding isolation. Perhaps Frau Salzmann was right. She sighed and gave in. But she had not the heart to pick the lute up again.

It occurred to her that their visits were becoming awkward, formal: they had already begun to grow apart. Often Yosef was gruff and short with her, but she could not reproach him. She would never dare to tell him of that conversation with Frau Salzmann. If he ever suspects, she thought, ever understands that Frau Salzmann is trying to separate us, he'll snatch my hand and march us both straight out of this house back onto the road. She shivered. She could not bear to think about traveling again, about the endless weary tramping with no home or hearth to welcome them. So when Yosef spoke sharply she only hung her head and said nothing.

Raising her hand to knock on his door late one summer afternoon, she realized it had been a week or more since she had last come. How had he been occupying himself? Perhaps a little learning, a very little; he could not concentrate, could not grasp the concepts, even simple ones. She remembered him slamming his fist against the table in frustration.

She had not known how to comfort him when that happened. Maybe his slowness was because he was not yet really well; or maybe it was another effect of the accident he would have to learn to live with. She wished the clerk in the bank would leave early. Surely if he had work, if he felt useful, Yosef would be happier.

She rapped lightly on the wood.

"Who is it?" asked a rough unwelcoming voice.

"Reina." Her own voice was timid.

"All right." Yosef sounded resigned, hardly pleased.

Lifting the simple latch, she pushed the door open.

Yosef had thrown wide both halves of the casement window to let in the late-afternoon brightness, for the waxed paper panes of the windows masked the blaze of the setting sun. The red-gold light brought a glow to the dark oak shutters folded back against the sides of the window recess, lit up the patterns painted on the plastered walls, and flashed from the satin surface of the heavy chest that still stood near the door. Above the open casements was a small circular window filled with roundels of glass; through this the sun flamed in dancing rings that stretched and lengthened along the broad beams of the ceiling.

Yosef was perched in the window recess, half-sitting on the sill, looking down at the people in the street, dots of people trailing exaggerated shadows as they scurried on inconsequential errands. As he turned to see Reina come in, the low sun caught his scarred face in a sharply angled maze of highlight and glancing shadows like cracked glaze on a badly fired tile. He looked more gargoyle than human, distorted into some freakish monster.

Shaken by this unexpectedly grotesque image of Yosef, Reina gave a small gasp, hardly more than a quickly indrawn breath. Yosef noticed.

"My own little sister," he said harshly. He turned back to the window, twisting away with an angry set to his shoulders. "You've become such a stranger that you shy away from me." He took a deep, rasping breath that sounded to Reina very like a sob. She ran to take his hand, but he drew it back.

"Yosef, it was the light," she said pleadingly.

Without answering he reached out and pulled the casements shut, one after the other.

Reina started to cry. Yosef made no move to comfort her. "You were so kind when we were traveling," she said miserably.

"How can you be so horrid, now? I always seem to say the wrong things to you these days."

On the folded shutters Yosef's fingertips drummed restlessly. "All right," he said suddenly. "I'll go."

"Go? Where?" Her hands clutched at his doublet.

Yosef heard the panic in her voice and despised himself for venting his ill-temper on her. "Reina," he said. He put his hand over hers where it held his doublet. "I'm sorry. I'm edgy — nothing to do, nobody to talk to. That's all. But I have to go. Just for a while."

She gazed up at him, strangely beautiful in the diffused glow, not the little sister, not the partner of his journey, but a third person, a child still, but a child for only a very little longer. He did not want to think about it.

"I promised Luis that I'd send ships to rescue everyone left on the island," Yosef said. "Until now, I wasn't well enough, and I wanted to wait to see if Ser Bruno's exercises did anything — "

"But it's far too soon for that!" Reina exclaimed. "I'm sure he meant months, at least."

Yosef flicked his hand. "It doesn't matter. I can't wait any longer to start collecting money for the ships. I have a responsibility to the children on the island and I've been shirking it." He spoke tensely.

Reina did not say anything in reply, but she gave Yosef a look that told him she knew the growing dread inside him, the dread of going unprotected from door to door, naked to the eyes and tongues of strangers. It was more than mere shyness. It was fear, fear of stares and comments and tactlessness and pity he did not want.

He did not mention any of these things. He had made a promise. The promise would be kept. What it cost him did not matter. But he was glad that Reina, at least, understood.

On the day Yosef began, the weather greeted him with its customary rain, with just enough of a shifting wind to slant the rain into his face no matter which direction he took. When he reached the first address, he stood dripping guiltily on the carpeted floor. Seated in a heavily carved Gothic chair, a portly man faced him across a massive table . Above the man the walls were hung with tapestries of hunting scenes, and Yosef found his eyes straying to the stag at bay. The stag was in rather better condition than the banker.

"I'm trying to collect enough to rescue over seven hundred children exiled from their homes and families," Yosef began. "It's a mitzva of pidyon shevuyim — "

"There was somebody here two days ago for the slaves in Corfu," interrupted the banker.

"These children are on the island of São Tome with no adults but priests and criminals, a thousand leagues from Spain, in a deadly climate — "

The banker reached into a small pouch and tossed a ducat onto the table. He waved a hand at it. "Go on; take it."

Yosef did not understand why the man should sound so encouraging for so little. It would take a lifetime to collect enough for one ship at this rate. With a muttered "Tizke l'mitzvoth" he accepted the coin and departed.

The next banker was more forthcoming, not with money but with advice. Leaning into his high-backed chair, the man gazed at the frescoed vaulted ceiling so high above him as to be hardly visible. His fingers caressed the carved knobs on the arms of his chair.

"You'd better daven for siyato dishmayo; you'll need it. Do you realize you're trying to assemble a whole fleet of ships? Who has that much money? A merchant can't spare his ships: his income depends on them. A banker can't give you money: money is his stock in trade. Without money he can't earn money. Do you understand me, boy?"

Yosef nodded.

"You're thinking that an office like this is a scandalous waste of money, aren't you? But if I don't impress my clients, they go to someone else. They don't want to take loans, but if I make it a respectable-looking experience, they're more willing to do it again. And the fancier the office is, the more highborn the customers, the bigger the loans, and the more interest. So don't get the idea that we use up what we have on luxury." He slammed down two coins. "We give!"

From all of the addresses in Milan Yosef received something, but it was discouragingly little. He borrowed from Herr Salzmann to go to other cities. After all, Milano's German Jews had had less contact with the Spanish refugees than the Italian communities. Perhaps contact with the Jews of Spain would encourage the Jews of Italy to donate more to rescue the children.

From Lodi to Cremona to Mantova he went, from one firm to the next, house to house, hardening himself to the glances he received. He did not expect too much of Lodi or Cremona; they were not the largest of cities. But in Mantova, a great business center with some of the oldest Jewish banking houses, he hoped to find a better response.

He stayed in the house of the financier Mordechai Finzi. It was less a house, he thought, than a palace. The luxury was overwhelming: carpets and tapestries, marble and gilding, armies of servants. His first impulse was to gape at the display like a simple rustic; he controlled himself with difficulty.

"Everyone lives like this," explained Mona Perna Finzi brightly, smiling at his awe. "Of course that lovely figured Genoese cloth is forbidden, but there are other fabrics. We all enjoy pretty things, don't we?

Mantova was his first encounter with the extravagant luxury of Italian life. He heard of the young man who gambled away three thousand ducats in a night; of the members of the exclusive tennis club who asked shayloth about playing there on Shabath; of the lavish theatricals presented at the slightest excuse; of the fabulous gifts presented to the dukes of various cities.

Yosef listened, bewildered. He remembered Saadya's conviction that catastrophe had overtaken the Spanish Jews because of their ostentatious luxury, the showy display of wealth. Yet these Italian Jews lived in a style that overwhelmed Yosef, who had been raised with wealth. Couldn't they see that they were asking for the same disaster?

Armed with Ser Mordechai's letter of recommendation, Yosef went on his rounds.

A secretary glanced at the letter, not bothering to read it. "Ser Mordechai's secretary churns these out by the score," he said. "Collecting for yourself, are you?" He gave the crippled boy a pitying look.

"No." Remembering Reina's hand on his arm, Yosef kept his temper. "For nearly eight hundred other children."

"Must be a very impressive institution," commented the secretary as he ushered him in. Yosef glared at his back.

Yosef described his mission to the prosperous merchant. The words had been spoken so often that they nearly said themselves.

"And where are these children?"

"On an island off the west coast of Africa."

"Good heavens, boy! The distance! The expense!" The man rolled his eyes. "What are they, Spanish refugees?"

"Yes."

Leaning forward, the merchant demanded, "Do you have any idea of how many Spanish refugees we're supporting here in Mantova alone? Or in the rest of Italy? Or how often people come asking for donations for them?"

"But pidyon shevuyim — "

"You forget the Corfiote slaves."

"I can't forget the children I left in that Gehinom!"

"You shouldn't forget that tzedaka goes to our own first. Your children will be the last on everybody's list." The merchant shook his head sympathetically. "Tell my secretary to give you 'chai.' It's more than I should, but I have rachmonus on you: you have a hard road ahead."

Your children will be the last on everybody's list. The words echoed in Yosef's mind as he made call after call. It was true. But it was not only other tzedakoth that came first, it was luxury and ornament, one extravagance after another. He recalled the tiny kehilla in Alger that had beggared itself to raise seven hundred ducats for pidyon shevuyim. Here, they no longer knew what self-denial and self-discipline meant.

No, that was not quite it. They understood the concepts well enough, but they applied them to being fit for the tennis courts, not to sacrificing for Torah or mitzvoth.

Because the Yomim Noraim were now so close, Yosef returned to Milano instead of continuing, as he had intended. When he told Reina, she threw her arms around him.

"Promise you'll stay until after Simchath Torah?"

He half-smiled down at her. It was good to have someone to

welcome him back. "I promise."

"I was so afraid you'd be away for the Yomim Tovim. I would have pined away with loneliness if you hadn't come back. I'm so glad, Yosef." She hugged him tighter. "I hated the way you looked when you came in; you looked so tired."

"I was."

"Then you need time to rest." She did not ask how well he had done. He would not have been tired if he had been successful.

With the arrival of Rosh Hashana, Yosef prepared himself for the elaborate tfilla. Already he had encountered the fondness the German Jews had for adding intricate Hebrew verse in what had been perfectly straightforward places. Nevertheless, he was taken unawares by the welter of piyutim that erupted into the service. Time after time, he was about to proceed when he was brought up short by yet another elaborate stanza, its thoughts trapped in the complex language. As well, the order of the tfilloth often disagreed with the machzor the Salzmanns had lent him.

He felt stupid, ignorant, homesick for a tfilla he knew, for people who spoke as he did, for a place of his own. Everywhere else the refugees had settled they had begun their lives anew; he alone did not seem to be able to start his life going again, like a water-clock that had run out of water.

All during that season Yosef ached to be off. The thought of São Tome preyed on his mind: every tfilla, every pasuk he learned, a casual comment — everything was a reminder of São Tome, and a reminder that he had not fulfilled his pledge.

Almost as soon as Simchath Torah was out, Yosef resumed his quest. The nights began to close in and the weather was no longer as mild as it had been a month before. Undeterred, Yosef went farther afield: Parma, Reggio, Modena, all cities with thriving Jewish communities. Again, people gave, but not enough. Never enough.

At night Yosef saw the faces he had left on São Tome pleading with him to rescue them. The dreams clutched at his heart and woke him to unforgiving darkness.

Begging for lists of wealthy Jews, he struggled through every address he had in Parma and Reggio. By the time he reached Modena he was exhaused. Desperation hounded him; he could not let himself stop. He was obsessed with the promise that had to be kept. As the end of Cheshvan went by, his fifteenth birthday passed as unnoticed as his fourteenth had been, when he had lain unconscious on São Tome. Forcing himself from one door to the next was all that mattered. Still it was not enough.

Determined though he was, he was tiring. Every muscle ached from the constant walking. His armpit was raw. His hand was bleeding. Every morning he rose sure that he could not endure another day of mud and pain and discouragement. Every night he lay awake consumed with guilt that he had not done more.

As he was leaving an office somewhere near the end of his list for Modena, he was suddenly so dizzy he had to lean against the wall.

"Are you all right?" a voice asked, sharp with concern.

"I will be, in a minute."

"They shouldn't send a boy like you, in your condition, to go out collecting," said the person indignantly.

"There isn't anyone else." Yosef wanted to let himself slide down the wall. He was so tired, he hurt so much, he only wanted to rest. There isn't anyone else, he thought. Fear sprang up inside him, the fear that he did not have the strength, the stamina, to keep on through the whole of Italy, the fear that one day he would have to admit defeat not because he could not raise the huge sum but because the labor itself was beyond him, and because there was no one else.

Counting over what remained of his loan from Herr Salzmann, Yosef judged that he had just enough to try Padova before returning to Milano. Sitting in an open cart that meandered along the roundabout route to Padova, Yosef dreamed of the del Banco financial empire in the city, dreamed of a donation that covered the whole sum. Hunched against the rain seeping through his cloak and hood, he dried out in inns at night only to be soaked through again.

In Padova he was directed to the house of the Conat family for lodging. The deep hoarse cough he stifled as he entered their door drew his hostess's attention immediately.

"How strong do you think you are?" Mona Leonora scolded

him. "Do think you're waterproof? On the edge of winter you want to wander in the rain with a cough like that? Sei meshuga, tu? Are you crazy?"

"Only Padova; then I'll go back to Milano." Yosef would have liked to stay and let the Conats take care of him. After a day of making the rounds of businesses, he found it was pleasant to sit in the evening listening to the Conats' son Avrohom learning with his father.

He liked Avrohom, only two years older than himself; he found Avrohom's ready smile and easy friendship reminded him of Luis. Avrohom attended Rav Mintz's famous yeshiva in Padova; his father was associated with it. Watching them learn together, Yosef thought he had never seen Torah so alive before. If it had not been beyond him he might have wanted to be a part of that life.

Yosef's stay with the Conats extended through Shabath. During the meal he told them, as he seldom did to anyone, of his own experience of São Tome, wanting them to understand the feeling of urgency that drove him. While the story unfolded Ser Rafoel looked thoughtful; but it was not until Motzaei Shabath that he drew Yosef aside for another discussion.

"There's something about this whole idea of sending ships that I find disturbing," he began. "You see, there's more to it than only the children and the island. To start with, the island is a Portuguese colony. Yes?"

Yosef nodded.

"Secondly, all of you were baptized: nominally, you're Christians from the Church's viewpoint. Thirdly, you were sent to São Tome by royal decree, weren't you?"

Another nod.

"Now tell me one more thing: are there Jews living in Portugal now?"

"Yes," Yosef answered readily, "all the native Portuguese Jews. The king didn't bother them when he seized the Spanish refugees."

"Ah," said Ser Rafoel. "Now tell me this: what would happen to those Portuguese Jews if the Jews of some other country financed an expedition to invade Portuguese territory

and kidnap seven hundred loyal Portuguese Christians who were
on a mission of the king's?"

Yosef stared at him without answering. His mouth felt
unaccountably dry. At length he said, "They wouldn't see it that
way. They couldn't." But his words lacked conviction.

"Wouldn't they?" Ser Rafoel asked softly. "And wouldn't
the Jews of Portugal be put in mortal danger?"

"Do you mean I'm simply to give up on seven hundred
children marooned in the middle of nowhere?" Yosef asked
desperately. "Just leave them with the priests and the fevers and
the degredados and the crocodiles? There has to be a way to
rescue them! I promised, don't you understand? I promised!" His
voice was rough, anguished. "They're waiting there for me. At
night I see their faces, pleading with me, reproaching me. How
can I tell them to go away, that there won't be any ships after all?
They're depending on me. I promised, I promised — " The cough
stopped him.

He did not even realize he was crying until an arm came
around his shoulders and Ser Rafoel was saying, "Come, sit down
in a quiet corner. You need time to think."

Yosef let himself be led and seated, but all the time in the
world would not have made his mind think of anything. When
Mona Leonora brought him a cup of hot spiced wine he looked up
at her blank-eyed, coughing a little.

"Drink it," she said kindly, "and then you'll go to sleep."
She stood beside him, watching him sip the steaming liquid, and
when he had finished she sent Avrohom to put him to bed. Yosef
went blindly, unresistingly. There did not seem to be anything
else to do.

In the morning he prepared to return to Milano.
Disheartened, he packed his traveling-bag, with the feeling that
nothing he did mattered any more. For a moment he held the
pouch of money he dared not use, money for pidyon shevuyim.
There were other captives to be ransomed; the money might as
well be used for them. But he had given so much of himself to
collecting it for São Tome. Something held him back from giving
it to anyone else. Someday, he thought, someday maybe it will be
safe to send the ships. He replaced the money in the traveling-

bag. He buckled his cloak at the shoulder and drew on the rough woolen hood against the rain. Slinging the bag across his back, he started for the door with tired steps.

What's the point? he thought. What's the point of doing anything? There was an empty sick feeling inside him, as if the idea of freeing the children of São Tome had been a living being that he had just seen slaughtered rather brutally.

"Don't blame yourself, Yosef." Ser Rafoel's voice stopped him. "You couldn't rescue the children because it wasn't the will of the Ribono shel Olam, not because you didn't do enough. Now isn't the time, or perhaps you aren't the person to do it." He rested his hands on Yosef's shoulders, trying to look into Yosef's eyes, but Yosef turned his face away.

"I've broken faith with them. What do I do now? I gave my whole being to trying to save those children. I forced myself to keep going when I didn't think I could move another step. How can I just go back to Milano and settle down as if I've never lived any other way?"

"What will you do there?"

"Herr Salzmann promised me a position as clerk in his bank." Yosef made a small sound of distaste. "Oh, I know I should be grateful for it. It's a good position and clean work, and considering how little I can do, I couldn't ask for more. But it seems such an empty sort of life."

"Of course," Ser Rafoel agreed. "A Jew can't find contentment in parnossa alone. The point of working is to earn enough money to support you so you can pursue your real career: learning Torah."

"Except that I can't learn, either," Yosef objected bitterly. "Nothing sticks in my mind."

Ser Rafoel's hand tightened unexpectedly on Yosef's shoulders. The shake he gave him was hard and angry. "Don't ever say that! If you threw yourself into Torah the way you threw yourself into this quest, it wouldn't matter if you remembered nothing! Nothing! You're expected to serve the Ribono shel Olam as well as you can with what you've been given. Don't measure yourself by others who have more; they're expected to do more."

Yosef looked at him in unresponsive silence.

"But of course," Ser Rafoel reminded himself, "you're not yet used to having limitations. Give yourself time. Only remember that the ikar, the important thing, is Torah."

Yosef shrugged. It did not seem polite to say that Ser Rafoel did not understand: that it was not enough to be contented with, to scribble meaninglessly in the banking-house in order to sit mystified at a shiur he could not follow. There did not seem to be any goal left for him, Yosef thought. He could not even devote himself to seeing to Reina's welfare; the Salzmanns did more for her than he ever could.

Ser Rafoel accompanied him out the door and a short way along the muddy street, then paused, as if expecting Yosef to say something. His head was half-bent against the rain.

"Thank you." Yosef could not think of anything else to say.

It seemed to be enough. With a smile Ser Rafoel embraced him. "Come back to us," he said warmly. "Tzeischem l'sholom. Go to peace." He went away quickly, picking his way through sodden rubbish in the street, shoulders up, head down.

Go to peace. It seemed a forlorn wish.

CHAPTER TWELVE

B Y THE FOLLOWING DAY the rain was mixed with sleet, chill and penetrating. Yosef huddled into himself, shrinking away from the heavy rain-soaked cloak on his back, condemned once again to an open cart. Day after dripping day passed. He could feel the cough settling heavily in his chest, clutching at him if he drew breath too sharply. At night his clothes steamed before the fire in some hostelry, but the dampness never left them.

Weary and discouraged and wet, he reached fog-shrouded Milano at last and made his way past the deep arched marble doorway in the brick façade. The street was gray-blanketed around him, dim, closed in, its sound muffled. He went in the discreet entrance at one side that led to the Salzmanns' home.

He thought wistfully that it would have been pleasant to feel that he was coming home. Still, Reina was there, and warmth and dry clothing and an end to travelling. He mounted the stairs one by one, too weary to do more than sink down on a chest when he reached the top.

From one of the rooms he could hear Reina's voice, singing a popular song. He recognized it: "L'amour de moy", quite pretty but with rather stupid words about love. He resented that song. It aggravated him because it was silly and shallow and false, and he had no patience with things that had no meaning to them. Perhaps that was the fault of having lived on São Tome.

He heard Reina break off in mid-phrase. Frau Salzmann's voice said something he could not distinguish, and then he heard Reina's clear "Oh!" There was more from Frau Salzmann.

"But of course I'd have to wait for Yosef to come back," Reina's voice carried well. "It ought to be his decision, too; he's my whole family."

Yosef stiffened. Reina was scarcely fourteen; surely they were not trying to marry her off! Sliding the strap of his bag over his head, he let it drop to the floor as he rose, tense with anger. The carpet on the floor muffled his footsteps, so when he entered the room the voices were coming from, both Reina and Frau Salzmann stared at him in surprise.

Reina flew to him. "I'm so happy!" she exclaimed, throwing her arms around him. "You've been so long and I've missed you." She drew back at once. "You're soaked through! Yosef, go and change!"

With a shake of his head, Yosef asked hoarsely, "What's going on?"

"Going on is hardly the way to describe it!" laughed Frau Salzmann. "As soon as you've changed we can discuss it."

"No. Now." The hoarseness made Yosef's voice sound menacing. He rested his arm protectively on Reina's shoulder.

"If you insist," Frau Salzmann conceded. "You see, an excellent shiduch has just presented itself. Now, I know — " she held up a hand to forestall his objections — "she's just a touch young, but we don't want to miss such a fine opportunity merely because of a few months."

We! Yosef controlled himself, feeling Reina's hand. "Who is the proposed chatan?"

"He comes from Pisa, and his name is Leone Massarano. Reina would probably want to call him Yehuda." She smiled indulgently. "Everyone likes him and he has a good profession."

"Which is — ?"

"He's a dancing-master," said Frau Salzmann. "A very good one, and very much in demand to teach the young ladies the newest figures."

Yosef stared at her. "A dancing-master! You'd marry my sister to a dancing-master! Is that all you think she's worth?"

"I think very highly of Reina," retorted the woman indignantly. "This *gentleman* — " she emphasized the word, suggesting that Yosef was not — "has a fine parnossa and is very personable. He has beautiful manners and excellent taste. And it's not everyone who's willing to take a girl with not a copper to her name." She sniffed. "And what's wrong with a dancing-master, anyway?''

"If you don't know I can't tell you!" Yosef yelled in her face. "What business is it of yours, anyway? I know what's right for my sister! Why don't you talk to me? It's my place to take care of her! Do you think because I'm crippled I don't have a mind? I go away for a few weeks and come in to find you scheming behind my back — '' He broke off, coughing. It went on for so long that he released Reina and groped his way to a chair to sit down until the spasm stopped.

Reina looked from him to Frau Salzmann. They both loved her, in their different ways. She did not know what to say to either one.

Herr Salzmann's deep tones boomed in upon them. "I should like to speak to the young man alone."

Sitting on the edge of his seat, his hand still gripping an arm of the chair, Yosef shot him a quick startled look. Reina gazed at the banker tearfully, while Frau Salzmann, white-faced, regarded her husband with gratitude before quitting the room.

"You, as well, Fräulein, bitte."

When Reina had gone, he turned to Yosef. "It was impossible not to overhear; I apologize." Pacing slowly across the room and back again for several minutes, he said no more until he stopped in front of Yosef. "When we took you and your sister in," he began, "we intended to regard you as our children as far as possible. For Reina, this has worked perfectly. She and my wife are great companions: they work together and enjoy the same pleasures. She's as popular with our friends as our own children would have been. With you, however, I feel we've been less successful.

"Perhaps you didn't really want parents, I don't know. But you don't seem happy in our house, you don't appear to enjoy our friends, and I don't feel that you want to be a part of our family. As well as all this, I've lent you a good deal of money and I've let you treat my home as a sort of boarding-house between trips.

"In return, you have not only hardly shown any appreciation, you've been unforgivably rude to my wife. I can only conclude that you would be happier if you lived elsewhere. You'll be welcome to visit at any time, of course." He paused.

"Would two weeks be enough time for you to prepare to go?"

"Two days will be sufficient." With a stiff bow Yosef left the room.

In his own bedchamber he found Reina waiting anxiously. As soon as he closed the door she asked, "What did he say?"

"I've been thrown out."

Reina gave a little gasp. "I never thought it would go so far!" She covered her face with her hands. "I might as well have stayed on São Tome for all the good I've done."

"Never mind," Yosef said comfortingly. "I'll be better off, able to live my own way without somebody looking over my shoulder wondering why I'm not behaving as he would." He did not tell her how much it hurt him to be told to leave; he did not mention how much more lonely he would be without her. "Only promise me that you won't let them even think of shiduchim for you until you're fifteen."

"Of course I promise." She gulped and sniffed, her eyes still wet. "Frau Salzmann is a dear and I love her but we don't always have the same taste. I knew the dancing-master wasn't for me." She looked up at Yosef as he stifled a cough. "You're coughing — you have to change out of these wet things. Surely Herr Salzmann will let you stay here until you've gotten rid of that cough."

"He will, but I won't. I'll be out of here by the day after tomorrow."

Reina gazed up at him in horror. "You're not fit to do it, Yosef! Think what a cough like that could turn into!" She flung her hands wide in despair. "I suppose you said that to Herr Salzmann because of your pride, your stupid, stupid pride. I wish you could use that pride of yours for good." She flung out of his room.

By suppertime the next day Yosef had steeled himself to confront Herr Salzmann. Waiting until the meal was over before he appeared in the family dining room, he saw the banker leaning back in his chair, enjoying a glass of wine to follow dessert. As Yosef entered, he glanced up and smiled a welcome. "The ladies have left me to my thoughts," he said. "Will you join me?"

Yosef held his head high. "I only came to ask you if you knew where I should go to find lodgings."

With an expression of distress the man set down his goblet. "I hadn't intended you to tramp the streets."

"I've done it before." He did not need to add, "when I had no home"; it was implicit in what he had said. He was being insulting.

"True." Herr Salzmann's voice was calm; he refused to be goaded. "But I've spoken to a very respectable lady who takes a few boarders. Her prices are reasonable and the rooms are quite adequate. She's a motherly sort; you'll be looked after." Herr Salzmann searched about his person for a moment. "I must have left the address on my desk. You'll have it in the morning. I think you'll be happy there." Seeming to remind himself of something, he added, "By the way, I said only that you wanted to be more independent. Perhaps it would be as well if that were your story, too."

For a time Yosef stared at Herr Salzmann. He had been rude to the banker and to his wife; he had shown little gratitude for the chesed they had shown him; he had been more concerned for his own feelings than for theirs. Yet Herr Salzmann still spoke kindly to him, still went out of his way to find him an appropriate place to live, and allowed him as well to save face in public by inventing a reason for Yosef to have left the Salzmann house.

"Ah — I forgot. The position at the bank is open. As soon as you feel well enough, you may start there."

"Grazie." Yosef had not expected this kindness, open-handed and undeserved. Feeling chastened, he bowed and left the room.

Before he could explain that a novice clerk should not have such an extensive wardrobe, Frau Salzmann had packed all of his belongings. He would have left behind the things he felt were unsuitable, but Reina caught him about to open the chest.

"Don't you see that you'd shame them?" she asked. "Everyone knows you've been living here like a son of the house. You can't appear in public looking like a poor man's son; it would reflect on the Salzmanns. Take it and wear it, not for yourself but for them."

Yosef gave in.

When he was ready to leave, the Salzmanns' man Alessandro

heaved Yosef's chest to his shoulder with a grunt. Yosef did not believe it was that heavy. Alessandro, he suspected, inclined to the theatrical. Despite the chest, Alessandro set such a good pace that Yosef was hard put to keep up with him.

The house they stopped at was smaller than the Salzmanns' and did not have the usual shop downstairs, though it was a very common arrangement. Almost as soon as the man had rattled the bronze fish that formed the knocker, the door opened. Letting the chest slide to the black-and-white marble checkerboard of the hall floor, he bobbed his head quickly and left.

"Hasty, isn't he?" remarked a voice dryly. "Baldassare, take the chest to the empty bedroom at the back."

The voice was very deep, almost like a man's, and Yosef was so struck by it that he paused momentarily on his way up the steps. As the servant who had answered the door departed with Yosef's possessions, the lady herself came into view.

Mona Benvenida Allemanno was a large woman, not fat but big-boned, tall, imposing. Framing her plain, bony face was a wimple so wide it suggested a sail. As she bore down on Yosef he had a fleeting impression of a benign canal-barge like those he had seen on the great waterway between Milan and the Adda. He guessed her to be in her late fifties, but her face was not the sort to show age clearly, so he could not be certain.

The woman did not react to his appearance at all, though she spared a sharp glance for the weather outside. "You'd better come in quickly," she advised him. "If it's not raining now, it will soon. Unless it snows. How I miss Firenze!"

While Yosef made his way inside, she regarded the rear of the entrance hall where the staircase rose gracefully, as though to assure herself that Baldassare had, indeed, taken the chest upstairs.

Turning back, she shut the door, saying, "There's an alcove here where you can hang your cloak, though if it's dry — if it's ever dry — you can lay it in this chest, if you like." Pointing to his right, she went on, "Over there is the tenants' living-room; you'll be eating there, as well. I think you'll want to spend a good part of your time there, just now, because of the fire. This is an older house, you see, and the bedrooms don't have fireplaces. Even those we do have are the old-fashioned ones with hoods."

She led the way to the staircase. "My other boarders are two young men who work in Herr Salzmann's bank. Dovid and Shimon: they learn together. Now," she said, stopping at the foot of the steps, "I'm getting too old to be running up and down these stairs so much. I'll have Baldassare show you your room, if you don't mind. Baldassare!"

Ascending behind the servant, Yosef realized that he had not actually had the chance to say a single word since he had walked in the door. He wondered if the woman always rattled on like that in her curious voice. Even if she did, he thought, he would be happier here than he had been at the Salzmanns'. Here he was free of social pressures, free of feeling obligated. He let his breath out in a long, silent sigh of relief — and set his cough off again.

The sound of coughing echoed around the hall, magnified by the marble floor and plaster walls. Baldassare came down to support Yosef where he balanced precariously on a step between landings, gasping for breath. When at last the coughing fit passed, Yosef clung to the balustrade for a few more minutes, shaken.

"What do you call that, young man?" came Mona Benvenida's deep tones from below.

"A cough, Madonna." Yosef replied meekly.

"A cough? I took it for an earthquake! It's a brocha you have the room over the kitchen; some of the warmth should come up through the floor. Baldassare, are there any stones heating?"

"A few, Madonna, in case someone wanted to go to sleep early."

Mona Benvenida gave a small "Ah!" of satisfaction. "Then show him to his room; be sure the shutters are fastened tightly; draw the curtains round the bed; but don't put him in before you warm the bed with the stones. I'll go wrap them now, and find something for that cough, and — " Her voice grew fainter as she moved briskly toward the kitchen.

Baldassare gave Yosef a toothless grin. "You'll be fit in a week, with her dosing you," he promised. "She won't tolerate sickness, not her. She likes taking care of people. You're not to mind; it's just her way. She won't bother you if you don't need it.

You don't mind, do you?"

Yosef knew that his cough needed attention. He knew, too, that he was tired and run-down and out of sorts with everyone. The thought of being fussed over a little seemed very pleasant. "No," he said, "I don't mind."

"And once he's in bed — " Mona Benvenida's voice followed them upwards — "he's not to get out!"

For a week that pronouncement stayed in force. In addition, Yosef was steamed and poulticed and dosed until the room smelled like an apothecary's nightmare. When at last Mona Benvenida let his two fellow-boarders in to meet him, they wrinkled their noses involuntarily at the fumes. As they approached him, Yosef examined the young men.

They were remarkably similar, though the hair of one was darker than the other's: pleasant-faced young men, both several years older than Yosef himself. Their hair was on the longish side, he noticed, and their doublets shortish, shorter, he knew, than his father would have ever permitted him to wear his. Fops, he thought with disdain. Fashion-conscious fops.

Smelling the cold freshness of outdoors on them, he realized that they must have come in from work, and only taken off their cloaks before coming to him. On the caps pushed well forward on their hair he saw a few snowflakes. Observing that both men wore short houppelandes, he concluded that the bank was chilly.

"Winter's come," announced the darker one with a smile. Reaching up to the high collar of his doublet, tight around his neck, he loosened the ties so that the fine linen underneath showed at the throat. "Hot in here." He nodded at his companion. "I'm Shimon; he's Dovid."

Dovid came closer. "Your cough's much better," he said. "I hardly hear it at all, now, in the night. Do you catch colds often?"

Yosef knew he meant well, that he was trying to be friendly, but the condescending tone made him bristle. "No," he said stiffly. "Only when I spend too many days in open wagons being sleeted on."

"Oh. Sorry."

There was a strained pause.

"Do you think you'll be joining us soon at the bank?" asked

Shimon cautiously.

"I hope so." Yosef's reply was discouragingly formal.

Shimon tried again. "I'm afraid you'll find life here in Milano rather boring. There are so few Jews here that we can't even get up any decent theatricals. Dovid and I were just agreeing the other day that we really long for a bit of adventure."

A bit of adventure. Adventure doesn't come in bits, Yosef wanted to tell them, it comes in great huge indigestible masses that make you sick and frightened and exhausted. Adventure leaves you crawling with insects and crying with pain, transforms you from an idealistic child to a savage creature that will do anything — anything — to survive. Adventure. His stomach turned over.

Enough years lay between him and these two young men to make them regard him as a child; yet he felt as though he were centuries older. I might have been like them, he thought, growing up in a world that valued fashion and sophistication; but while they've been playing at life I've been living in deadly earnest. What on earth do I have to say to them? What do we have in common? I can't even remember how they think.

"Thank you for visiting," he said, unaware that his reply to Shimon sounded like an abrupt dismissal because he had spoken none of his thoughts aloud.

Glancing at Dovid in surprise, Shimon seemed to be at a loss as to what to say. Dovid looked towards Yosef. "Refua sheleima." He drew Shimon with him towards the door. "Our rooms are on either side of yours, if you feel like visiting." The words were cordial; the tone was not. The door closed behind them with a firm snap.

Long after Yosef felt he ought to have recovered, Mona Benvenida kept him in the house. Two weeks, three weeks. Weeks of board and lodging that he had not paid for. There was money owing to Herr Salzmann, as well. Yosef had a horror of debts. He could not escape the memory of the debts that had destroyed Papa's business those last few months in Spain. The worry about the money owed preyed on his mind.

"I have to start work," he protested to Mona Benvenida. "I ought to have been at the bank two weeks ago."

Mona Benvenida had allowed him to sit in the kitchen because it was warm. He was there now, watching her bend her tall figure down to check the frumenty that was working on the hearth. Ruddy-faced from the fire, she glanced at him and shook her head.

"Are you comparing yourself to Shimon and Dovid?" she asked, replacing the cover on the pot. She sat down on a settle near the fireplace.

Yosef understood that she referred to their robust health. "I suppose," he admitted reluctantly.

Mona Benvenida looked at her big hands as if wondering why they were not busy with some household task. "Yosef, Shimon and Dovid have been brought up in comfortable homes, well-fed, well-dressed, well-educated. They don't know what hardship means. I don't know much about you — only what Herr Salzmann felt I needed to know: that you're one of the Spanish exiles, that you had a long, difficult journey, and that you and your sister arrived last Tamuz not in the best of condition. I was told only a few details of your journey."

"I was brought up in a comfortable home, too."

"Yosef, you left that home in 1492. It's the very end of 1494 now. You've had two and a half years of illness, poor food, injury, exhaustion. I appreciate the fact that you've survived, but you have to realize that you've put too much strain on your health to take it for granted any longer. You'll miss more time from work later if you don't take the extra time to recover now. Do you understand me?" She looked at him sharply.

"Yes, Madonna." Yosef gazed at the tiles at his feet, but what he saw was a small pink gecko stepping delicately across a rough woolen blanket after a straying ant.

"Good." She rose and moved to her tasks about the kitchen. "Next week I'll have Ser Bruno examine you."

"Ser Bruno?" Yosef flushed with embarrassment.

"What's wrong?"

"I promised faithfully that I'd do the exercises he gave me and — I haven't."

Mona Benvenida laughed. "Start today," she advised, "and when he asks you can honestly say you've been doing them. But you'd better report to me every week that you've continued, or I'll tell Ser Bruno the truth!"

"Yes, Madonna." Yosef did not laugh in return. He was not feeling light-hearted; a grimness seemed to have settled into his mind and he could not find the energy to shake it out. At every turn there seemed to be another limitation he had not anticipated. Now he had to take care of himself, like an old man trying to eke out a few more months of feeble existence. He reached for his crutch and went back upstairs to his room.

The mood was still on him when, a week later, the doctor pronounced him fit for work. As soon as Ser Bruno had gone, Yosef went to the chest in the alcove in the entrance hall, flung up the lid and pulled out his cloak. With an impatient motion he shook out the month-old folds and, throwing the cloak over his shoulders, fastened the buckle. He tried to let the lid of the chest down silently but it slipped, and banged. The sound fetched Mona Benvenida.

"Does your cloak have a hood?" she demanded as she bore down on Yosef. "Wear a hood. And a scarf, too. It's bitter outside. And pattens on your shoes to keep your feet out of the snow."

Yosef glared at her rebelliously.

"You won't be conspicuous," she assured him, understanding his look. "You don't know how to dress for a Milanese winter; why, you don't even know what winter is, where you come from."

Obediently Yosef did as he was told. Once out the door, he was amazed at the cold in the damp wind, and the heaviness of the wet snow that stuck to his pattens in icy lumps. All the way to the banking-house he had to keep stopping to knock clear the bulwark of soggy snow that built up in front of his dragging foot. From indoors he had seen the snow and thought it beautiful, had been eager to go out in it; but long before he stood in front of the familiar brick facade the novelty had been lost in annoyance.

Passing the private entrance, he went by one of the ground-floor windows with its heavy iron grille, and turned into the deep marble doorway. He had not been through that doorway or up those steps since his arrival and he felt oddly shy, particularly when he realized that it was mid-morning and there would be customers already. Taking a deep breath, he went in.

With relief he saw that, for the moment, there were no prospective borrowers in the spacious room. He could stand where he was for a little while and look around him.

He remembered the veined marble floor that Reina had fainted onto. Around the walls pilasters broke the severity of the smooth plaster and framed two frescoed sections that faced each other across the room. His gaze followed the pilasters to the coffered ceiling, the squares between the beams painted and gilded. A lowbacked settle and two coffer-maker's chairs stood ready for patrons waiting their turn at the U-shaped counter that occupied the far end of the room. Behind the right leg of the counter there was an uncurtained doorway, but what was beyond it Yosef could not tell. Sitting at the counter, money-purse and record book at hand, Shimon glanced up.

"Ha!" he exclaimed. "Dovid! Back to your old place! We're not short handed any more!" To Yosef he said with a smile, "One of us has to be at the counter at all times. As soon as Dovid's here I'll show you where to hang your cloak."

In a moment Yosef was led through the mysterious doorway behind the counter, was divested of his outerwear and shown the little clerk's office that lay between Herr Salzmann's sanctuary and the public room. If the sun had been shining, the small space would have been bright, for there was a generous window that faced the courtyard; but even on this gray day the desk was well lit. Dovid came and showed him what he was to do; Herr Salzmann threw open his office door and bellowed a welcome; and Yosef set to work.

It was not long before Yosef became familiar with his duties, and life at the banking-house and away from it settled into a routine. During the week he devoted himself conscientiously to his work, remembering Herr Salzmann's kindness and wanting both to show his appreciation and to fully earn his wages. On Shabath he ate at Mona Benvenida's table, rested for an hour, and then went to visit Reina for the rest of the day.

He would have liked to see more of her. Every visit to Reina warned him how quickly they were growing apart. For him there was no going back to what he had been before São Tome; Reina, however, had become again the cherished daughter of a wealthy home. She had not wanted to grow up, he knew; she had been forced by events to be strong and unafraid. Now that she was safe, she seemed to have closed off that part of herself that had been capable of nursing children as they died, of facing a perilous voyage, of even killing. She did not want to be that person. All she desired was to be a child for a little longer, to be silly and afraid, to be dependent and cared for.

Again and again Yosef remembered her as she had been on the journey: courageous, sensible, dependable. He remembered her restraining hand on his arm. He remembered what she had said about "gam zu l'tova" that Motzaei Shabath in the field near Pavia. Like Mama, Reina had been tough and strong when it was necessary. Yet now she was no more than the little sister he had laughed at in Spain, no more than a little girl. Of the person he recalled from the journey there was no trace.

He had nothing to say to this child. When he came to see her he let her babble on about the lute, about friends and parties, about the Salzmanns. He nodded and commented appropriately. But when she asked after his own affairs, he told her only that there was nothing new. How could he discuss with this child his frustration at his failure to rescue the children? What could she understand of his isolation, his loneliness, his dissatisfaction with the life he led? As he had watched the last ships drift from the quay in Lisboa, he watched Reina draw slowly away from him.

The unvarying routine of workday and Shabath blurred the passage of time: each day was much like the one before, slipping past unnoticed until a Yom Tov would bring Yosef up short, shocked at the way whole months had dropped behind him. Spring came, and summer. Mona Benvenida no longer badgered him about scarves and cloaks and hoods; occupied with her visiting grandchildren, she trusted to the mild weather and his commonsense and left him alone.

At first he was pleased to escape the nagging, to come and go as he pleased, unhindered; and then he discovered that he missed it, and was vexed with himself.

He remembered the Conats in Padova: how Mona Leonora

had fussed over him, how Ser Rafoel had tried to guide him. There was their son Avrohom, closer to his own age than anyone else he had met in Italy. He had been friendly. Ser Rafoel's parting words came back to him: "Come back to us ... Go to peace." In Milano he had not found peace, only an uneasy truce with himself. But he wanted to go back to them.

It occurred to Yosef that the Yomim Noraim were very close. He had not forgotten the uncomfortable experience they had been for him the previous year. He would not be in Milano for that season again, he decided: he would go to Padova, to the Conats, where he had felt less ill at ease than he did in Milano's community. He made the requisite arrangements.

Reina was shocked. "In Padova! But I thought we'd have so much extra time together during the Yomim Tovim after davening."

Davening. Meldar had been their word. She did not even think in Ladino any more. He could hardly wait to leave Milano.

❁ ❁ ❁

Ser Rafoel embraced Yosef in welcome, then held him away from himself for a moment. "You look better," he pronounced. "Better — and worse. You're healthy, but you're discontented."

Yosef shrugged uncomfortably. Ser Rafoel saw too much. "I'm working in the banking office," he said.

"And how much do you learn?"

Yosef looked away. He did not learn. The local shiur was given in Jüdisch, very rapidly. The two clerks already learned with each other: they were on the same level, and far beyond his own. He intended to buy a chumash, but he had hardly finished repaying Herr Salzmann's loan, and even the new printed seforim were not cheap. And the truth was that he was too depressed to make the effort in any case.

"But if you learned, you'd be happier." Ser Rafoel sounded exasperated. "You can't expect to be satisfied with nothing but parnossa to live for." He considered the problem. "At least, while you're here we can learn with you. I may still have a couple of Chumashim my father printed in Mantua. You're welcome to one if you promise me you'll discipline yourself to learn Torah every day."

Discipline. So very long ago Yosef recalled he had been proud of his self-discipline: acting like a young grandee in the midst of poverty, driving himself in the fields, forcing himself through a few more addresses in the cities of Italy, resisting discouragement on the long journey. He did not seem to have any discipline left now. Except for the little he expended on work, it seemed to have leaked out of him through some unsuspected crack. He could not even be bothered to stand straight.

"I can't promise. I don't know if I can any more," he said at last.

Mona Leonora had appeared. "How can he think when he's still so tired from traveling here?" she scolded her husband. "Don't bully him; let him rest."

Afterwards Ser Rafoel did not return to the subject, but he and Avrohom went out of their way to learn with Yosef at his level, at his speed. It was terribly difficult for everyone. Every word, every concept had to be explained over and over before Yosef could grasp it. By the afternoon of the first day of Rosh Hashana he was exhausted.

Leaning his head on his hand, he pleaded, "Can't we take a break? I won't have any strength left for tfilloth tomorrow at this rate."

With a laugh, Ser Rafoel agreed. "Avrohom, bring the siddur. Yosef ought to see it." When the volume arrived, he went on, "Avrohom has been working at this for some time. I'm quite pleased with it." Opening it at random, he laid it before Yosef.

After one glance, Yosef stared at Avrohom. "You made this?"

"You don't have to look like that," laughed the young man. "I didn't do it overnight!"

Yosef returned to the siddur, page after page of clear, neat script, decoratively executed yet perfectly legible. The wonderful vivid decoration held the eye: flowers and leaves, delicately shaded, sweeping round upon themselves on graceful curving stems, the spaces between sprinkled with tiny gilded suns. Golden-edged panels enclosed the words of each title page of tfilloth and megilloth.

"Did you live in Firenze?" Yosef inquired.

"No, I just like the Florentine style." Avrohom tapped a page. "Do you think it's too florid?"

Yosef thought of his crude, laborious copying on São Tome. "I'm not qualified to offer an opinion," he said. "Except that it's beautiful."

Avrohom nodded his thanks. "When the time comes for shiduchim — and I'll be eighteen in a few months — I want to show that I can earn a decent parnossa."

"But with *your* head, you'll probably have wealthy fathers falling at your feet."

Avrohom laughed. "Yes, but I don't want their daughters. Most of them think of nothing but clothes and furniture." He sobered. "I'd rather have a girl who won't expect me to attend theater parties and drape her in Chinese silks, even if it means my learning less time and having to earn a living. What's — "

He broke off abruptly and reddened. "Excuse me," he said, and left the room.

Yosef looked at Ser Rafoel in puzzlement. "What's wrong?"

"It's not really proper for a young man personally to inquire after prospective kallos," explained his host. "What is your sister like?"

"My sister!" Yosef had not imagined that Reina would be under consideration. He remembered the adage that one should look at the girl's brothers to judge her character. "She's not like me," he said hastily. "She's pretty and sociable and domestic — "

From his description she sounded ordinary and a little shallow. Yet she had been so different. "But on São Tome she worked in the infirmary, where as many children died as lived; she came with me when I wanted to escape, though she was afraid; she could say *"gam zu l'tova"* when I couldn't," he added helplessly. "And then we came to Milano and she was a little girl again. It's as if she were two different people. I can't understand it."

After a pause Ser Rafoel said, "I think I can. You share the same strength in discipline, but she uses hers differently. She closes off parts of herself that she doesn't want bothering her: the part that's afraid, the part that's childish, the part that's adult too soon. When she felt she needed more childhood before she had to leave it behind for good, she simply sealed away those months she had spent being adult. And when the time comes, she'll open that door. Do you see?"

Yosef nodded, but hesitatingly.

"Do you think Avrohom would like her?"

"How should I know? I've never understood people. I don't know anything about shiduchim. I made Reina promise she wouldn't let the Salzmanns consider shiduchim before she was fifteen and now I'm doing it. I'm only fifteen myself. I don't even know what's to be done. You'll have to tell me."

So Ser Rafoel took charge. Bearing the siddur, Yosef returned to Milano after Simchath Torah; a month later Avrohom paid Reina a visit — and it was a shiduch. Amidst mazel-tovs the chasane was set for Teveth.

Instantly Frau Salzmann devoted herself to planning the affair. Although she planned to invite the entire Milano Jewish community, the Conat family and a number of yeshiva bochurim — to make it more "lebedik" — the Salzmann house was more than adequate to accommodate the chasane, and she felt that her expertise at such occasions would be on display. Nor was Reina's dress forgotten.

Well-muffled in a warm cloak, Reina was borne off on a sunny winter day to choose the cloth for her wedding dress. At the draper's, she watched as bolt after bolt of beautiful fabrics appeared on the table. Silks and brocades, satins and velvets lay in tumbled richness before her. She fingered the materials; she loved the feel of them and had never seen such variety of magnificence. Camalote, grecisco, dami and ciclaton from the Arab countries; fabrics printed and streaked, silks from Lucca, figured cloth from Genova. Even in Spain they had never dressed as extravagantly as this.

If she had remained on São Tome she would have been wearing the simplest of cloths, coarsely woven linen or perhaps cotton if they had been able to obtain it, unbleached except by the sun, or dyed the dull brown that was all they had managed. How could she luxuriate in such opulence when the others had so little?

"Perhaps something a little more restrained," she suggested. The draper gave her an amazed look. "I'd like to be able to wear the dress quite often afterwards. We'll be living very modestly," she explained. "Wool might be a good idea."

The princely fabrics were wisked away and replaced with others less dazzling and more to Reina's taste. "Now, this is lovely," she said, lifting the edge of a soft grey wool.

"Yes, it is," agreed Frau Salzmann tartly, "for a woman of sixty. Try again."

Reina laughed and turned to some cloth of a pleasant shade of green.

"How romantic!" exclaimed the draper. "Green for true love."

Reina jerked her hand away. Minstrels' nonsense had no place in a Jewish marriage. Before her the tints and shades rainbowed across the table: how could she choose? She wondered which one Avrohom would have picked, with his eye for color. In her mind's eye she could see clearly the flowers on the pages of the siddur: deep blue with a hint of green, and a warm rose-pink. And in front of her lay a fine, soft wool of exactly that same warm shade, not weak, though not as bright as madder-rose. She held it out, knowing it was right. "This."

Frau Salzmann heaved a sigh of resignation. "No doubt we can dress it up with the best lace with a little gold thread in it, but I wish I could see what you have against looking really fine for your own chupa."

Taking the older woman's hands in her own, Reina squeezed them affectionately. "Tell me, Tante," she said gently, "if you had been on São Tomé, if you had left behind hundreds of children who had nothing, if you had a brother who looked like Yosef, wouldn't you feel a little bit guilty at 'looking really fine' for anything, ever again?"

Frau Salzmann's arms went around Reina and held her close. "I thought you had forgotten all that," she said.

"I turned away from it; I didn't want to remember," Reina answered softly. "It's time to grow up now and let it come back again." She paused. "May I have the cloth I chose?"

"Of course." Frau Salzmann dabbed at her eyes. "Of course."

CHAPTER THIRTEEN

OUTSIDE THE SHUTTERED WINDOWS the late-afternoon winter gloom shrouded the streets, but inside the Salzmanns' house, candles and torches lit the rooms to daylight brightness. Guests milled around, elbowing each other good-naturedly as they tried to find the best view of the chupa. One of the musicians was tuning his lute in preparation for the ceremony: a series of soft plucking sounds, hardly audible.

Inconspicuous in a corner, Yosef watched the assemblage, an onlooker safely out of the way. A few years earlier, he would have expected to be in the forefront of things, organizing and managing, supremely confident, supremely officious. The thought hurt less than it might have a year ago.

So much about the chasane, as they said it, was strange, he mused. The chatan — choson — under the chupa wore, for some unknown reason, a kittel. Perhaps it was another of the peculiar Ashkenazi minhagim. Reina was escorted in, heavily veiled, and led around and around Avrohom.

"What's that for?" Yosef asked the man nearest him.

"Minhag," the man shrugged. "Minhag avoseinu b'yodeinu. She goes around three times. Nice number."

Despite his advanced age, Rav Mintz had come from Padova to Milano to be mesader kidushin; his Ashkenazi accent was very pronounced. Between the accent and the unfamiliar nigunim, the brochos were almost unintelligible to Yosef. For a moment a wave of homesickness for his own minhagim and his own language swept over Yosef. It was good that Reina seemed unbothered.

Before he expected it, he heard the muffled crack of breaking glass. Calls of "Mazel-tov!" filled the room as people pressed back to let the young couple through, Reina almost invisible among the bobbing headdresses of well-wishing ladies, Avrohom laughing and no longer white-faced. Yosef stood back with the rest and watched them pass him by.

Until the seuda began, Yosef stayed in his quiet niche. He felt self-conscious, with so many strangers about. Later, when there was music and dancing and everyone had had a sip of wine, there would be too much to do for people to notice him and point and whisper curiously.

It was not long before the festive meal was announced. The Salzmanns led their guests to tables laden with all the dishes the occasion demanded: salt herring and mortrews and fresh roast bream; capon pasties and a meat brewet; roast meats with at least six different sauces, broth with plenty of sops in every serving, spiced meats and frumenty, fritters and rissoles and sweetmeats. Course followed course, the progression broken only by a flurry of speeches and droshas. At length the meal ended with platters of sweets and confections made, no doubt, by the expert confectioner brought in for the occasion to create the spun-sugar sculptures of eagles that decorated each table. Dry whole spices were served round to help the digestion, and not long afterwards the gathering "benshed" over spiced wine.

From the next room came the sound of the musicians. They had played softly throughout the meal, but now the doors were thrown open, and the music grew in volume, inviting everyone to the dancing. While the women remained at the tables, laughing and chatting, the men went out to continue the festivities. Together Avrohom and Reina went into the room to preside over the celebration.

From a quiet corner Yosef watched Reina and Avrohom sitting side by side, smiling happily at the dancing and at each other. The young men danced and leapt, twisting and turning, twining in and out, growing ever more lively and excited. The singing and handclapping all but drowned the genteel tones of the lutes and recorders. Yosef found himself smiling at the contented couple. He was still smiling when someone tried to pull him out of his recess to join in the dancing. Resisting only a little, he let himself be led along. But as he neared the dancers Yosef felt a strangeness; he sensed, rather than saw, the sudden restraint his presence cast on the rejoicing. His smile flickered out.

He dragged his arm free of his jovial captor and went from the hall into the courtyard. It was very dark there; the stars that had sprinkled the night sky only a little while before had been blotted out by clouds. A fine, misty rain had begun to fall. Yosef stood hatless in it, staring into the darkness. From behind him the sounds of revelry flowed out of the hall, washing around him like a tidal flood, yet leaving him untouched and dry.

He had been a fool, forgetting for even a few moments how he was set apart. He thought bitterly that he could not even celebrate his own sister's chatuna without spoiling it. In front of him the iron gate leading out of the courtyard gleamed dully, drawing him towards the street that lay black and silent beyond it. He wanted that darkness, that cloak of invisibility. Slowly he moved forward into the shadows.

For most of the night he roamed aimlessly through the deserted streets of Milano unchallenged, unmet. Even the footpads left him alone, as though he really had become invisible. Sometime in the gray predawn he let himself into Mona Benvenida's boarding-house and went softly up the stairs without waking anyone.

As he changed he realized he had left his cloak at the Salzmanns' house; until then he had not felt the cold. He went as usual to shacharith, and to the banking-house, and worked as diligently as ever. Shimon and Dovid were a bit surprised to see him there so early, but they said nothing; and when he went upstairs to Frau Salzmann for his cloak, he accepted without comment her remark that "one shouldn't be so mazed with simcha that he forgets to take care of himself."

But if Yosef's simcha was marred, the rest of the Jews of Milano rejoiced wholeheartedly not only at seeing an orphan satisfactorily married, but with the expectation that Reina's unhappiness was behind her. Every night another family gave the new couple sheva brochos, families Yosef scarcely knew but who felt close to Reina. Dutifully he attended each night's feasting; dutifully he smiled and exchanged pleasantries; dutifully he appeared at his desk each day. He was grateful for work. He did not feel adequate to further socializing.

All through that week Yosef found his thoughts wandering toward Reina's departure. Don't be silly, he told himself, you hardly know her any more and you only see her on Shabath; there's no sense in getting worked up for only four hours a week of missing someone you can hardly talk to anyway. For a short while he could keep himself firmly logical, thinking that way; and then he could not bear it any longer, for Reina was all he had, and he was losing her. He bit the inside of his cheek savagely and turned his face aside to keep the ledger book dry.

The night he had spent roaming the dark streets of Milano had started a heaviness deep in his chest. At the sheva brochos and at home where Mona Benvenida could hear, he stifled the cough that developed. He remembered that cough; he knew it from a year ago when he had brought it with him as he entered Mona Benvenida's door for the first time. Recalling her treatment of the cough, he did not want to give way to it, to be robbed of a single one of his remaining minutes with Reina.

With something like relief Yosef found himself at last in the street outside the Salzmanns' house, his hand on the shoulder of his new brother-in-law. Cloaked and hooded against the weather, Reina clung to his left hand as they stood looking at the wagon laden with gifts and household necessities. He had spoken all the conventional good wishes; he could not trust himself to say anything further to Avrohom. Behind him he could hear the elder Conats taking their leave of the Salzmanns. There was a quick pressure on his right hand as Avrohom left him to say farewell to Reina.

Reina held Yosef's hands. It was as difficult for her to speak as it was for him. At last she said, pleadingly, "Let Mona Benvenida look after you, Yosef. I can't bear to think of you on your own. I wanted to do so much for you."

"I'll manage. You don't need to worry about me."

"Try to be sensible — " Her voice broke. She bit her lip, looking up at him. "Don't get wet, you know how all your colds go to your chest. And try to remember that people have feelings." She rested her cheek against his shoulder, briefly. "And write, and come to visit us."

"When the weather is better." He watched her climb into her

place in the wagon.

Ser Rafoel said nothing; only he kissed Yosef on both cheeks and embraced him and held his arms for a moment in a firm grip that was full of compassion. And then, all at once, they were in the wagon and it was swaying ponderously down the street and out of sight and Yosef was alone outside the marble doorway of Herr Salzmann's bank.

Coming to himself with a start, Yosef returned to his desk and his ledgers as if nothing out of the ordinary had happened, as if he had not that hour watched his last link with the half-remembered life in Spain disappear with his blessing.

That evening he let himself cough unhindered and Mona Benvenida heard him at it and scolded him to bed. He went meekly, not out of obedience or because he wanted to be fussed over, but because he did not care any more what he did. Whatever was done to him he accepted unresistingly, staring unseeing at the blank plastered wall opposite the foot of his bed, and saying little.

Eventually Mona Benvenida allowed him out, and he went back to work. From time to time the close-written figures would blur and he would gaze in front of him with unfocussed eyes, but he was conscientious the rest of the time. If Herr Salzmann noticed the odd lapses he understood, and made allowances.

Only four hours a week, Yosef had told himself; but he had not understood how his whole life had been built around those four hours, how his weeks had passed featureless except for that time he spent with Reina. Now Shabath afternoons, too, faded into that monotonous unvarying rhthym of his existence, drifting away as he dozed fitfully or wandered aimlessly from room to room, kept indoors by the winter chill.

Considerate and sympathetic, his fellow-boarders made friendly overtures again, though Yosef had never welcomed their companionship. Yosef could scarcely rouse himself to respond. Rebuffed once more, Shimon and Dovid shrugged and retired, resigned and just a trifle resentful, and left Yosef to himself.

But Yosef was not altogether alone. More and more the sack of coins deep inside the chip-carved chest in his room preyed on his mind. The promise he could not keep gnawed at the back of his thoughts, and where once he had dreamt of São Tome only occasionally, now his sleep was haunted every night by the faces of the children of the island of crocodiles.

Early one Friday morning when everyone was seated at the breakfast table, one of the boarders gave vent to a gargantuan yawn. The other clerk answered it with one of his own.

"I know how you feel," he commented, reaching for more cheese.

"Haven't you two been sleeping well?" inquired Mona Benvenida.

"Oh, *we're* doing fine," replied Shimon, with a glance at Yosef. "It's the interruptions."

Yosef was only half-listening as he prodded the food on his plate and wondered how little he could eat without attracting Mona Benvenida's attention. He had not had much of an appetite for a long time.

"I don't understand," the landlady was saying.

"It's him." Shimon bit decisively into his bagel. "He's got to be the loudest dreamer in Milano. Wakes us up almost every night, sometimes twice. I realize that you have to get along with all kinds of people, but I think there are limits."

Yosef, his eyes on his plate, heard Mona Benvenida ask, "How long has this been going on?"

"Must be since the beginning of the winter," said Shimon vaguely.

"A little after Chanuka time or so," supplemented Dovid.

Yosef slid off the end of the bench and picked up his crutch. The next thing would be a public questioning, he was sure. He had gotten as far as the hall when Mona Benvenida caught up.

"Have you been having nightmares?" she demanded bluntly.

Yosef looked at the floor. "Yes." She might be well-meaning and good-hearted, but he was not going to spill his feelings into her lap. He had to escape soon anyway or he would be late to work.

"I'll give you an extra quilt. You're probably cold; it isn't surprising, you're so thin. If you ate more it would warm you up, too. I'll make sure you have some chicken soup tonight."

"Thank you." He made his escape. He did not want chicken

soup or anything else, but he did not want to argue with her, either. The soup would go to waste, and that was a pity, but there was no stopping Mona Benvenida. There was no stopping the nightmares, either.

The day continued in the same track it had begun. On the way to work Yosef missed his footing in the mixture of slush and rubbish that slicked the street, and fell full-length in the filth. Although he cleaned off what he could, he was glad to have his small room where he could work unseen. The mishap made him late, and Herr Salzmann commented disapprovingly, being in a mood as grim as the overcast sky because he had discovered gross errors in Yosef's work of a few days earlier. Horrified, Yosef devoted the morning to correcting the mistakes and rechecking his previous two weeks' work.

It was a tedious labor. The nightmares had broken his sleep so badly that time after time Yosef realized with a start that he had nodded off for a minute or two. Not until early afternoon could he begin work for that Friday. Only half-awake, Yosef tried to hurry; the quill split and blotted the page; and Herr Salzmann emerged from his office to see Yosef alternately trying to rub his eyes into wakefulness and repair the damage to the ledger.

The beard that had flowed so expansively over Herr Salzmann's chest looked wiry and aggressive. A stern expression hardened his face and the generous mouth thinned. Rising, Yosef shot him a glance of hopeless desperation.

"What's gotten into you, boy?" snapped the banker. "You used to be so dependable." He gave Yosef a keen look. Almost at once the man's face softened. "Is something wrong with you? Your face looks sucked in on itself." Without waiting for an answer he ordered, "Put these things away and go home; it's only an hour's difference, anyway. And tell Mona Benvenida that I want her to take a good look at you."

But it was erev Shabath and Mona Benvenida was busy; Yosef said nothing. At the seuda that evening he took care to be unobtrusive, although he could not, in the end, escape the chicken soup she forced on him. Too exhausted to delay going to sleep, he went to his room and got ready for bed in a dazed, fumbling way.

The first of the nightmares came only an hour later.

He saw Reina, drawing away from him slowly, slowly, ever further until she was hardly a speck in the distance, while he dragged after her calling, "Reina! Come back! I need you!" until she was gone.

Voices, a dry rustle on the wind: "She left you as you left us, Yosef." Whispering, whispering: "Where are the ships, Yosef?"

Faces, one after another. Saadya: " ... can't allow it ... too risky ... "

His own voice: " ... the ships will take you all ... "

Eyes, burning eyes in a throng of faces, and the voices: "the ships, the ships, Yosef! We're dying! Where are the ships?"

He flung out of the dream to wakefulness. In his throat there was a dry scream starting. He lay rigid with guilt, wide-eyed and unmoving, afraid, as always, to fall asleep again. But he was too tired to resist drifting off. Dream after dream jerked him awake, shuddering. He had never had such a dreadfilled night.

By morning he had had an hour's unbroken sleep around dawn, but his heart was still beating frantically and he could not seem to catch his breath. Half-asleep, he stumbled to schul and pinched himself awake for long enough to finish the davening and hear Parshas Zachor. Afterwards he went back to Mona Benvenida's table for the second seuda of Shabath, not consciously — he was too tired to think — but automatically because he had done it regularly, like a deliveryman's horse.

After the meal Yosef retired to his room to rest, but he gave up after half an hour, too tense to sleep, too fuzzy-minded to be truly awake.

By the time he came downstairs again the table had been cleared, and the two clerks were learning together out of a sefer that had replaced the dishes on the white cloths. As he passed the door to Mona Benvenida's own apartments, he noticed that it was slightly ajar, and he glimpsed the lady herself, eyes closed, her head leaning against one wing of a high-backed chair, her hands resting in her lap.

Across the black-and-white squares of the floor of the foyer he made his way, took his cloak and fastened it with the buckle at the shoulder, and continued toward the front door. His hand was actually resting on the wooden panels of the door when he remembered that there was nowhere to go any more. He had been unthinkingly following his unvarying routine of so many months: the meal, the short rest, the walk to the Salzmanns' house, an afternoon with Reina. But Reina was gone.

Reaching up, he slowly undid the buckle at the shoulder, catching the heavy material as it slipped off. It had not yet dried completely from the morning's drizzle; he could not lay it away in the chest yet, so he hung it up where it had been before. He did not know anybody. He could not learn. He stood where he was and wondered what to do.

From somewhere in the house he heard footsteps approaching, tapping on the marble floor. "Yosef?"

He stared blankly at Mona Benvenida as though he had forgotten who she was. "Shabath shalom, Madonna," he said vaguely, trying to bring his thoughts into focus.

"I want to speak to you." She led the way to the door he had seen ajar and motioned him in. Leaving the door open, she sat down and nodded to Yosef to do the same.

As he obeyed he glanced around this room he had never seen. Although it was as airy as his own, it was sparsely furnished, and with pieces that were by no means the best, that were nicked and dented with long use. Besides the tall chair he had seen earlier, two of the usual backless seats, a table and a bench stood in the large room. On the floor a worn carpet kept the chill of the stone from the feet. Yet against one wall he saw a bookcase filled with more seforim than he had ever found in one place.

Following his gaze, Mona Benvenida smiled. "For many years my husband served in the house of Yechiel da Pisa, in Firenze, as the tutor for his children and to copy seforim for him, as well as odds and ends of paperwork. Naturally, he made copies of the seforim for himself, too. He used to work at this table and learn on it with our sons; our daughters and I used to sit sewing to the sound of their Torah. All the children are grown and married with families of their own, now. Since my husband died, no one learns on the table any more, and the seforim sit collecting dust. I couldn't sell them, though I might have been able to live comfortably on what they would have brought, and not had to take boarders; but so much of my husband is in those seforim that I think I would have sold everything else first before I could bring myself to offer the seforim to anyone."

She leaned back and closed her eyes. "My dear, I'm an old woman and perhaps I've become a bit odd, but I miss having someone learning on that table. Now that you have these hours free on Shabos afternoons, maybe you'd be willing to spare a little time to oblige me?" Her eyes opened and fixed on him.

"I?" Yosef made a scornful sound. "Once, I might have been able to learn well enough to satisfy you, but now? Since my accident I'm like the man who had to have something repeated four hundred times before he got it. I'm sorry." He shifted in his chair and began to get up.

"But surely you learn something, anyway." protested Mona Benvenida. "*Mishnayos? Menorath Hamaor? Ayn Yaakov?* When do you read over the parshas hashavua? Or prepare for shiurim?"

"I sit at the shiur between mincha and maariv in the schul, but I don't get much out of it."

"I see." She sounded disappointed but sympathetic. "Well, I'm a silly old woman. Forgive me." She surged to the door and threw it wide. "Enjoy your afternoon."

His afternoon. What would he do with his afternoon? He might as well satisfy an old woman's whim as waste the time with nightmares. She would be content if he merely read the sedra aloud. What had Ser Rafoel said? "If you threw yourself into Torah, it wouldn't matter if you remembered nothing," He need not go even that far.

He looked up at Mona Benvenida, waiting patiently by the door. "If simply reading the parsha out loud would be enough, I could do that."

"Of course!" She nodded so vigorously her wimple flapped like a great white bird about to take flight. Moving quickly to the seforim, she extracted a Chumash and placed it, open to the proper sedra, on the table. "I won't sit over you," she said; "I'll be in another room."

When he had seated himself on the bench, with the sefer open in front of him, she stood looking at him from an inner doorway for a few minutes. "Yes, that's how it ought to be," she said softly. "The table was lonely; the seforim were lonely; and maybe a foolish old woman was lonely, too."

Hesitantly he began to read. ואתה תצוה את־בני ישראל ויקחו ... ... אליך שמן זית זך. At first he understood most of the words, but as soon as he reached the description of the garments of the kohanim he was lost in a maze of forgotten terms.

What's the sense of just saying words? he asked himself. But he had promised Mona Benvenida her performance; he would not stop. Doggedly he plowed ahead, disciplining himself to keep on through one meaningless pasuk after another.

"... if you promise me you'll discipline yourself to learn Torah ... " Yosef heard Ser Rafoel's voice. Discipline? I used to be disciplined, Yosef thought, and what good did it do me? What do I have to discipline myself for? To pretend to myself that I still have my self-respect? Why pretend? I'm crippled and sickly and thick-headed. What use am I?

He dragged his eyes back to the page. "... ufitachta alav ... " he went on, "kodesh laShem". Holy to Hashem. Comprehension struck him. This is where the kohanim are consecrated to Hashem, he thought, where they become more than ordinary people because they've been set aside for their special duties: they become kohanim, kodesh laShem.

Raising his head he gazed toward the light that filtered through the translucent windowpanes. Kodesh laShem, he said softly. All Jews are kdoshim laShem. There is a maimed, useless person named Yosef; but there is another Yosef who is a Jew with different tasks that have little to do with the body that houses him. My self-discipline was all for myself, for my own goals, like the Jews I scorned who disciplined themselves only to be fit for tennis.

"The ikar is Torah." It was Ser Rafoel's voice again. "If you threw yourself into Torah — " And there was Saadya quoting the Menorath Hamaor: "The people of our times are hungry for food and thirsty for wine; they do not hunger or thirst for the word of Hashem."

Yosef sighed. Disciplining himself for Torah, for learning and mitzvoth and midoth — that was an aim far beyond his own goals that had been so easily reached. But I have to discipline myself in Torah now, he thought, to use that part of me that is kodesh laShem, because other than that I am nothing but a disintegrating body that is hardly worth tolerating.

Finishing the sedra at last, he drew a long breath of relief, like a swimmer coming up for air. Every week, he thought, Shabath after Shabath, I'm going to have to come in here and drag through the parsha, not for Mona Benvenida but for myself. I'll have to force myself to learn during the week in the evenings, even just a little. Maybe the *Menorath Hamaor*; Saadya was fond of it, and he was only twelve when he learned it. I might be able to cope.

In the days that followed, Mona Benvenida appeared to be gratified to find her sitting-room table occupied more often than on Shabos alone. Few words passed between her and Yosef. Withdrawn, uncommunicative, Yosef came to learn and departed. He did not enjoy learning. How could he, finding every word a stumbling block, knowing he would recall almost nothing? He learned because it was the only field of endeavor open to him, and because he found life insupportable without something to strive for.

He told Reina nothing of this in the vague impersonal letters he wrote. He felt he hardly knew her, that she was no longer his sister but Avrohom's wife. In return she sent cheerful chatty notes that might have been written to anyone:

> " ... We are all well and happy and busy setting up house. The weather has been no doubt the same as yours. There was no decent salt to be had this month and we had to use the dirty gray stuff just like the peasants. There really is nothing else to say. Are you well? Are you taking care of yourself? ... "

Reina loved him still, but she was not comfortable writing letters.

Having paid off his debt, Yosef found he had more money than he needed for his few wants. He thought of Avrohom, learning for as long as he could afford to, and Reina, managing carefully to run her household on as little as possible. Saving up the excess salary for a month, Yosef sent it to Reina, pleased that he could help out. He unfolded her letter in return:

" ... so we will keep what you have sent this time and we are grateful for your gift, but you must not make it a habit. You must think of your own future because we will not be able to help you out very much if it ever becomes necessary, chas v'shalom, although you know there is always a place for you with us ... "

CHAPTER FOURTEEN

WINTER PASSED INTO SPRING, spring into summer. The glutinous mud of the roads dried and baked in the sun to pottery firmness. With the good weather, Mona Benvenida's grandchildren arrived, sent by their parents to delight their grandmother for a week or two at a time. They had arrived the previous year, too, Yosef's first in that house, but he had kept so much to his own room that he had hardly noticed them, except as minor disturbances at some meals. Now, however, he sat exposed to them as he tried to learn.

It was a strange sensation to have children around him again, strange and painful. He was reminded too forcibly of his unfulfilled pledge to rescue the children on São Tome. That memory and his dislike for children kept him remote from them, aloof and unresponsive. He was displeased and close to being annoyed when his concentration was broken by a small curly head that popped up under his elbow.

"Will you show me alef?" demanded the child.

Yosef glanced down with distaste at the little boy of about five who craned up from under the edge of the table. He was just the age of the children he remembered who distracted one from more important matters and got underfoot when one was in a hurry. About to give the child a brusque reply, Yosef stopped. What important matters did he have? And what did he have to hurry to? He could not move that fast, anyway. And they were, after all, company of a sort. So long ago Reina had said that he could not see how terribly alone he was. So terribly alone. The child was still waiting patiently for an answer.

"All right," Yosef said at last, "come up. Sit here by me."

Obediently the child joined Yosef on the bench and was shown the letter. "Now beis," he ordered. Yosef obliged. Leaning down, the child peered under the edge of the table and said, "You can, too, Miri."

"What, another one of you?"

The little boy nodded. "My little sister is there. She's almost three."

"Does she want to sit here, too?" Yosef did not know whether to feel besieged or amused.

There was a whispered conference under the table, and the curly head reappeared, followed by that of a little girl, her fine hair tied back severely. Standing on the side of her brother that was farther from Yosef, she leaned shyly against the bench.

"Do you want to sit here?" Yosef asked her. She gave her head a tiny shake and pressed against her brother.

"She's afraid of your face and your arm," explained the little boy.

Yosef gave the child a stricken look and turned his head away. As clearly as if it had just happened, he could see cold food spilling out of a dropped bowl, a boy jerking away in terror. "I don't blame her," he said quietly, not wanting to frighten her more.

Yosef felt the boy slide off the bench. A moment later he heard him say reproachfully to his sister, "You made him sad, Miri. That was very naughty."

A sorrowful sniff answered him. The bench quivered slightly as a small body squirmed up onto it. Yosef felt a light touch on his left arm and a ticklish whisper in his ear: "I'm sorry."

Turning his head in the direction of the whisper, he saw the little girl balancing on the edge of the seat, one small hand resting on his shoulder, the other supporting her against the table. Carefully he put his good hand across to steady her.

She touched her fingers to his scarred face timidly, as lightly as the flutter of a moth. "Does it hurt?" she asked.

"Not any more."

In deep silence she regarded him intently. "Are you good?" she asked at last.

"Sometimes. Not always."

"Neither am I," she admitted frankly. Lifting her hand over his face, she scrutinized him for some time longer, then overwhelmed Yosef by laying her cheek against his in wordless sympathy. Sliding confidently into his lap, she grasped the Chumash. "Show me alef."

As he bent over the sefer with the little girl, his stern expression softened. Patiently he pointed out one alef after another. She had an insatiable appetite for alefs, although the letter beis did not interest her at all.

"Alef!" she exclaimed, delighted with each one. "Alef!" She pointed to one by herself. "Alef!" Twisting around to give Yosef a brilliant smile, she slid off his lap as suddenly as she had arrived and vanished under the table. Her brother, at the doorway to the inner room, beckoned to her.

"Miri!" called Mona Benvenida from within. The little girl trotted after her brother.

Yosef returned to the words in front of him, but instead of the page he saw Miri's considering face and felt again her cheek against his. Hardly aware of what he did, he touched that side of his face with wondering fingers. She was so straightforward: she had made him feel sad, so she was naughty; she was sorry and tried to make him feel happier, so she was good. Nobody had told her it wasn't polite to stare; she stared until she was satisfied, and then she accepted him as he was and did not need to stare any more. He thought of adults and their sidelong glances and murmuring behind their hands.

From the other room he could hear Miri saying proudly, "I know alef!"

"Do you? Let's see," Mona Benvenida replied. "Which is alef? You do know! Who taught you?"

"L'uomo brutto," said Miri.

L'uomo brutto. The ugly man. From someone else that description would have hurt. But Miri meant it simply as identification, the way one would say "the boy with red hair" or "the girl in the blue dress", pointing out a person by some superficial tag. It had nothing to do with how she felt about him.

Not realizing how well her deep voice carried, Mona

Benvenida was saying in a low tone, "You must remember always to be very kind and gentle with him because he has been hurt."

"I know that," the little boy said disdainfully: "his face and his arm and his leg."

"That's what you can see," said his grandmother. "But he has been hurt here as well" — Yosef did not need to guess where on her grandson her hand rested — "and that takes longer to get better than anything else."

Something tight within Yosef eased: he relaxed from the tension of being constantly on guard against people's insensitivity. Mona Benvenida understood; he was safe here. She had known that he had felt alone and embattled; and she had given him a refuge.

Remember that people have feelings. Reina's words crept into his thoughts. How had Mona Benvenida known what he needed? Had she sensed it out of simple motherliness? Or had she, too, been hurt? He tried to think back to all the conversations he had had with her, concerned that he might inadvertently have said something to wound her more. There were so many words to sift through; he could not remember them all, in any case. And perhaps she had not been hurt at all. He sighed. It was so hard to think that minutely. It was so peaceful here in her quiet sitting-room. And he was so very tired.

Inch by inch the late afternoon sun stole across the table, creeping over the open Chumash as if surprised to find it not in use, playing over Yosef's head pillowed on his arm, lighting up his gaunt face, tranquil with sleep untroubled by dreams. The children tiptoed past him on their way to play outside; but Mona Benvenida stood gazing down at him as he slept, the child who, more than any of her own children, needed someone to care for him.

On weekdays when Yosef returned from work, Miri and Yom Tov, the little boy, ran to him and brought him into their grandmother's sitting-room. When he ate, they sat one on either side of him and picked the choicest bits from the serving platter, laying the pieces solicitously on his trencher. To please the children, he ate what they gave him, scarcely realizing how much more he consumed than he had before. In the evenings, after

Mona Benvenida had seen to it that her grandchildren left him in peace for an hour or so of learning, he entertained them until their bedtime, saying silly things and being an appreciative audience for their happy nonsense.

He glanced up once to see Mona Benvenida regarding him steadily. It did not make him bristle, as someone else's gaze would have. With a smile he asked, "What is it, Madonna?"

Her face creased benignly in return. "I was thinking that you have a very pleasant smile, my dear, and that I never used to see it."

Still smiling, Yosef looked down and stroked Miri's smooth head and Yom Tov's curly one. "I suppose I didn't find much to smile about before I knew these two. It's funny," he went on softly, "I was so sure I didn't like children."

"Yet you're a born teacher; you have the patience and the love for little ones." Mona Benvenida shook her head. "You're wasted in an office. Why don't you teach, as my husband did?"

Yosef's smile faded. "Madonna, your husband was a lamdan. I couldn't teach much beyond alef-beith because I know so little myself. It's a pity; I would have liked it." He stared in front of him briefly, watching a fleeting dream fade, then gave himself a slight shake. Smiling up at Mona Benvenida again, he shrugged. "Never mind. It doesn't matter."

After an extra week's stay, Miri and Yom Tov departed, to be replaced by others of Mona Benvenida's grandchildren. Each time there was the children's investigation, then the acceptance, and Yosef grew accustomed to it knowing that the end would be the same as it had been with Miri: friendship and compassion.

With adults, however, he was as wary as before, avoiding people he did not know, reserved and short-spoken. At the banking house he was grateful for his inconspicuous corner overlooked by the clients in the grand waiting-room.

He was surprised when he found Dovid next to him, nudging him with his elbow. "Lucky you. Your turn."

Yosef raised his head from the interminable accounts. Through the main room, towards his tiny office, came a man in early middle age, well-muscled and very handsome. His hair and beard flowed into each other and his bushy eyebrows overhung his eyes like awnings.

"The Sforzas' pet artist," explained the clerk. "Il Moro doesn't pay him very regularly, and he's got an expensive bee in his bonnet about flying. He's been here other times. Usually he has to wait, so he sketches us. He hasn't seen you before."

"I don't need him to tell me I look like a freak." Slipping from his bench, Yosef made for an inner door that led to a corridor.

"You there! Wait!" came a commanding voice.

Half-turning toward the right, Yosef threw the man a look of both resentment and entreaty.

"Excellent!" said the man as he whisked out paper and crayon. "Stay like that; it won't be long." He was at work before he had finished speaking, the crayon oddly at home in his left hand.

Ignoring both artist and subject, the other two clerks attended once again to their clients. In the silence, Yosef could hear the diligent scratching of their quills and the soft whisper of the artist's crayon on the paper. Held in his place by the artist's authoritative command, Yosef stayed leaning on his crutch, motionless. Sunlight streamed through the tall windows in a great broad band, the dust motes within it sparkling like particles of gold.

"All right; you can go, now."

Without so much as a glance at the artist, Yosef returned to his place and resumed his work.

From the counter Dovid gave him a curious stare. "Aren't you going to look at it?"

"I have work to do."

"It's all right; Salzmann won't mind. He finds the fellow entertaining." The clerk gave him a friendly nod. "Go on, we all do."

With a sigh of resignation Yosef left his place a second time and went to where the man stood gazing at him.

Holding out the paper, the artist asked, "Do you want it or shall I keep it?"

"I don't care." Yosef did not look at the sketch.

The man examined the drawing. "It could come in useful for

a fresco of 'Our Lord' healing the sick or some such thing."

"If it's all the same to you, then," said Yosef, holding out his hand for the portrait, "I'd rather have the picture than have my face on some monastery wall."

"Don't you want to see it?"

"I know what I look like." Yosef's voice was bitter.

"Do you?" With a sudden movement the man thrust the study of Yosef's face directly at him.

Familiar features stared up at him from the paper. He saw the face of a half-grown youth, a face whose wounds had healed to hard, tight sunken scars that pulled the upper lip into a grimace and wrenched one eye into the suggestion of a leer. It was a face that was, to Yosef, monstrous in its mutilation, the face of a pirate or a beggar. Yet as he examined it, the face seemed neither hideous nor grotesque. There was a directness, an openness in its expression. The mouth was firm but not harsh. The gaze of the eyes compelled respect. It was not a handsome face, but it had dignity. Yosef had never seen himself like this.

He could feel the artist's delight in exploring the unfamiliar contours, the angles and shapes and planes: a child's sense of wonder. The man had no interest in whether the face was ugly or beautiful, only in capturing the subtlety of line and shadow.

"You made it look as if — as if it were a face worth having," Yosef said in wonder.

"I drew what was there. Every face is worth having. To an artist, every face is worth drawing. I like to think that I see as the Creator does: that every face is beautiful in its own way, beautiful in its individuality. Do you understand me?"

Yosef continued to stare at the portrait. If it had been someone else, he thought, not himself, he would have liked him. Into his mind came another face, vivid and mobile, of a child on São Tome; and he could hear himself shouting, "Don't call yourself ugly!"

Every face is beautiful.

Once, there had been a boy named Yosef who was handsome and whole, but that was a different person, as separate from himself as all the thousands of other Yosefs in the world. He was a Yosef with an arm and a leg that did not work, and a ruined face that was worth having.

Without warning, Saadya's words came back to him: "You're not trapped inside your body, Yosef, you're trapped inside your mind." The strange thing was that they had both been right: he *had* been trapped, though neither of them had seen how, trapped into being elegant and dignified and capable and respected, trapped into being like Papa. No: trying to *be* Papa, until the accident made it impossible. He had been whole and strong and handsome, and he had been trapped. Now he was scarred and crippled and he was free.

He smiled at the handsome artist as he handed the paper back, a sweeping, soaring smile like a bird's flight. "It's a very good picture, Ser — "

"Leonardo." The man tucked the paper away. "If Herr Salzmann lends me what I need, I'm planning more of my flying experiments. Would you like to come along to watch?"

Yosef glanced down at his leg. Flying, for someone who could hardly walk? So? What did that matter? he asked himself. He laughed quietly and looked at the artist again. "I might," he said. "Why not?"

He thought that perhaps the man Leonardo was about to say something when the door to Herr Salzmann's office opened. The banker's voice was booming jovially, "One of our clerks is a Spanish refugee, too. You ought to meet him. Yosef!"

As Yosef moved obediently toward the office, Herr Salzmann and his visitor emerged. The man beside the banker looked competent but tired, as though he would have welcomed a quiet place to settle and a peaceful life.

"Herr Gascon is hoping to re-establish the business he used to have in Spain," explained Herr Salzmann. With a cordial nod to the man at his side, he asked, "And your family? How do they like moving to Milano?"

"I have no family." Herr Gascon's voice was heavy. "I lost my family in Portugal. My wife died in the king's prison while we waited to be sold into slavery, and my children — " He stopped for a moment before he could continue. "They took my children from me. I never found them again. People said that many children were sent to some far tropic island, but — " Leaving his words to trail off, he shook his head. "Sometimes I wonder why I'm bothering to start up the business again."

The look the man had was not tiredness, Yosef understood; the man was beaten down like grain after the hail. Within him Yosef felt a quick sharp pain at the man's desolation. He knew that lost emptiness. Wanting to help, he asked, "Did you ever hear the name of the island? Might it have been São Tomé?"

Life sprang into the dull eyes. "You know of the place?"

Do I know of the place, Yosef thought. Do I know of that place where I left my friends, where I left whatever remains of the eight hundred children? Do I know of the place that marked me for the rest of my life? "I was there," he said.

The man's hands snatched eagerly at Yosef's doublet. "My Chava, my little Eliezer — did you see them?"

"Senhor." Yosef's voice was gentle. "There were eight hundred children. I couldn't know them all — I was there only a short time."

"You were rescued; perhaps they were rescued." The man was desperate for hope.

It was hard to disappoint him. Shaking his head slightly, Yosef said, "They were not rescued; I was not rescued. I escaped." He did not mention Reina.

"You ... escaped?" Herr Gascon's grip on Yosef's doublet shifted to the fabric at his neck. "You escaped, and you reached safety. And what have you done for the children you left behind?"

Yosef could not meet his eyes. What have I done? he asked himself. There is a little sack of golden coins in the bottom of my chest, doing no one any good. I did my best, and it was not enough. What have I done for them? He turned his face aside. "Nothing," he said, very low. He felt the material at his throat tighten in the man's hands.

"Nothing?" Herr Gascon's face twisted. "You came here, you were safe," he said hoarsely, "but you cared nothing for eight hundred children? You didn't know their names. You didn't lift a finger to help them. You just washed them out of your mind like sweat out of a handkerchief?"

His fingers clutched hungrily at the fabric, gathering in

doublet and laces and shirt, pulling Yosef towards him. Suddenly he roared, "You have the chutzpa to lounge here in a marble office and swaddle yourself in silks and velvets while my children wear rags and die of fever at the end of the earth? What kind of Jew are you, without chesed, without rachamim? You —!" His voice was thick with contempt and disgust.

Without warning Yosef felt his clothing released. Caught off balance, he did not see the man's open hand blurring towards him. But he felt the savage blow to his face, heard the sharp smack as the hand struck against his scarred cheek. If the wall had not been only a few inches behind him, Yosef would have fallen. White-faced, he struggled erect again to face the man. For an instant their eyes met.

Shaken, Yosef caught his breath. He had never seen such eyes: staring, wild, consumed with longing for the lost family, inconsolable.

I drove myself, Yosef wanted to tell him, I tried but I was prevented, I tried but I did not succeed. Forgive me. He felt the tears in his eyes. Forgive me. Forgive me. "Forgive me." He hardly realized he had spoken aloud.

"Forgive?" raged the man. "Forgive betrayal? Forgive abandonment?" His hands, outstretched, trembled. Herr Salzmann laid his own hand on his arm.

He can never forgive me, Yosef thought. There is nothing left in him but grief and hatred and madness, and I have stirred it up again, standing brazen before him, surrounded by uncaring opulence. He looked down at the heavy velvet of his clothing, looked around him at the marble and fresco and gilding. Slowly he turned away, moving past his desk, through the small door behind the counter and into the ostentatious reception room. He made his way among the waiting clients, frozen into uneasy silence, and out between the massive wooden doors. He went carefully down the steps, one by one, because he found he was shaking all over and he was afraid he would fall.

No one came after him. No one called him back. He stood briefly by the fine marble archway of Herr Salzmann's bank; then he plunged into the stream of people in front of him in the street.

Halfway through supper that evening Frau Salzmann

glanced at a note that had been handed her and made a puzzled sound. "Why should Mona Benvenida think I know where Yosef is?" she asked her husband.

Herr Salzmann's face fell. "There was a most distressing incident at the bank today." He cleared his throat.

Frau Salzmann sat up straight in her high-backed chair as her husband told her what had passed. "Why couldn't you have sent somebody after him?" she begged, distraught.

"After being publicly shamed? I thought he wanted to be left alone! We all did! Wouldn't you?" bellowed Herr Salzmann, as upset as his wife.

There was a silence. "Reina!" Frau Salzmann said suddenly. "He must have gone to Reina! You'll have to write immediately and explain, and tell Yosef that that poor man understands now."

"Of course." Herr Salzmann mopped his face with relief.

But Yosef had not gone to Reina.

In the marble office the quills scratched restlessly without him. In vain Mona Benvenida listened for his step at the door. His room remained untenanted; the bench in her sitting-room stood empty once more, and under the table he had learned on her grandchildren bickered. After a while Mona Benvenida closed the door between her sitting-room and the hall with the black-and-white marble floor. Some weeks later she cleared his room and eventually let it to someone else. For a long time she kept the contents of the chip-carved chest, but at last she packaged up his belongings and sent them to Reina: the fine clothing he had not wanted, the printed Chumash Ser Rafoel had given him, and a small pouch of florins and ducats and lire that had never been enough.

Despite the Salzmanns' exhaustive inquiries, there was no word of Yosef. Whether he had been murdered by some footpad or had merely left Milano on a stray farm-cart, they could not discover. They knew only that Yosef had vanished.

CHAPTER FIFTEEN

FF THE COAST OF AFRICA, on a half-forgotten island that was neither successful enough nor disastrous enough to attract the king's notice, a young village spread itself cautiously across the hillsides: still there were children on São Tome.

Sheltering from a shower under a wild-mango tree, Luis and Chanan stood side by side looking out over a broad meadow. They presented a strong contrast: Luis, stocky and broad-shouldered, was a full head shorter than Chanan, who had grown into a young giant.

"It just seems such a waste to leave it, when it would be so easy to clear and plant it," said Luis tentatively, "but you'd be the one in charge, so if it bothers you, I'll forget about it." He rubbed his young beard uncomfortably.

Chanan considered the question, sniffing absently. A tall Kino tree nearby was in bloom, its cluster of pale yellow flowers lavishing vanilla fragrance on the moist air. "The place doesn't do anything to me," he said at last. "It looks pretty different in any case, with all the shrubby undergrowth. No, it's only when I think about Yosef that I — " He broke off. "It doesn't seem possible that it's not six years yet since it happened; it feels like about a thousand. What did you want to plant here?"

"Not sugar cane!"

They both laughed. It was a standing joke: they had all had enough of sugar cane, working in Don Alvaro's fields.

"Maize, I think," Luis went on. "Since I got that sack of seed from the new lands, I've been keeping an eye on how it does. I think it shows a lot of promise: easy to grow, good yield, plenty of ways to cook it. I'd like to see it become our cash crop, too."

"Dreamer."

"No, I don't think so. Chanan. We've accomplished a lot in the last couple of years. I can really see us earning enough to buy us all passage back to civilization."

"If the new donatario lets us go."

"Well, that's not in his hands, anyway; it's up to the Ribono shel Olam."

The rain subsided to a few heavy drops rattling on the leaves above them. Luis looked across the field to the waterfall and the begonia-carpeted rocks at its foot. Even if it did not affect Chanan, being here made him feel uneasy. But the maize would change it. He could picture it now, standing tall with its drooping leaves and stiffly upright ears, all the way to the river's edge.

Together they started back up the hill, along the road of hard-packed earth, its top layer a little muddy from the shower, but drying quickly. Six years before, it had been scarcely more than a trail.

"I think you want to get back more than any of us," Chanan commented as they walked.

"You know my parents were killed because they were Marranos."

"Yes."

"What happened to them made me want to be openly, completely Jewish. I don't know why; I just felt it ought to be that way."

"Maybe to make their deaths worthwhile?" suggested Chanan.

"Maybe. I don't analyze things the way Saadya does. But I don't have any dreams other than leaving São Tome. Everything I do to build up the colony is only to make us prosperous enough to escape it."

"I know." For a time Chanan was quiet; then, abruptly, he said, "Saadya wants to see you, Luis."

"What for?" Luis asked, only half-attentive.

Chanan shrugged. "He just gave me the message."

Luis slapped at a mosquito. "I suppose he wants me to find another poseik. I wish he'd realize that we all have to do jobs we don't like from time to time."

"Like?" Chanan was indignant. "It's not a question of 'like',

Luis. You're straightforward and easygoing; you can't even imagine being as intense as Saadya. He thinks. He worries. He's under tremendous pressure to be right, every single time. Can't you feel what it's like never to be allowed even one mistake? How many mistakes have you made since you've been parnes? Dozens? More? You expect to make mistakes, don't you? He can't."

Luis stared. "Why the sudden passionate defense?"

"I'm worried about him." Chanan kept his eyes on the roadway. "He made me move my bed in near his last week. And he had to get himself drunk on palm wine to get to sleep."

The regular tramp of Luis's feet stopped. "What's going on?"

"I don't know." Chanan glanced up. "You're not as close to what's happening as you were before you were married; you live separate from the rest of us. You don't realize how much I deal with just because I'm nearby and you're not. But I can't deal with this."

Luis saw the tiredness in Chanan's face. It was true, he reflected, that he had been letting Chanan do too much while he enjoyed being a husband and a father. And though I owe so much to Saadya, he reproached himself, I've neglected him because I didn't want to be bothered with his pleas to be replaced as lamdan. I don't even know what it is that Chanan can't deal with.

"Chanan," he said. He had been silent for so long that Chanan started at his voice. "If you catch me slacking like this again — "

"I'll let you know." The grin was friendly.

Reaching the compound, they found Saadya sitting in the shade learning from the original Chumash that had come to São Tome with the children. The copies were distributed and well used, but this one volume he never allowed away from himself.

"You wanted to see me?" Luis asked, trying to examine Saadya unobtrusively. He seemed healthy enough.

"Yes; I wanted to show you — " Saadya led Luis into the small thatched hut nearby: Saadya's own quarters. Lifting a solidly-constructed coffer from the floor, Saadya set it carefully on his table and raised the lid.

Luis looked at the interior of the chest with surprise: the whole inner surface was lined with sheets of metal, tin, at a guess. He watched Saadya remove several thin books from the coffer. They were bound clumsily in what seemed to be goatskin; a faint goaty odor still clung to them.

Opening one volume at random, Saadya pointed to the pages covered with writing in his fine, meticulous hand. At the top of the page he had put "Ship: *S. Maria da Esphineiro;* number of children: 102; number of dead: 10." There followed a listing of the ten names with as much information to identify them as he had apparently had available. A few were complete: "Bathya bath Miriam v'Avraham, surname Silvera, born Tortosa, age nine and a half." But on this page and the rest, as Luis turned them over, there were many entries that were pathetically vague: "boy, aged approximately six years, light brown hair with slight curl, believed to have spoken with Barcelona accent."

"I recorded the shipboard deaths first," Saadya explained. "Then the later ones: they have the date of petira written beside them. But after that time that you told me about the very little ones, I started to write down everybody here, with all the information I could dig out of them." He closed the first book and opened another, again lists of names. Here and there, at the end of an entry, he had written "niftar", with the date. "If anyone ever comes," he said hesitantly, "or if someone here leaves … " He let the words fade.

Opening a third book, Saadya went on, "In here are the zmanim, the Jewish and secular dates for all the Yom Tovim and so on, for the next thirteen years. Most of this is Moshe-ben-Nachman's work — you know, the red-haired boy who helps me. He has a marvelous mind: he can take any date you ask for, and tell you the secular date, the day of the week, and I don't know what else besides. The other things are the two original siddurim —I keep the Chumash in here, as well — and a journal of sorts that I've been keeping; it has events and sh'eiloth and my tshuvoth." Without looking at Luis he replaced the volumes in the coffer, secured it, and returned it to its place in silence.

"And the metal keeps insects out, I suppose?" Luis asked.

"Yes."

Luis waited for him to continue, but Saadya had wandered to the doorway and was standing silhouetted against the brightness beyond, facing away from him. "Why did you decide, now, to show me all this?" Luis asked at last.

Saadya seemed to give a tiny jump, as though Luis's voice had recalled him from somewhere else. After darting a quick embarrassed glance at Luis, he did not look at him again as he answered. "I — I don't think I'll be keeping records for much longer," he said, a blunt, abrupt announcement.

So it's the same complaint as usual, thought Luis, annoyed at the wasted visit. "I've told you before, there's nobody else. You can't quit."

"I know that. I'm not quitting." Saadya sounded defensive. "But my — my mind doesn't seem to agree."

In two strides Luis was next to Saadya, laying his hand on Saadya's arm. With a sudden shiver for a reason he could not yet comprehend, Luis asked, "What are you trying to say?"

Saadya twisted and siezed Luis's hand with both of his own, clutching it tightly as if a thing unseen were dragging him away. "Luis — " He looked at Luis's comfortable ordinary face. "I — I keep finding myself in the most wonderful place — a meadow of long grass with wild flowers scattered through it, dry in the summer heat as it used to be at home. Every time I find I'm there I throw myself down in the grass with the feeling that in that place I'm free, unburdened — you can't imagine the relief, Luis — and all I do is lie on my back under the clear blue sky and listen to the chirping and buzzing of the insects, and the birds singing, and wish it would never end and I could stay there always."

"Where is this place?" asked Luis, puzzled.

Saadya stared at him, unblinking. "Nowhere, I think, except in my mind." Some of the coarse linen of Luis's shirt was caught in Saadya's grasp; he rubbed it slowly between his thumb and forefinger, a pinch of reality. "Try to understand, Luis: whenever I'm in that other place I keep remembering that I have a duty, a responsibility, here; and I fight against the part of me that wants to stay, and I come back. But each time the struggle is harder; each time the part of me that wants to stay grows stronger, and the part that remembers duty grows weaker. So I wanted to show you what was needful today, because — because tomorrow I may not be here any longer."

A sea of profound horror seemed to break over Luis. He felt as though he reached across a gulf to speak to Saadya. "Aren't you frightened?" he asked, trying desperately to hold Saadya back from that other place.

Saadya shook his head, only a very slight movement. "Perhaps I should be, but — how can I be afraid of feeling so much at peace?"

Luis could not stop himself picturing the thing Saadya would become in Luis's world: he saw him being dressed in the morning, fed by someone at mealtimes, led unresisting about the compound, standing where he was left, sitting where he was put; a body only, with no will of its own because Saadya was lying in a peaceful meadow where no one would ever find him.

"Saadya, if I could get you off the island, if I found you passage on the next ship, would you — would you stay away from that place? Would it be all right if you left São Tomé?"

"I — don't know."

"Could you keep hold of us here long enough to find out?"

"If it didn't take too much time — maybe." Saadya's voice was tinged with regret as he saw the wonderful dream being wrested from him. "But how — ?"

"I'll find a way, Saadya, I promise. I swear it to you." As gently as he could, Luis released his hand from Saadya's. "If I go down to see the donatario now, I'll have word for you by late tonight. Promise me you'll still be — here."

"Yes." As he moved aside to let Luis pass, Saadya added, in a rush. "Luis, I — I'm sorry. I did my best — at least, I think I did — "

Luis turned back. He did not know what prompted him to put his arms around Saadya for a moment as though he were comforting a very small child. "You did, Saadya; you did more than anyone."

Luis walked away quickly, toward his own hut, the oldest in a little village of married couples that was gradually springing up. "Shmone-esre l'chupa, at eighteen — marriage." He remembered Saadya, very embarrassed, quoting that to him on his eighteenth birthday. Except for Nechama, whom he dealt with, he had had no contact with any girls; so he had asked her to marry him, explaining awkwardly that he did not know anyone else. He could still hear her laughing at his elegant proposal. But she had married him anyway, and did not seem to have regretted it.

Holding the baby out to him, Nechama met Luis at the door. "If you talk to him, you may get a smile; he's just learned how."

Accepting the baby, Luis looked down at his b'chor with a gaze that mixed wonder and delight and sadness. They had called him Gershom so that nobody would ever forget that they did not belong here on São Tome, that all the Judaismo they had was only a shadow of what it was meant to be.

He looked at Nechama. She seemed gentler and more motherly, though he was sure that if he mentioned it to her she would laugh and say she had only put on weight. "He won't smile at me," he said.

"I'm not surprised, you staring at him so seriously. You have to smile at him first," she laughed.

Luis smiled experimentally. An answering rubbery grin lit up the tiny face, and Luis laughed at it. "Do I look like that, I wonder?"

Nechama's expression told him that he did, and she was very pleased that their son did, too. "Did you find Chanan?" she asked. "When you left, you were searching for him."

"Yes. We went to inspect a meadow I want to plow up." He gave the baby back to her. His face sober, he went on, "And then I went to see Saadya and I — " He swallowed. "Saadya's not well; he needs to get away from here."

"I know," Nechama said quietly. "I felt something, a wrongness, at the pidyon haben. Is it worse, then?"

"Much worse." Luis took a deep breath. "I'm going down to the port now, to see the donatario. I won't be back till late; will you be all right?"

"Perfectly. And if I'm lonely I can ask Esperansa to keep me company."

Almost at once he was gone.

By the time Luis reached the town, the sun was low in the sky. Turning toward the donatario's palace, exactly as it had been when he first saw it in 1493, he looked at the veranda, half-expecting to see Don Alvaro slumped in an armchair, listless and fever-ridden. But the chair stood empty: Don Alvaro had died six months earlier. And now the new donatario had taken his place.

Luis knocked at the door. "He's at the clearing," someone's voice came languidly from within.

The clearing: Luis knew where that was. Don Fernão de Melo had been on São Tome only two weeks, and already his plans for the island were plain. Outside the town, he was starting to build slave-pens.

Nearing the work site, Luis thought about the ugly business. He had seen the half-dead Kongo blacks that Don Alvaro had brought in; he had heard the captains of slave ships that provisioned at São Tome complaining of the number they lost on the journey to Portugal. Now Don Fernão de Melo would make São Tome the central clearing-house for the whole African traffic in human misery.

He saw the man now, striding eagerly across the open area, his sharp, dark features alive with impatience to see his ideas at work. Against the rampant forest growth the naked earth was a stark scar. Luis caught the donatario as he approached the edge of the barren stretch.

"Senhor de Melo."

The man stopped and turned very deliberately to look at Luis. His expression said as clearly as words that Luis did not matter and what he wanted did not matter. He had no place in Don Fernão's plans for the slave trade, so he did not exist. "Well?"

Luis looked around him at the open expanse, the activity, the distractions for de Melo. Here, de Melo would not even listen; he would be visualizing the slave-pens, heaving with black bodies, and would pay Luis no attention. "In the donatario's house, if you please," said Luis firmly.

The man flicked him an annoyed glance. "Come see me after sunset."

"I have a two-hour walk home, Senhor."

The donatario's eyes strayed again to the activity before him. "It can't be that urgent," he said shortly.

"I'm afraid it is, Senhor."

"It had better be," snapped Don Fernão irritably. "I'm losing a good hour of work here on your account. People don't work without supervision."

Luis noticed a blandly inquisitive young man detaching himself from the confusion of laborers: the Crown inspector. He remembered the man. Only a week before he had visited the Jewish compound "just to have a look around", as he had put it. Now Luis nodded toward the man. "Perhaps Don Valentim Fernandes would do you a favor, just for that hour?"

"Possibly."

Almost holding his breath, Luis watched de Melo confer briefly with the inspector. He had to keep the inspector away from his discussion with Don Fernão: no hint of leaving must reach official ears or the government would certainly take steps to prevent it. He saw Fernandes nod, and Don Fernão turn back; and he let his breathing ease. It was safe; the two of them would be alone.

Once behind the desk, the donatario sat impatiently, leaning a little forward, away from the low curved back of his chair.

"Well?"

Through the open door the low sun poured a flood of light between them. Luis stared across the brightness. Left to stand, like a peasant come, hat in hand, to beg some trifle from his lord, Luis stumbled over his words as he asked, "Are there any ships for Portugal due to call here soon, Senhor?"

"I don't know. When they come, they come. I'm no diviner."

"But is it likely that there might be something soon?" Luis persisted.

"Reasonably likely." The donatario's eyes narrowed. "Why are you so interested?"

"My — my aide isn't himself, from too much pressure." Luis's voice was strained. "If he leaves São Tome, he may recover; but if he stays here he'll demoralize the colony." Please understand, Luis appealed silently, understand that it's not because you've just arrived and we're trying to take advantage of you, or because we think you're weak or stupid.

The narrowed eyes met Luis's. "Are you telling me you've

got a lunatic up there?" At Luis's hesitant nod, he went on, "Isn't dying good enough for you any more? Don Valentim says there are only six hundred of you left — oh, never mind, I see your point; you can't have somebody like that running around."

For a few seconds the donatario tapped a forefinger thoughtfully on the desk while he considered the request. "You've got to see my side," he said at last. "If I let one go, am I opening the floodgates to a rush of requests? I don't doubt you'd all like to leave."

Luis stared at him uncomfortably. He had wanted to work up to that idea slowly, but de Melo had seen it at once. Saadya would have been a better negotiator; he understood this kind of maneuvering. "Yes, we would," he admitted. "But this one boy — "

"Oh, I understand it's a matter of some urgency, and there should be no difficulty in sending him away quite soon — as long as we can come to an arrangement about the rest of your colonists. After all, Don Alvaro came with a commission to populate the island; surely you don't expect me to agree to its depopulation."

"What arrangement?" Luis asked suspiciously. He stood tense and fearful, conscious of how much all the children were at this man's mercy because of Saadya's need to escape.

Don Fernão sat back in his chair. Delicately fitting his fingertips together, he began, "You know what my plans are for Sao Tome, don't you?"

"The slave trade." Luis could not keep the revulsion out of his voice.

The donatario laughed. "You're still very idealistic. Now look here: the king has cut back our production of sugar cane to keep the market price high. If São Tome is to be profitable, I have to find some other enterprise. Now, the slave trade is obvious: the island is well-located, and the ships stop here for provisions anyway. Do you know how the system works at present?"

"Only vaguely."

"Along the coast of Africa there are savages who sell us the enemies they capture in war. If they run out of enemies, a number of the chiefs aren't above selling their own people as well. The captain of each slave ship negotiates independently with these chiefs. It's tedious and time-consuming.

"What I propose is to assign my own staff to take care of these negotiations along the coast, to use a fleet of ships of my own to bring the slaves here, and to sell this stock, suitably culled, to the slave ships, naturally for a higher price than they would have paid on the mainland. But I'll save them time, trouble, and wastage; the ships will be able to make more journeys per year, and the slave trade should expand tremendously.

"Now, everybody knows you Jews are sharp dealers; you have haggling in your blood. I want your men to be my representatives to the chiefs — for a commission, of course."

"Men?" Luis gaped incredulously. "We're only boys. I'm the oldest, and I'm scarcely nineteen."

The donatario stared. "Do you mean to tell me that you were nothing but a bunch of little boys six years ago when you virtually held Don Alvaro to ransom?"

"No more than little boys," Luis agreed soberly, thinking of the children as they had been then, homeless, frightened, lonely, but determined to cling to their Judaismo. "But, you see, we threatened him with our own deaths, and we truly believed we would do it; and, Senhor, if you believe in yourself that completely, others do, too."

"I see." Don Fernão began to rise. "It seems that we have nothing to discuss, then."

"I think we may." Luis spoke so sharply that the donatario's head jerked up. "What do you mean to feed your slaves on while you wait between ships?"

"There's quite a lot of grain grown here."

With a firm shake of his head, Luis explained, "That's mostly our grain; we depend on it. When we came we were too young to clear and plow, so Don Alvaro's men did it, down here, obviously. We're only just beginning to work the land near our compound. However," he hurried on, thinking as he spoke, "we've been experimenting with maize. Now, maize doesn't need the usual furrows; it's planted in hills. Even the girls and the very little children can do that, and that would free the rest of us to clear further land. We could offer you quite a lot of maize very shortly."

"And in return?"

Luis felt his jaw harden. "You let us leave."

"But that leaves me without a food supply again," the donatario objected, "since the grain depends on your labor, too. Of course, if enough of you were to remain, enough to assure me of maize for all my needs, we might have something to talk about."

If enough of you were to remain. No! Luis cried out inwardly at the injustice of it. More than any of the children, he wanted to escape São Tome, not to find family but simply to be again in a Jewish community. His taste of Judaismo had been so brief! He hungered for it, thirsted for it, as no one else in the colony could. But how could he ask anyone to stay on São Tome without staying himself? He was parnes. The parnes must set the example. The parnes must lead.

But I didn't want to be parnes in the first place, he argued silently.

What does that matter? he answered himself. Hashem made you parnes because you were the right one for the office and the time.

The right one? I'm not the right one. Yosef would have been.

Yosef has been gone for a long time. There is no one else, now.

Luis felt the slow, inescapable advance of a future he had never even let himself consider. He wanted to flail and struggle, but there was nothing to fight against, only a few ripples licking at his feet. And when the great waves came, it would be too late. He bowed his head in defeat. "Enough of us will remain."

The donatario said something approving that Luis did not listen to, and added, "They'll have to leave a few at a time, not to be too conspicuous. Once Don Valentim is off the island, you can make arrangements with the captains of the slavers to take your people to Tangier or Arzila — after the maize starts coming, naturally."

Luis nodded mechanically. Still shocked at the swiftness with which he had condemned himself to São Tome, he was turning to leave when he saw Don Fernão raise a hand to stop him.

"A moment," he said smoothly as he reached into an iron-bound chest next to him. In his hand there was a folded sheet of paper. Passing the letter to Luis through the orange glare of the setting sun, he remarked, "This was found in Don Alvaro de Caminha's effects. It seems to be addressed to one of your people. I'm afraid the seal was broken in error."

Luis took the proferred letter. The seal had not been broken in error. It had been deliberate. The letter had been read. He looked at de Melo and saw that the man knew that Luis realized that he had lied,and that de Melo did not care. Somewhere inside Luis the suspicion grew that the letter held something that mattered a great deal to all of them.

A letter. Looking at the thing in his hand, his indignation gave way to puzzlement. In the whole colony, nobody had ever received a letter. Government communications were addressed to the donatario; church missives went to the remaining friars in their tiny monastery in the port city. There was no one to write to the children and no way for them to communicate with Jews now that the Jews had been expelled from Portugal. Yet in his hand he held a letter. A letter for whom? He turned it over wonderingly and read the careful writing on the other side.

It was addressed to his wife.

"Thank you," he said to the donatario coldly. With the most minimal of bows Luis left the office and started home.

A letter. A letter to his wife. No, not to his wife, to Nechama de Lamego, her maiden name. Someone had written to her who did not know she was married, or perhaps the letter had been sent long ago from somewhere very distant. Her parents, maybe.

He hoped the news it contained was not all bad. He would have liked to read it. It crackled tantalizingly against his chest inside his doublet where he had pushed it. He would not read it. Even though Nechama was his wife, he would not open it.

Let it be good news, he thought. Please let it be good. My own news is bad enough.

Although it was still hot, only a golden glow in the sky remained of the sun; the short tropical dusk was beginning. As he climbed the long slope home, he heard birds and monkeys calling sleepily in the fading light. On he walked, through the twilight and into the night. Long before he reached the compound owls were calling, and flights of bats flapped across the road to unseen fruit trees. The moon rose, nearly full, and shadows streaked and stained the ground under his feet.

Nechama had laid the baby in the basket. She was waiting for Luis, but she had sat down beside the basket, one hand resting on its edge with unconscious grace, and she was watching the sleeping child with such absorption that she did not hear Luis's light footfall as he came in. Not until he was standing by her did she look up, her face soft in the glow of the lamp on the table.

"I didn't hear you."

"I know." He gazed down at his son. What kind of Jewish life had he given him, imprisoned on São Tome?

Rising, Nechama asked him, "Will he let Saadya leave?"

Luis did not look at her. "Yes, and others, too. For a price."

"What price?" Nechama's voice was sharp with fear.

Now he did turn his eyes to her face. Let her be strong, he thought, I need her to take it calmly. "Some of us have to stay behind," he said heavily.

Nechama did not say anything. She only stood staring at him, staring as if she had been spellbound motionless. "And of course the parnes has to stay, too," she whispered at last. After a while she knelt down beside the sleeping infant. His thumb was stuffed firmly into his tiny mouth. "Poor baby," she said softly. "Poor, poor baby."

Luis watched her stroke the little bald head. "I can't deal with people like that," he said miserably. "I'm not devious enough. Saadya could have, before he was so nervous. Maybe Yosef ... He backed me into a corner. I had to make a bargain. He wouldn't take anything else."

Nechama rose quickly, gazing up at Luis with compassion. "I'm sorry, Luis. It's hardest for you, having to give up what you wanted most. Don't you be the one to tell everyone and make it seem pleasant. Let Chanan do it, Luis; it's not fair that you should have to do that, too."

"No." His chest felt tight. "I'm parnes, not Chanan. I've

been letting him do too much of my work already. It's my place to break this to the others, not his. My responsibility. How I feel doesn't matter." He sat down at the table and put his hands over his face. Inside his doublet the letter crackled.

Shaking his head, he rubbed his sleeve across his eyes and, reaching across the table to where Nechama had sat down, laid the letter in front of her. "All the way home I was thinking about this and then I forgot it when I came in the door. Don Fernão says they found it in Don Alvaro's effects. It's addressed to you."

Cautiously, Nechama turned the paper over to see for herself. "It is," she whispered. "Why?"

"I don't know. Read it." He gave her the ghost of his usual grin. "It can't be very bad, whatever's in it. It's practically history, the letter's so old. Nearly two years, at least."

For a minute longer she held back. Then, swiftly, she unfolded the paper and smoothed it flat. She caught her breath. "Reina!" She clutched at the letter as she skimmed through the lines of neat Hebrew script.

"She tells about their journey — Tunis ... Gen-Genova ... Milano ... People in Milano took them in ... Reina's married! Her husband is still learning ... the first baby died but she's expecting again — I hope it was all right — the baby must be two by now ... Yosef did try to collect money to rescue us, Luis ... she writes 'and then he simply disappeared' — I wonder if I should tell Esperansa; nobody knows what happened to him. Poor Reina! — the money is in Fas, being held for us. The money and the letter, passed from one person to the next all the way from Padova to Fas ... " She laid the letter on the table in front of Luis and moved away.

Luis glanced only at the last part, the part about the money. There was a great deal of it, by São Tome standards, and certainly they could arrange to get hold of it. They had money to buy or bribe their way off São Tome. But the letter had been opened. Don Fernão had read the letter. He had known about the money in Fas when he maneuvered Luis into bargaining away his life and the lives of perhaps a hundred others in exchange for something he might have bought. There was a bitter taste in Luis's mouth. He felt sick. He got up and went out.

The stars blinked coldly at him and the moon gave him a

chilly stare. Under the trees that sheltered the couples' houses it was very dark.

So much was at stake. The Inquisition had been invited into Portugal. How long would it be, Luis wondered, before the Inquisition reached the colonies? All of the children had been baptized. Nominally, they were all New Christians. How long would it be until their eroded Judaism lay under siege?

They were not accustomed any longer to having the friars looking over their shoulders. Frei Domingo's death a few years earlier had been the final blow to the Church's plans for them. Without his determination the friars let their useless outpost in the children's compound crumble under the termites, while the friars moved down to the town. How would the children resist the Inquisition?

He remembered Rosalia's secretive kashruth; he recalled the few scraps of observance his parents had taught him. Had he condemned those who would stay on São Tome not only to this imprisonment but to life as Marranos in addition? Luis, alone of all of them, understood. And Luis was parnes.

He saw, now, why it was that he had been forced into that office. The Inquisition would assuredly reach São Tome one day, but he would see to it that his colons was prepared. Suddenly he was sure that Don Fernão would never have let any of the children leave, despite the money in Fas, if the overriding consideration of food for the slave trade had not made it worthwhile to bargain away some of his captive labor force. Luis's fumbling statesmanship did not matter. Hashem had intended this to happen.

And to me it seems black and dreadful, yet I must believe it is all good and right. I must have emuna. He sighed. Sometimes emuna was very hard to have.

In a little while he would go to Saadya and tell him he would be leaving São Tome and he must not let himself visit the peaceful meadow again. That was a good thing: that Saadya would escape. He must concentrate on that.

In the morning he would tell the others that some of them would have to remain on São Tome, would have to make themselves hostages so that the rest could go free. They would look at him, the parnes, and they would ask, "And will you stay, too?"

And he would smile because he was parnes and he had to smile, and he would say lightly, "Of course."

Only afterwards he would go away to some quiet place in the forest and stand with his face against a tree for a long while, thinking about all the things he would never see again. And then he would come back and be as he always was, with a ready grin and a friendly word. He would be no different from the way he had been before, because he was parnes. He did not have the right to be Luis any more.

He would only have to take care not to stand too long at night under the trees near the couples' houses when the ground was streaked with moonlight; he would be careful not to remember this night. In time, perhaps, the ache in his chest would lessen and he would learn to be content with what he had been given.

Of course.

CHAPTER SIXTEEN

LEVEN YEARS AFTER Don Fernão had made his bitter bargain with Luis, Esperansa stood in a cemetery in Fas and saw her mother buried. One by one, men filed past. One by one, each tossed a handful of earth into the open grave. Dry-eyed, she watched them and listened to her brothers and sisters sobbing quietly.

She thought back to the day she had come at last to Fas and had found her family, as she had dreamed she would. But it was not at all as she had imagined it. For one thing, Papa was dead years before, dead of starvation in the fields outside Fas. For another, all her brothers and sisters had lost everything in their wanderings and were only now struggling to rebuild their lives: there was no wealth now, only utter, abject poverty. And for a third thing, Mama had been mad.

She looked at the grave.

Mama is there, she thought. Mama is dead. After nine years she is never going to keep me awake at night again, or interrupt every meal, or call me constantly for things she doesn't need. I will not have to pretend any longer that we have a retinue of servants, while I do all the work myself. I will not have to go hungry so she can have the fine foods she thinks we can afford. I will not have to lecture myself on the mitzva of kibud eim. I will not have to wonder when it will end. It has ended. Mama is dead.

It was strange that there was no sense of release, no sense of freedom, as though she had been a part of Mama's life for too many years to change overnight to a separate person. During the shiva week she sat tense and alert, expecting her mother to call her at any moment; and then she would remember that Mama was gone, and she would relax; and forget again, and sit like a coiled spring.

She sat unobtrusively, out of the way, alone with her thoughts. Only her sisters' friends came to be menachem aveil; she had none of her own save one old woman from next door. Esperansa had never had a chance to meet anyone except, perhaps, the butcher and the vegetable-seller, who both hated her because she haggled viciously over cheap meat scraps and bunches of wilted greens.

Her thoughts were bitter ones. I came to Fas a girl of seventeen, she reminded herself. Suddenly I'm a woman of twenty-six and nine years of my life have disappeared. When did I ever have one moment to myself, except when old Lalla Rahel next door took pity on me? Were all my sisters and sisters-in-law working so hard that they couldn't spare me one day a year to draw breath uninterrupted? From the day I arrived I nursed Mama, nursed a fretful invalid who refused to acknowledge poverty. I catered to her whims, I was enslaved to her. My family made me their sacrifice and I was helpless, as I was always helpless against them.

After the shiva week was over and everyone had gone away, Esperansa opened the door of her mother's deserted room, the room that shammed wealth while outside it the house stood bleak. She looked at the empty bed hung with Oriental silks and brocade, at the heavy draperies muffling the tiled walls, at the tooled leather on the floor and the carved bedside table that stood upon it. For so long this extravagant room had been strewn with Mama's shawls and veils, with extra coverlets of every thickness, with Mama's fancywork and embroidery that she incessantly took up and threw down. The room was oppressive with memories.

Turning her back, Esperansa shut the door and went into the room she had cooked and sat in, expecting to find herself alone. But Lalla Rahel was there, waiting for her. The old woman gave her an understanding look.

"What happens to me now, Lalla Rahel?" Esperansa asked bleakly. "They'll shut up the house in a few days. Where do I go?"

The old woman cocked her head to one side and regarded Esperansa silently with bird-bright eyes.

"They'll expect me to live with them, I suppose," Esperansa answered herself, "to live their lives and put mine away forever. I don't want that. But what else is there?"

"A cousin of mine," said Lalla Rahel unexpectedly. "In Tunis. Her husband is away for months, sometimes, on business. Now that her parents have moved to Constantinople — no doubt they believe that talk about Spain's designs on North Africa — she wants a companion."

"Tunis?" asked Esperansa. She knew she looked as frightened as she felt. Her face showed everything. "It's very far," she said hesitantly.

"Yes," agreed Lalla Rahel. "Far enough to start again."

It was surprising how swiftly the idea became fact, how quickly Esperansa found herself bidding farewell to a cluster of disapproving older sisters and brothers.

She watched as someone tied her single bag of belongings onto a camel. Climbing on, she clung precariously as the camel rose, throwing her forward and then back. Some distant relative of Lalla Rahel's had business in Tunis and was traveling with the caravan. Her camel, firmly led, started off behind him.

Laden with dried fruit, the camels in front of them stretched their ungainly legs and swayed along the ancient route to Tunis. Tlemcen, Alger, Constantine: names of cities she had never known, now each one a Shabath spent en route.

As she rode, Esperansa thought of the disdainful glance her own camel had given her when she had mounted it for the first time. Did it know she was being foolish? It had the same superior look her brother had had on his face when he had told her that. And her sisters: wiser, more worldly, more confident; so considerate, they thought, of her welfare. How horrified they had been, how insulted that she refused their homes to go to a stranger's.

Perhaps I am being foolish, she thought. Why am I suddenly trying to be independent? All my life I've wanted only to belong to someone, to be protected. I don't want to make my own way in the world. I ought to have stayed in the house of one of my sisters and been safe.

I must have been foolish, listening to Lalla Rahel tell me I was so capable and responsible that I'd do well in Tunis. I was so capable and responsible when I came to Fas that I was rewarded with nursing Mama all by myself for nine years. I don't want to be capable and responsible.

And now it's too late and the date palms of Tunis are in sight and in a little while I'll be starting the same trap all over again.

Oh, Ribono shel Olam, help me, I've been so very, very foolish.

And then she was there and she was standing with her one bag outside a blank door while the caravan went on without her. She raised her hand and knocked.

The old man who opened the door to admit her gave her a friendly smile as he led her along a hallway and around a bend. Just through an arched doorway, Esperansa found herself at one corner of a covered passage that ran around all four sides of the central courtyard. Narrow, graceful columns that seemed too light to carry the weight of the arches above them separated the walk from the open area in the center.

"If you will wait in the courtyard, I'll tell Lalla Mazal that you've arrived," he said, and left her.

Esperansa stepped timorously onto the brick paving. She was so cold; the sun felt good on her shoulders. I shouldn't be so cold, she thought, it's only the end of Cheshvan. I'm frightened. I daren't let myself wonder what Lalla Mazal is like. I've got to think of something else.

At the opposite side of the courtyard, in the angle where two lines of columns met, a fig tree thrust up through the paving to spread its branches wide. Moving nearer, Esperansa gazed up at it. It was a very large fig tree, larger than one might have expected. With bricks running right up to its trunk, it should have been stunted.

A fig tree. She remembered Paloma telling her about her fig tree before she died. Oh, Paloma! she cried silently. The ache she had felt then came back without warning. Paloma. Nechama. Reina. With a rush the faces from São Tome came flooding back around her, children she had played with grown to people who were married now, all of them together in a crowd of memories.

"Esperansa?"

She did not know where she was for a few seconds. It would not have surprised her to turn around and see Nechama standing smiling in the sun behind her.

But she had never seen this woman before, slender, pretty, her robe flowing gracefully about her. She moved easily, lightly, her hands outstretched in welcome.

She's younger than I am, Esperansa thought, startled, but she has a husband and a home. I'm twenty-six and I have nothing, not even friends. All my friends are on São Tome. I wish I had stayed there, even sickly and ailing and feverish, among people who knew me, people I loved.

Pushing her thoughts away, Esperansa turned to the strange woman and smiled. "Lalla Mazal."

Lalla Mazal gave her something to eat and showed her to her room, saying she would wait until the next day to discuss Esperansa's duties. Esperansa's eyes followed the woman as she walked away, along the upstairs gallery, around two sides of the square to the steps leading down to the ground floor. A faint echo of Lalla Mazal's voice wandered up from the entrance passage, then the sound of the front door closing as someone went out.

From where she stood, in the doorway of the room, Esperansa could see part of the courtyard below through the railing of the gallery. As Lalla Mazal stepped across the herringbone-laid bricks, a little boy of about six came flying out to meet her. She stooped and gathered him into her arms, and he clung to her in return. Esperansa turned away.

In the morning Lalla Mazal divided the household chores between the two of them. Long before Lalla Mazal expected her to, Esperansa had finished her share and begun scrubbing the tiled floor of the room they had eaten in.

"You don't have to do that," protested Lalla Mazal when she discovered her at it. "We have a woman who comes in to do the heavy cleaning."

"Oh." The strokes of Esperansa's brush did not change. Without glancing up, she said, "I just thought the floor needed cleaning too badly to wait."

"You were right, but — " Lalla Mazal gave her a peculiar look. "You're so capable I can't understand why you didn't find a more rewarding position," she remarked. "Being my companion isn't very demanding; I don't know what you see in it."

You're so capable. Capable and responsible. I don't want to be capable and responsible. I don't want to be independent. I don't want a more rewarding position. I want to be safe.

She gave the tiles a vicious swipe. "Oh, simply personal taste, I suppose," she said casually, just too late for it to sound as natural as she had intended it to.

Lalla Mazal was perceptive enough to realize that it was not a subject Esperansa wanted to discuss. After a pause she said, "I'm planning on going out soon. Would you like to come?"

"Yes; I'm nearly through." Esperansa glanced up at Lalla Mazal. "Will you be taking your little boy?"

"Chushiel? No; he's with his melamed now." She slipped away.

When Esperansa was finished she rejoined Lalla Mazal. As they crossed the courtyard on the way to the door, she was reminded of her original impression of the fig tree: that it was larger than she expected. She asked Lalla Mazal about it.

"Oh, it wasn't always bricked up like that," she answered. "When I was little it had quite a large patch of open ground around it. But when all the Sicilian refugees came — in 1492, you know — my parents took in as many as they could and, needing all the courtyard space, they ran the bricks over that open patch. With the paving and the children climbing it and people banging into it, we didn't think the tree would survive, but it did, and the odd thing was that it gave far more fruit afterwards."

" ... a whole crop of figs ... " Esperansa could hear Paloma's whisper. "The taste of Gan Eden," she said softly.

Lalla Mazal laughed. "Well, no, they taste quite ordinary. I suppose lush living just didn't agree with it."

"And we, too, we Jews," Esperansa said pensively, "we fruit better when times are hard; we run too much to leaves and gashmiuth when things are easy for us. Like the fig tree: lush living doesn't agree with us."

Lalla Mazal looked at her thoughtfully. "It does seem that way, doesn't it," she agreed, "though you can go too far in the opposite direction, I think. You'll see what I mean in a little while."

Ibrahim, the old man who had first admitted Esperansa, was waiting for them, and together all three walked through the mellah, Esperansa carrying a basket of food, Ibrahim with a brazier and a small sack of charcoal.

"I had to be sure to go now," Lalla Mazal commented conversationally, "because these things are for Chushiel's melamed, and I wanted to be sure he'd be out. He lives with only the barest necessities; he gives away most of his earnings." She nodded at the brazier. "It will be cold enough for that very soon. If I ask him if he needs one, he'll refuse it, so I have to deliver it while he's away."

"And anonymously," added Esperansa.

Lalla Mazal laughed. "Well, I think he knows who's doing it, but I suppose if he can't prove it he can't protest."

"But maybe it's a vow of some kind."

"Oh, I'm careful not to do anything that looks permanent. The brazier comes at the beginning of winter and leaves at the end; as far as he's concerned, there's no guarantee that it will arrive the next year. Except for the food, which he really does need, everything I bring is left in the same manner. And here we are," Lalla Mazal added.

They stood before the doorway to a small outbuilding, a nondescript storage structure. "Put the brazier down, Ibrahim, and open the door," said Lalla Mazal.

"He lives in a storeroom?" Esperansa was horrified.

"It's a little dark, but apparently quite livable," the other lady assured her. "Come in."

The morning sunshine flooding in after them showed Esperansa the room with a light that was brutal in its clarity. Only the most essential furniture stood on the earth floor: a simple bed, a table, a small bench, all in the European manner, all of the very poorest, all pushed firmly against the wall. A water jar stood humbly in a corner; a few rough shelves housed a meager collection of utensils and a single worn-out siddur. From the one small, high window, a ray of light fell on walls that were uncompromisingly bare, save their pale mottling that pleaded vainly for a coat of whitewash. Nothing was out of place. The room was perfectly neat. The bed was made. The dishes were clean.

The picture of her mother's room flashed into Esperansa's mind as she had last seen it: painfully tidy, divested of everything that made it look lived in. That room was filled with wealth, this one with poverty; otherwise they had the same feeling. It was the feeling that the tenant had already died. Yet at this moment the melamed was teaching Chushiel. The man must be very old, she thought, to be so ready for Olam Haba; this is the home of an old, old man who has cut nearly all his ties to this world and is waiting only for death. She shuddered slightly. "I couldn't live like this."

"You shouldn't. Neither should he." Lalla Mazal's tone was very definite. "But you can't live other people's lives for them, can you?" She bent down to feel the blanket on the bed. "I'll send Ibrahim with an extra blanket next week. Would you unpack the basket onto the table, Esperansa?" she added, turning to see if anything else were needed.

Ibrahim spoke. "Where should I put the brazier?"

"By the table, I think," said Lalla Mazal, considering the question. "Where do you imagine he would want it, Esperansa?"

"Oh, by the table, I suppose; he can always move it if he wants it elsewhere."

"Not easily," objected Lalla Mazal; "he's crippled."

Esperansa's eyes moved slowly around the barren room. From every side she seemed to feel a sensation of creeping age and decrepitude moving inexorably toward death. She had seen enough death. She had lived nine years with that deliberate, irresistible progress toward the grave. She felt as though those interminable years that she wanted to forget were crawling back upon her as she stood in this place, this joyless place empty of everything but the last brief breath of an ancient, crippled man.

"May I — may I go out?" she whispered.

Lalla Mazal shot her a startled glance. "I've never seen anyone that color!" she exclaimed, catching at Esperansa. "You certainly shall go out, into the sun." She pulled her through the door. "Are you going to faint, do you think?"

Esperansa shook her head.

"Then I'll just finish up and we'll go home." The woman

darted back inside and returned moments later with Ibrahim at her heels, the basket in his hand. "How are you feeling now?"

"I'm sorry," Esperansa said. "I'm all right." The pallor under the olive skin dissipated gradually, but not quickly enough to satisfy Lalla Mazal.

"You'll take a rest when we're home," she ordered.

"I'm not ill," said Esperansa. "I was being silly."

"Silly! Silly doesn't turn you white. No, I'm not even going to ask. You'll take a rest and be careful for a day or two." And that was all she had to say on the subject.

From then on, Esperansa had a horror of the melamed. Whenever she knew he was due to arrive she moved away from the rooms near the door, and while he was teaching Chushiel she kept to the part of the house farthest from the man's presence. She did not want to be near him. She did not even want to think of him. Yet she could not help musing on the odd fact that he was an excellent teacher, according to Lalla Mazal's account. And Chushiel loved the man. It seemed contradictory that the child so full of life should be deeply attached to the man so devoid of it.

Some weeks later while she was sitting, as usual, as far as possible from Chushiel's learning, Lalla Mazal bustled in.

"Esperansa, my dear," she began, "will you do me a particular favor?"

Laying down the fine sewing, every minute stitch precise, she looked up. "What is it?"

"Well, it's the melamed."

A chill stole down Esperansa's back and made her shiver. Had the old man died suddenly? She said nothing.

"He wants to meet you. Not you, exactly," Lalla Mazal rushed on, ignoring Esperansa's tight little gasp, "but he heard you called today and the name — "

Who had called? Ah, it must have been the cook, up to her elbows in dough, kneading — Esperansa cut the thought off. "No," she said.

"Wait. Listen to me." Lalla Mazal settled herself beside Esperansa and put her arm around her. "Let me tell you what he said to me. He heard you called, and he stopped short.

" 'Is there someone named Esperansa here?' he asked.

" 'Yes; she came to live with us recently,' I told him.

"He went on a few steps, very thoughtful, then turned to me and said, 'I once knew a child named Esperansa. No doubt she died years ago, and no doubt I'm being foolish, but do you think I could meet this child who lives with you, because of that other one?'

"He spoke so hesitantly my heart went out to him. Come into the courtyard to him, Esperansa."

"No," she said. "Not to him."

"Think, Esperansa. He has suffered so much since the expulsions, yet I have never known him to ask for one single thing. Now he has made a small request: to meet a child with your name. Perhaps the name reminds him of some little happiness he had long ago. Have pity on him, Esperansa; he has nothing and no one."

She turned her head away. "But I'm not a child," she said pleadingly.

"You're so tiny; you could pass for one. Let your braids down; that's all that's needed."

He has nothing and no one. Esperansa tried to imagine a little girl of fifty of sixty years ago. How could she be like that unknown child? But it was such a small thing, and his life was so bleak. With slow, reluctant hands she reached up and undid her braids, letting them fall over her shoulders as she had when she was young, her small face framed between them.

Past one doorway after another she clung to Lalla Mazal's comforting arm as they followed the upstairs gallery to the stairway. She dared not look down into the courtyard. At the foot of the steps she stopped and sheltered behind Lalla Mazal in the covered passage and gazed through the archway at this strange old man.

The melamed was by the fig tree. Dressed in the same dark robes every Jew of Tunis wore, he stood leaning on a crutch, waiting patiently. He did not seem to be looking at anything; rather, perhaps, he was dreaming of that Esperansa of long ago, the child she did not know. But she did know her after all, she thought, with a sharp bite in her throat. It was herself.

For the man she saw was not aged, but scarcely older than

she was. A black beard followed the line of his jaw, framing a cluster of scars that furrowed his face. Esperansa drew a soft, deep breath, remembering a boy who sat like a wounded falcon, restless, alert, with bright fierce eyes, who shouted at her like an eagle screaming defiance. But the fire, the aliveness, was gone.

She scrutinized this man, trying to read what he had become, but she could not learn much. Only she saw that his eyes were very kind.

Slowly she moved away from Lalla Mazal and stepped out of the shadows, through the archway. As soon as she entered the courtyard the man's quiet eyes fastened on her and did not leave her. In their gaze there was a question, she knew, but she could not answer it.

"Come here, child; I won't hurt you," said the man gently. "Do I frighten you?"

The question struck Esperansa like a blow. How many children had shrunk from him, that he asked such a question before anything else? Yet they must have learned very quickly that there was nothing fearsome about him.

"I was never afraid of you, Don Yosef, even when you shouted at me," she said. Her voice was scarcely above a whisper.

He looked at her keenly for a long minute; then, smiling, he said, "Like the cook." She had never seen him smile. It changed his face like the dawn breaking. "It is the same Esperansa, isn't it?"

"Yes; only a little older."

"I think we're both 'a little older.' Is that why I didn't recognize you?"

Momentarily she turned away, to pin up her braids with embarrassed haste. "My hair was short, then."

"Of course — from the fever. I remember, now."

On first seeing Yosef, Esperansa's impression was that he had been hurt, that she must deal gently with him. Yet she discovered that it was he who looked at her with compassion, now. He gazed so steadily at her that she thought she ought to feel uncomfortable, and did not understand why, instead, she felt at peace. "You still stare, too," she smiled.

"Instead of speaking," he said. "There is so much I want to

put into words, but none of it would be proper for me to say to you."

A long silence fell between them, not separating them but drawing them close, though they did not move from their places. In the stillness they could hear Chushiel being roundly scolded for some piece of naughtiness. The sound of it made Esperansa feel utterly alone.

Half to herself, she said, "I have no one to shout at me any more."

"I would shout at you for the rest of my life, if it would content you." He stopped short, as if his own words had taken him by surprise.

She darted a swift, shocked glance at him. He was not smiling, now; his face was serious, his eyes fixed on her with the same intensity she remembered from long ago. The fire was not gone after all. With all her being she wanted what Yosef offered her. It would content me, she wanted to say, it would content me entirely.

But he had changed; he was not the boy she remembered. All she knew of him was that he wanted to care for her and that his eyes were kind. She turned away. I have to be sensible, she told herself, I can't answer him until I know more. Besides, quite likely I've misunderstood his meaning altogether. She looked up at him. He was taller than she remembered.

"I'm sorry," he said. "You must think I'm mad, asking you to marry me when we've only just met after fifteen years. You couldn't have been more than six or seven then; you must hardly remember me."

"I was nine, Yosef, and I've never forgotten you." She could not look away from his eyes. "But you're so different."

"From the boy who was proud and tactless and so full of himself there was no room for anybody else? I hope so." He hesitated before he added, "You do realize that you're different, too?"

"Oh, yes," she said bitterly, "very capable and very responsible."

"No." His voice was quiet. "Very lonely."

"It's easier to bear than what I had for nine years before," she said defiantly.

The intent gaze wavered slightly. After a while Yosef said, "Is that my answer?"

"No — I don't know — I can't — " she struggled desperately. He wanted to care for her. His eyes were kind. But was he sane to live as he did, in that barren house? "I saw how you live," she said at last.

"It worries you?"

She nodded.

"Just before I came to Tunis, a man accused me of swaddling myself in luxury while his children on São Tome lived comfortless. It was not true, but he thought it was; and the thought that someone could be so heartless, so devoid of rachamim toward his own lost children caused him dreadful anguish. I never want that to happen again. That's all."

In her mind's eye Esperansa could picture the melamed's stark, room. It had become beautiful. She did not need to know anything more.

"For the rest," he was continuing, "I'm happy teaching Torah; I live quietly and have few wants; and Lalla Mazal takes care of any needs she thinks she finds. So I discipline myself to be content."

"And are you?" she asked gently. She knew he was not; she could see the longing in his eyes.

For a few moments he looked down at his left side. "I would have liked to have a wife, a home, a family — the things other people seem to take for granted. No doubt I'll learn to be content without them, one day."

"I won't let you!" She was half-laughing, half-crying. He was trying so hard to be content with the very little he had been granted. "Yosef! Shout at me!"

Lifting his head slowly, he looked at her searchingly before he spoke. "Are you sure, Esperansa?" he asked.

"Quite, quite sure," she said happily, her cheeks wet.

The wonderful, transforming smile broke over his face. For a long time he said nothing, only gazed at her. "I think I ought to warn you," he said after a while, "that I shout very, very softly."

CHAPTER SEVENTEEN

ORE THAN A YEAR had passed since they had been married, and it was winter again. Rain drummed on the tiles overhead. Yosef and Esperansa sat on either side of the brazier, close to the warmth of the glowing embers. On the table before Yosef lay the new Torah commentary of Don Yitzchok Abarbanel, open to that week's sedra. The baby had fallen asleep in Esperansa's arms, and she held the child against her, reluctant to separate herself from the tiny, trusting infant. On the earth floor there was a sudden splat of water: the rain had found its way in. Rising, she laid the baby in her cradle and put a bowl under the leak, with a cloth in it to muffle the sound. His concentration disturbed by the movement, Yosef glanced up from the sefer.

"It will be a cracked tile, I suppose," she said comfortably. "We'll have to have someone in tomorrow."

With a brief nod, Yosef returned to his learning. His gaze, moving back to the pages, was caught by the sight of his left hand lying half-curved on the pages to hold them down. He had never regained the use of that hand. He felt a pang of regret for the many things he could not do. It was Esperansa who moved furniture, who fixed what was broken, who had whitewashed the house inside and out before she had had the baby. He would have liked to make her life easier: if he had been whole, he would have done all of these things and more. He reached across and unbent the useless fingers with a sigh.

Esperansa came and tilted the lamp slightly so that the last of its oil ran towards the flame. "What is it, Yosef?"

"Nothing." He looked up at her with a smile. "I was forgetting what I learned from the artist that last day in Milano."

Milano. Long before, he had told Esperansa what had happened in Milano. It had felt good to let it come out of him at last, but he had been sorry afterwards when he saw her, white-faced, knuckles pressing against her lips: he had not known she would take it so to heart.

But she had only asked, after a while, "Did they ever learn what became of you?"

"Perhaps. I write to Reina; I sent something once to Mona Benvenida; either may have told them."

"Oh, Yosef! You must write to the Salzmanns. They're such good people — "

Only because he did not want her to be unhappy, he had sent the letter. And the Salzmann had sent the set of Abarbanel as a marriage-gift. Such good people ...

He watched her move away and take up her spinning before he returned to the sedra. Later, when he closed the sefer, he saw her still standing by the brazier, her face ruddy in its dim light, the spindle twisting in the shadows by her feet. She was staring into the darkness before her as though she could see something he could not.

"What are you thinking, Esperansa?" he asked gently.

Without turning her head she answered, "Only that our children will never really be able to understand what São Tome was like, no matter how much we explain. And in their turn, they'll only be able to tell their children a little, and they'll understand even less. In a few generations, people will have forgotten all about it."

"You're sorry?"

"I think so. I would have liked it to be remembered, if only to teach future generations what we learned about luxury and sacrifice."

"They wouldn't learn, anyway; each generation has its own tikun."

He saw her shiver suddenly. "But there are so many still on São Tome. I don't want them to be forgotten." It was almost a plea.

"Listen, Esperansa," he said, compassionate. Opening the sefer to the pages he had just finished, he moved his fingers down the line until he found the words. " מגורשי העברים מילדי ורבים ספרד ..., ' " he began, " 'Many of the children of the exiled Spanish Jews were forcibly converted by the king of Portugal. He sent them to that island fourteen years ago. They were all children with no defect, boys and girls ... ' They won't be forgotten, Esperansa. As long as people learn Chumash with Abarbanel they will remember São Tomé."

She sighed. "And we can do no more for them than to live well the lives they gave us. It seems so little."

"It was all they wanted for you." He wanted her to understand, to be at peace, to be happy. She had been so desolate when he had seen her first in Lalla Mazal's house. "Esperansa — " perhaps he should not ask? — "for yourself, Esperansa, are you happy, now?" He got up and went towards her, his foot dragging across the earth with a faint whisper.

"Very." She glanced at him and back to the thread between her fingers. "And you, Yosef? Are you content?"

Standing near her in the semi-darkness he looked down at her bent head and thought of the comfortable homelike things she had brought with her, dishes and pots, blankets and cushions. He listened to the rain on the tiles, the plop of the leak, the soft sound of the spindle's motion against her dress, a little singing from the nearly spent brazier, the baby's small, satisfied sucking. All familiar domestic sounds, reassuringly commonplace. The spindle-shaft reached the ground and the spindle stopped.

"Yes," he said, "well content."

Glossary

All entries are in Hebrew unless otherwise indicated. Because the story takes place in many lands, the same Hebrew word has sometimes been transliterated in more than one way, to approximate the local inflection and accent.

Adar: twelfth month of the Hebrew calendar (Feb.-Mar.).

ahavath Yisroel: love of one's fellow Jew

alef: first letter of Hebrew alphabet

Ashkenazi: of Germanic origin

aveira: sin

Ayn Yaakov: collection of non-legal sections of the Talmud

Baruch Habo: "Blessed is he who enters;" traditional expression of welcome

Baruch Hashem: "Thank G-d!"

bath: daughter (of)

b'chor: firstborn son

beith [or, beis]: (1) second letter of Hebrew alphabet; (2) house

Beith Hamikdash: Holy Temple in Jerusalem

ben: son (of)

benched [or, benshed] (Yiddish): recited Grace After Meals

bitachon: faith in G-d

bitte (German): please

bochurim: youths

brocha (pl., brochos): blessing

Chacham: (1) wise man; (2) specifically, a rabbinic authority among Levantine (Sephardic) Jewry

chai: literally, life. It is customary to give charitable donations in multiples of eighteen units of currency because the Hebrew word chai has a numerical equivalent of eighteen.

chas v'shalom: "Heaven forbid!"

chatan [or, chasan; choson]: bridegroom

chatuna (or, chasane): wedding

chesed: act of kindness

Cheshvan: eighth month of Hebrew calendar (Oct.-Nov.)

chinuch: education

Chol haMoed: intermediate days of Pesach and Sukoth

Chumash (pl., Chumashim): any one of the Five Books of Moses

chupa: marriage ceremony; specifically, wedding canopy under which ceremony takes place

chutzpa: audacity

cruzados (Portuguese): Portuguese currency

daven (Yiddish): pray

degredado (Portuguese): convict pardoned in return for dangerous service to the crown

destino (Ladino): destined

dinim: laws; specifically, Torah laws

Don (Portuguese): Sir

donatario (Portuguese): colonial administrator

Elul: sixth month of Hebrew calendar (Aug.-Sep.)

emuna: belief in G-d

erev Shabath: eve of the Sabbath; Friday

fidalgo (Portuguese): noble

Fräulein (German): Miss

Frei (Portuguese): Brother

galuth: exile

gam zu l'tova: "This, too, is for the good!"; an expression of faith in G-d when one has fallen upon ill fortune

Gan Eden: Garden of Eden; Paradise

gashmiuth: materialistic values

gedolim: prominent Rabbis

Gehinom: Hell

Genova (Italian): Genoa

gorita (Ladino): skullcap

gracias (Spanish): "Thank you!"

grandee (Spanish): nobleman

gravana (Portuguese): dry season

grazie (Italian): "Thank you!"

halacha: Torah law

Hashem: literally, the Name; G-d

Hashem Yithbarach: "G-d, Who is Blessed"

ikar: main point; important principle

Judaismo (Ladino): Judaism

Juderia (Spanish); Judiaria (Portuguese): Jewish quarter

Jüdisch (German): Jewish; Yiddish

kallah (pl., kallos): bride

kappl (Yiddish): skullcap

kehilla: (1) congregation; (2) organized community

kibud eim: honor for one's mother; specifically, the Torah's commandment that one honor one's mother

kittel (Yiddish): ceremonial white robe

kohanim: male descendants of the priestly family of Aaron

kriath-sh'ma: prayer recited before going to sleep for the night

Ladino: a Judaic-Spanish dialect, written in Hebrew letters

Lalla (Arabic): Mrs.

lamdan (pl., lamdanim): Talmudic scholar

learning (English): Throughout this volume the word learning is not used in the sense of passive acquisition of knowledge, but in the sense of intensive study — specifically, of Torah.

lebedik (Yiddish): lively

limud: intensive study (see also, learning)

lulavim: palm branches used in the Four Species on Sukoth

machzor: prayerbook for Festivals

Madonna (Italian): "My lady!"

marath ayin: an act performed in a way that can be misinterpreted as either wicked or illegal

maror: bitter herbs; specifically those used at the Pesach seder

Marrano (Spanish): a Jew, converted to Christianity under duress, who secretly adhered to Judaism

mazel-tov: "Congratulations!"

megilla (pl., megilloth): a scroll; specifically, Megillath Esther, the Scroll (Book) of Esther read on Purim

melamed: teacher of young children

meldar (Ladino): pray

mellah (Arabic): Jewish quarter in Arab lands

menachem aveil: comforting the bereaved

Menorath Hamaor: a collection of aggadic (non-legal) sections of the Talmud, arranged by topic; compiled by Rabbi Yitzchak Aboab of 14th century Spain (first printed edition, Turkey, 1514)

midoth: character traits; ethics

minhag (pl., minhagim): long-standing custom; specifically, a religious custom

minhag avoseinu b'yodeinu: "We follow the customs of our forefathers!"

Mishnayoth [or, Mishnayos]: the body of Mishna, first codification of Torah and Rabbinic law, which forms the basis of the Talmud

missionario (Portuguese): official priest of a mission

mitzva (pl., mitzvoth): (1) Torah commandment; (2) religious obligation

Mona (Italian): Madam

Motzaei Shabath: departure of the Sabbath, i.e., Saturday night

niftar: deceased

nigunim: liturgical melodies

Nine Days: first nine days of Hebrew month of Av; intense period of mourning for the destruction of the Temples

n'kama: revenge

Padre (Spanish): Father

parnassa [or, parnossa]: livelihood

parnes: community leader

parshath hashavua [or, parshas hashavua]: weekly Torah portions for synagogue reading pasuk: Biblical verse

Pesach: Passover

petira: death

pidyon haben: ritual redemption of firstborn son

pidyon shevuyim: ransoming of captives

piyutim: liturgical poems

por favor (Spanish): "Please!"

poseik: halachic authority

psak: legal decision

Purim: Feast of Lots

rachamim; rachmanuth [or, rachmonus]: compassion

rav: Rabbi

refua sheleima: complete recovery

Ribono shel Olam: Master of the universe, i.e., G-d

rotzon: will; desire

s'chach: covering for sukoth

schul (Yiddish): synagogue

sedra: see, parshath hashavua

sefer (pl., seforim): book; specifically, a religious tract

Senhor (Portuguese): Mr.

Ser (Italian): Mr.

seuda: meal

Shabath [or, Shabos]: the Sabbath

Shabath Shalom: traditional Sabbath greeting

shacharith: morning prayers

shalach manoth: gifts of food exchanged on Purim

Shalom aleichem: "Peace be with you!"; traditional greeting

Shavuoth: Feast of Weeks

sh'eiloth [or, shayloth; shaylos]: halachic questions

sheva brochos: weeklong festivities following marriage

shiduch (pl., shiduchim): a match which will hopefully lead to marriage

shiur (pl., shiurim): class; lesson

shiva: (1) seven; (2) seven-day period of mourning

Shvat: eleventh month of Hebrew calendar (Feb.-Mar.)

siddur (pl. siddurim): prayer book

simcha: (1) rejoicing; (2) joyous occasion

Simchath Purim: "Joyous Purim!"

siyato dishmayo: Heavenly assistance

Sukoth: (1) Feast of Tabernacles; (2) uncapitalized, the booths used during that Festival

taanith: fast day

talith katan: literally, small talith; four-cornered, fringed garment worn by Jewish men, usually under the outer garment

Tamuz: fourth month of Hebrew calendar (June-July)

Tante (German; Yiddish): Aunt

Tehillim: Psalms

Teveth: tenth month of Hebrew calendar (Jan.-Feb.)

tfilla (pl., tfilloth): prayer

tikun: spiritual improvement or rectification

tizke l'mitzvoth: "May you be worthy to perform [other] mitzvoth!"; traditional blessing for one who has just performed a mitzva

Torah: (1) Scripture; (2) the Pentateuch

tshuva: repentance

tshuvoth: responses to sh'eiloth

tzedaka (pl., tzedakoth): charity

tzitzith: fringes attached to the talith

yeshiva: institute of Torah study

Yomim Noraim: High Holy Days

Yom Tov (pl., Yomim Tovim): (1) holiday; (2) a boy's Hebrew name

zman simchatheinu: "Time of our rejoicing!"; a reference to the holiday of Sukoth

zmanim: seasons or special days of the calendar

zocheh: worthy